'This is a charming book, th
what happens to the central
lives, everyday worries, reco
of human relationships, as v
Hazel Southam, author

'It is a gifted writer who can ..... a book that is both gentle and soothing and yet also profound and deeply soul stirring. With *The Perfect Companion,* Jo has done just that. Among her lyrical descriptions of cathedral spires and nesting falcons are carefully crafted, believable character studies. She takes us inside the minds and hearts of her main protagonists; we live out the challenges to their faith and walk with them, we learn from the scriptures they learn from, we see the things God reveals to them, both in the supernatural and the natural, and we share their doubts and uncertainties. This is a beautiful book, about ordinary people being called by God to live out their faith more openly, to rely on Him more closely, to open up their hearts to those in need around them and to see God respond when they step out. I believe this book is God inspired and timely. It speaks to us all, when we get bogged down in the ordinary, to not forget just how extraordinary we can be in God.'
Joy Margetts, author

'Jo has captured the difference that a deep Christian faith makes to a very ordinary, even mundane life. In Maggie she has created a gentle character who, in the midst of sometimes tough circumstances, finds courage to allow herself to be changed by God's grace – and to change others' lives too. The Perfect Companion is shot through with the redemptive hope that comes from watching out for God's work in everything.'
Lisa Cherrett, editor and writer

'A reflective yet realistic story that is brim-full of peace and a sense of God's love; thoughtfully written and hauntingly beautiful.'
Sheila Jacobs, editor and award-winning author

The Perfect Companion

Jo Sheringham

instant
apostle

First published in Great Britain in 2024

Instant Apostle
104A The Drive
Rickmansworth
Herts
WD3 4DU

British Library Cataloguing-in-Publication Data

A catalogue record for this book is available from the British Library.

This book and all other Instant Apostle books are available from Instant Apostle:

Website: www.instantapostle.com

Email: info@instantapostle.com

ISBN 978-1-912726-76-9

Printed in Great Britain.

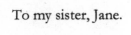

To my sister, Jane.

Acknowledgements

Thank you to the publishing team at Instant Apostle – Nicki Copeland, Sheila Jacobs, Anne Rogers and Nigel Freeman. Also, many thanks to friends and family who read the book in its early stages, and who in their encouragement have been the perfect companions.

Go forth into the world in peace;
be of good courage;
hold fast that which is good;
render to no one evil for evil;
strengthen the fainthearted;
support the weak;
help the afflicted;
honour everyone;
love and serve the Lord,
rejoicing in the power of the Holy Spirit.
And the blessing of God Almighty,
The Father, the Son and the Holy Spirit,
be among you and remain with you always.
Amen.
(Book of Common Prayer 1892, 1928, modified)[1]

Encourage the disheartened, help the weak, be patient with
everyone. Make sure that nobody pays back wrong for wrong, but
always strive to do what is good for each other and for everyone else.
Rejoice always, pray continually, give thanks in all circumstances;
for this is God's will for you in Christ Jesus.
(1 Thessalonians 5:14-18)

---

[1] This version, with slight modifications for the purpose of this book, is based in a collectionofprayers.com/2016/08/01/go-forth-into-the-world (accessed 4th July 2023).

Contents

Go Forth

Sharp pinnacles of slate grey stood fast against the driving rain. The falcon pair, lifelong companions, shuffled together, closer still inside their ornamental alcove. It was not good weather for hunting. Ancient stone cathedral spires adorned by clusters of budding crockets, which for the most part had remained unsullied by the elements, now found themselves blackened by a century of pollution. A grime-ridden atmosphere, formerly from the spew of factory pollutants, and more lately from the constant chug of city traffic billowing up from below, had left its mark.

For the most part the spires had had little to do with the worries of the world beneath them. They required nothing more than the sun when it shone like a forever friend; and the wind as it hurried back and forth like a mother rushing to gather her clan for a journey; and sometimes the occasional novelty of a shower of hail or snow. Any sporadic interruption by a storm or strike of lightning had been survived. Birds and wildlife were few but faithful, passing through as visitors or residing as tenants. Over the centuries, human contact had been as rare as any blue moon.

Though the spires had been painstakingly birthed by hammer and chisel, rope and pulley, by those referred to as craftsmen, only on the odd occasion since had the spires been touched by such ministering skill. Perhaps one day their soiled stonework would be encased in a temporary cage once again. If so, then this time it would be a scaffold of bold steel as opposed to a precarious wooden one. Another generation of brave craftsmen would conquer their peaks. Equipped with appropriate tools, brushes and chemical substances they would work, determined to reveal a fresh layer of gleaming stone which promised to blaze through.

But this was not that day and, try as it might, the efforts of the incessant rain achieved nothing; it could not even scratch the surface of the spires' tainted shrouds. Instead, this was a day for the cathedral pinnacles to study the journeying train of cloud, which, in its desperate hurry to be elsewhere, never seemed to come to an end. The concentration of human activity in the wet streets below held no interest for the falcon pair. Busy people beetled around, shielded by a host of colourful umbrellas; criss-crossing between road, traffic and lesser buildings. For them the rain was something to be dodged and avoided and hurried through because, unlike the stone spires, it threatened to pierce their fragile armour.

Unknown and unheeded by anything above, one such human figure hesitated under the Norman arch that framed the open door of the cathedral, shaking out their dark-blue umbrella from within the folds of their grey, woollen cape. Here was a woman: diminutive, and currently a member of that vast collective known as middle-aged. Behind spectacles, her eyes flicked up and down, back and forth; from the recalcitrant umbrella at the end of her fingers to the steady rain; and then across to the lively puddles, as if she were not at all sure who or what would come out on top. She muttered in anxious tones and tutted at her own incompetence against such a day.

It had been a short service with few attendees and she was not alone in her anxiety to leave the cold, cavernous building and head for home. The Canon who had read the early morning lesson, guiding the small gathering through the Christian words, had already left the building through another door; a door only accessible to those who held office there, whose affiliation to the stonework was more than just passing. But he too would at some point or other have to face the weather.

The woman had finally managed to raise her standard against the pounding elements and, with a mixture of trepidation and resolve, she sallied forth. Her footwear was not best suited to the ever-deepening puddles, but right now there was little she could do to counter the problem. After all, on waking that morning she had heard the forecast on her radio, so she should have been better prepared. From the doorway, her tiny figure in the grey cape – a canvas shopping bag swinging in one hand and the navy umbrella raised in the other – could be seen scurrying across the cobbled square with unbroken focus; like an insect clutching its hoard, following a well-worn trail to reach its own particular hole in the ground.

The words from the benediction were still fresh in her ears: *'Go forth...'*

They were words that had not been spoken lightly or softly like the rest of the regular Tuesday morning service beforehand, which to her ears at least had been barely audible. The Canon had, as with a sudden passion and as if a light had all at once dawned in his unconscious mind, rallied and cried a battle command; as if the sparse congregation in the pews were instead an assembly of stalwart troops ready for war. She recalled the preceding moments when she had been mulling over the passage of Scripture they had just read, and on which the Canon had spoken. Nothing he had said had been particularly memorable; nevertheless, she had read the words and absorbed their meaning and thought about how they might fit into her day. However, when the service was reaching its conclusion and he had begun to speak the words of the all-too-familiar prayer, she had looked up and seen a light blazing from his eyes. It had even seemed to surprise the Canon himself because he had faltered for just a moment before repeating the words:

'Go forth...'

Had he lifted his arm at this point? She couldn't quite remember, but in her mind's eye he certainly appeared to do so.

She had felt herself lifted as the words radiated like blasts of sunlight, out across the gathered few.

Here she was, she thought, a small, sort of nothing person; a flimsy, weak creature, with little to show for her years thus far. Furthermore, the very fact that such a description did not bother her too much was perhaps a woeful addition to the picture. And yet here she was, going forth.

The cobbles shone with rain and therefore in her hurrying she still took care. Lifting the brim of her umbrella every so often, she checked for obstacles and for other pedestrians who might be crossing in front of her, or be driven by the rain towards her. She intended to catch a bus straight home, as this was her day off. In her intention she would not be thwarted, despite the lure of a coffee shop with steamed-up, whorled windowpanes and a wafting, warm aroma. This was not enough to drag her off course. The temptation was only slight, as she was not accustomed to entering coffee shops alone for the sole reason of enjoying a cup of coffee, in and of itself. She might arrange to meet a friend once in a while, but it was not something she was in the habit of doing.

There was an air about her which belonged to another age. Maybe it was the cape, or her understated style of dress where bold intrusions of colour were rarely a feature. But it was also more than her appearance. On first impression she seemed mousy, perhaps even a little twitchy and nervous. Nevertheless, in character she was quiet and steady; resolved in her daily patterns, thoughts and beliefs.

The main road running down from a central crossing point which had always marked the centre of town was now before her. Water gushed along the gutters, urgently seeking the slots of a leaf-free drain. In actual fact it was no longer a main road, more of a diverted back road, as the four main streets that crossed in the centre had long since been pedestrianised. The original straight road now curved around a newly refurbished block of flats, instead of carrying on up into the town as it used to do. Turning back on itself to circumnavigate the centre and bear away the constant flow of traffic, like rainwater in the gutter, the road veered south of the town where it split, breaking into smaller tributaries.

It was just a short walk for her to turn left, up towards the main shopping area, then, at the curve of the road, where it was halted by a rank of bollards, she could follow it round. Where once she would have had to cross through city traffic, she could now cut through, between a row of taller buildings, to the main bus station.

The route was more than familiar and her usual wait of just a few minutes remained unchanged. At least here in the station there was shelter, and standing in line as the number twenty-four pulled into its bay she could fiddle with her umbrella, shake it dry and arrange the fabric back into folds. It was almost imperceptible; the small number of passengers shuffling forward, each one covertly eyeing the next at their shoulder as they ensured that the unwritten rules of British queuing were adhered to. There was a far greater number of passengers alighting from the bus than there was waiting to get on. It was the time of day to be embarking on errands and shopping and business rather than leaving the town centre to be going home. The woman wondered if she was the only one who had just attended a church service.

Rainwater from both above and below had already seeped through her sturdy lace-up shoes. She felt it beginning to squish into her socks, between her toes, as she stepped up into the bus and scanned her monthly pass. It was strange, she thought, that you didn't really sense the infiltration of water while walking through the rain; it was usually only when you stopped or got out of the weather that it began to draw your attention.

She moved to the middle of the bus and sat down in an empty two-seater, next to a misted window, where someone on an earlier trip had casually drawn a love heart with a question mark tucked inside. She didn't usually sit at the front of the bus, as those seats – the information on the printed notices stated – should be left for the elderly, wheelchair users or parents with prams and buggies, and she rarely sat at the back of the bus (unless space was limited) because once or twice she had got into difficulties with some less socially inhibited passengers: either that was just their nature or they had been aided in their lack of inhibitions by rowdy peers or intoxicating substances.

She heard herself sigh as the bus began its laborious, beeping, reversing manoeuvre out of the bay and then as it lurched forward to head out of the station. *'Go forth…'*

She thought that the bus was perhaps rather like herself in its effort to *go forth*: it was cumbersome and unenthusiastic but, nevertheless, focused and resigned to the task ahead. Though perhaps these were not quite the right words she should use to describe herself: cumbersome implied bulkiness and awkwardness, and from a physical point of view she displayed neither of these traits. However, this was sometimes how she felt inside. She was all too aware of her ineptitude and clumsiness when it came to communicating with others, and she so often seemed to get it wrong in social situations, as if she were dressed in ill-fitting clothing. Unenthusiastic: yes, she had to admit that when it came to *going forth*, she was not bubbling over with excitement, ready and alert to relish any given opportunity to speak about who she was and what she believed. She was so much like the bus. On the other hand, when it came to being focused and, at the same time, resigned, she had to conclude that she was both, though definitely one more than the other. Her faith was true and solid. Although at times she felt the onslaught of doubt, pouring down upon her like the pelting rain, attempting to seep into her soul, she understood the commitment involved. Inevitably, assuredly, she was resigned.

'Go forth…'

After twenty minutes of stop-start city travel, the bus turned a corner like a pachyderm spinning tightly on a coin. Then, as if catching a fresh wind, it gathered a little more speed. Perhaps it could make it to the end of the street without having the bother of halting for passengers. Unfortunately, the stop halfway up the street was where the woman needed to get off. She pressed the bell to alert the driver, almost feeling an odd though momentary pang of guilt at having to disturb the flow. Pulling up sharply, the bus stopped and the woman, murmuring her thanks to the driver, stepped down onto the pavement. There was another drawn-out battle with the umbrella.

Glancing along the street, she walked back a few paces and turned down an alleyway which was well hidden by overgrown shrubbery and a broken fence panel. There were no familiar cats to greet her today as they had better things to do than venture outside in such dismal weather. The passage led her to the back of a terraced housing block, past a row of garages, until she finally found her own back gate. It was a tall wooden gate that had once been painted light blue but now looked as if it had been stripped of all colour, dismissed from service while begging for reinstatement. Because the paint was peeling and old, and the gate was swollen and bloated, it was difficult to open. The woman heaved it with her shoulder as she had done hundreds of times before, and with just the right amount of pressure it sprang open. Pushing it to with her back, until it was forced into position within the frame of two delinquent posts, she sighed, staring up at the brick, mid-terraced, Edwardian building that was her home.

It was too wet to stop for any length of time and examine the tiled roof and the crumbling chimney block, which she shared with next door, or at the past-their-best double-glazed windows and the small kitchen extension, which had once been the outhouse or perhaps the coal hole. The curtains, both upstairs and downstairs, were open, so that meant that the carer had arrived on time and was either still here or had already finished getting her mother washed, dressed and breakfasted. Maybe they could both sit together, the woman and her mother, and have a cup of tea and talk about... what would they talk about? The weather? The bus journey? The neighbouring cats?

The terrible long hours of wakefulness during the previous night? There was so much to talk about.

The woman took the few steps up to the back door, resolute against the falling rain, and shook out her umbrella one last time under the overhanging mantel that shielded the step into the kitchen. Taking a deep breath, she roused herself to shout a bright and breezy, 'Hello! I'm home.'

She reopened the umbrella, which she hadn't quite closed, and set it to dry on the kitchen floor in front of the sink. It was not the best place to put it, as the kitchen was narrow; however, she would be the only member of the household requiring a clear passage to the sink. If she needed to reach the taps, she would just have to lean over the umbrella.

Littered across the open worktop were the tell-tale signs of a recently prepared breakfast: a pan and a wooden spoon, thickly coated with warm, sticky porridge, which smelt sweeter than it should have. There was also a still-open box of porridge oats, a plastic-squeezy bottle of golden syrup (cap off completely) and a quarter-full container of semi-skimmed milk. There was no sign of the dried fruit portion that was supposed to go with the porridge. The woman hoped that the carer had not yet left and would at any moment appear through the doorway into the kitchen from the open dining-through-living room beyond, with the intention of putting all these items back in their place. Of course, she could do that herself, but as she had already on numerous occasions tried to explain in an email to the care company, that was not the point. Tightening the top on the milk, replacing the cap on the syrup bottle and tucking down the lid of the porridge oats box, she put everything away and then reached across, over the umbrella, to run some water into the pan and set it to soak in the sink.

Hearing voices all at once from the room beyond, she felt annoyed with herself for not checking first to see if the carer was still there, and now there was the awkwardness of having dealt with the objects on the counter before the carer had had the chance to come back and finish off the task. She could of course brush it off as if she had just been helping out – at least she didn't have to face sending another email – but she still felt the niggle that she had crossed some sort of line into no-man's-land between client and service provider, where one felt obliged and indebted despite having paid.

It was all part of the whole picture in which she now found herself. Her elderly mother needed looking after, so she had come back home to live with her. She could not cope with the full requirement of care on a day-in-day-out, week-in-week-out basis (they called it 24/7), therefore, when she had to go to work, or when certain commitments called on her time, or when she needed to just get out of the house, a care contract had been organised and a routine established. It was not ideal, but then, why on earth should she ever expect the ideal? Life just wasn't like that. Maybe for some people it was; maybe for others life was perfect and joyous, a never-ending celebration. Maybe that's how certain people behaved, as if by living that way they could convince themselves it truly was the case. However, she was not aggrieved at this because she just knew it wasn't. No matter how hard you worked, or how much money you had, or how many people loved and thought about you, things still went wrong. So the not-so-ideal was the working norm and, to a degree, it did just that – it worked.

'Good morning, Alana.' The woman greeted the carer who was pouring out a cup of tea for her mother after successfully seating her at the small dining table just inside the doorway from the kitchen.

'Good morning, Maggie.' The carer smiled back at her. 'Is it still raining out there?'

'Yes, I'm afraid so. It doesn't look like changing either.'

'And, *"Good morning, Mother."* Yes, I'm still here. Still eating my porridge. No fruit today…' The old lady was sitting at the table, spoon midway towards her mouth, shaking her head at the whole sorry affair. 'You're always out these days and I get lumbered with this foreign one here, and there was no fruit today, again.'

The woman and Alana exchanged glances.

Maggie whispered to Alana, the carer, 'I'm sorry.' An apology sprang more readily from her lips than anything else.

'You should be...' muttered the old lady between a mouthful of fruitless porridge. The elderly lady's hearing was extraordinarily keen at times.

The carer smiled and rolled her eyes a little. They both retreated into the safety of the kitchen and Maggie hoped Alana wouldn't notice that she had already put everything away.

'I'm sorry about the fruit, but I could not find the usual container,' the carer began, her slight Eastern European accent flavouring her speech.

Now it dawned on Maggie. 'Oh, it was me.' She put a hand to her forehead. 'I'm sorry. I just remembered. I bought some new packets of apricots and raisins yesterday and I completely forgot to put them in the container ready for today. I washed it out but forgot to fill it.'

'No matter. She will be fine.' Alana flicked her hand as if motioning the concern away. 'If everything's OK then I will just write notes in the book and I will be on to my next call.'

'Yes, of course. Everything's fine,' replied Maggie; she could see that the carer was confident she had done nothing amiss and was keen to stick to her schedule. Perhaps, Maggie wondered, the carers found that sometimes it was more than just the elderly person or client who needed placating and reassuring.

Maggie realised that she still had her cape on so unwrapped herself and began to settle back into the home. She reached for the kettle and, finding that it was already full enough for one cup, flicked the switch. She heard the carer's singsong voice call out a final goodbye to the old lady, who was beginning to fall asleep over her bowl of porridge, and then the front door shut behind her. The daughter was now alone with her mother, and from the kitchen window she watched the rain streak the windows while she waited for the kettle to boil and wondered when the garden would produce any further signs of spring.

'Go forth...'

There it was, just for a split second. She saw the light, or rather she sensed the light, the same light that had suddenly graced the expression of the Canon at the end of the service that morning. Stepping off the bus and walking up the steps to her back door it had felt like a whole other world away. But now, was it really just that, another world, where she went for a bit of spiritual comfort? She knew there was more to it. That was what she truly believed but, if she was honest, for the most part she found that sometimes that belief was only hanging on by a thread. Today? Today it had been different: today she was the same person as yesterday, yet today she felt herself believing a little bit more.

The kettle had boiled, so she made herself a cup of tea and took it through to sit with her mother.

Into the World

Her mother took slow, ponderous mouthfuls of the syrupy porridge which clung to the bowl, and the spoon, and her chin, with positive determination. She would not submit to any attempt at cleaning up until she was quite finished. Her daughter knew that and so resisted the urge to pick up the paper napkin and wipe away the persistent globules of porridge.

The television had been left on at the other end of the long room that stretched towards the front of the house, away from the table where mother and daughter were both sitting. Maggie could see the screen, although the sound was indistinct. It seemed that switching the television on was like a gasp of relief in an awkward, tense situation: the relief of the normal and the ordinary, restoring a sense of the everyday. It didn't have to be closely observed or listened to; however, without its constant presence, chatter and comforting noise, a house was in danger of thinking for itself, and then who knew what might happen.

To her knowledge, it wasn't that her mother had requested it to be switched on (that wasn't in the care plan), and it certainly wasn't Maggie who had asked it to happen, as it did without fail on the mornings when the carers came. She wondered if it was in fact similar to the phenomenon of queuing: another unwritten rule, a social expectation. Nevertheless, neither of them minded that much and it was certainly nothing to send an instructive email about; after all, they could easily switch it off themselves. Maggie knew that her mother was not shy in coming forward when it came to complaining about something amiss. However, when she thought about it as she did now, it was a strange intrusion into their lives. She herself liked to watch television when there was something worth watching, but she couldn't bear it to be forever droning on, like an uninvited guest who sat on the sofa, immovable; conversing, spouting – partying raucously, sometimes – with anybody and everybody, whether they paid attention or not.

The more serious early morning news-style programme was drawing to a close with the subtle blending of several far less noteworthy items. Of course, Maggie thought, who was she to judge whether one thing was more important than another? She noticed that the atmosphere in the studio, the snappy presenters and the expert commentators and guests were becoming increasingly jocular and frivolous. Also, she noticed, everyone appeared to be in on a conspiracy to wear bright red – dresses, ties, lipstick, shoes – all matching, and she wondered whether this was normally the case or just a visually happy coincidence. Along the bottom of the screen ran a ticker-tape, informing each and every household of the most arresting events of the day, just in case you got too carried away with all the fun they appeared to be having on the studio sofas and forgot the real news happening in the world.

All at once the words she had heard so eloquently and so passionately proclaimed from the medieval pulpit in the early morning service came back to her. As she watched the glossy red lips smile and natter across the television screen in their living room, she heard the Canon declare once more:

'Go forth into the world...'

What was real – or rather, what was more real than the other: the soft, sugary drama played out on the modest flat screen, tucked into the corner where the bay window curved round to meet the adjoining wall? Or the words that had been thrown towards her as a lifeline when she had sat silently in the pew?

It didn't end with *going forth*; that was only the beginning.

'Into the world...'

She thought about the world, her world, and how it unfolded each day, bringing news, challenges, monotony, confrontation, comfort and battle. The particular Bible passage that the Canon had read out to them earlier on in the service was from the Gospel of Matthew, chapter 28, verses 16 to 20, right at the end of the book. It was commonly titled 'The Great Commission' where Jesus, just before His ascension to heaven, spoke His final words to His disciples as the Son of God here on earth. Contained in those words, explained the Canon, were command, truth and promise, all of equal importance and, in fact, so he had strongly implied, those three things were inseparable.

The command to all who choose to believe in Jesus was to – yes, she knew it – go forth. The truth was in what Jesus said about Himself: 'All authority in heaven and on earth has been given to me.' The promise was that those who follow would never be left alone. Yet for the daughter, sitting there with her aged mother, who was quietly embalming herself with porridge, the world, both serious and superficial, flitting before her on the screen, was not a picture that seemed to fit with the Lord's Great Commission. That world was not her world. Although she was a follower of Jesus, she did not feel like a disciple. The two spheres jarred, clashing and flinching if she attempted to bring them together. So how could she *go forth into the world* if she felt lost, straddled between the two?

'There,' declared her mother as she pushed the slimy bowl away from her. She reached for the napkin to dab at the corners of her mouth with little realisation that a face flannel and some warm water were more in order. Maggie let her begin the process with the inadequate piece of paper while she fetched a soapy, wet facecloth from the sink in the downstairs toilet, which was situated off the kitchen. She came back to the table just as the scale of the problem was dawning on her mother who, with an utterly defeated piece of tissue, had found herself unequal to the task.

'Here, let me help you, Mum.' The daughter gently attacked the sticky remains on both her mother's chin and hands.

'You don't need to fuss so much. I can manage perfectly well!' her mother remonstrated, as was her wont; nevertheless, she allowed the ministrations to continue: the spirit was feisty but the flesh was ill-equipped. 'Now, then, I want to watch some television. Will you switch it on, please?'

The daughter opened her mouth to reply that it was already on – hadn't she heard it? – when thankfully the possible confrontational consequence of such an answer was quickly recalled, halting her. Instead, she helped her mother to stand, positioning her walking frame to the left of the chair where the old lady had been sitting. With one hand at her back while the other edged the chair away, she waited as her mother steadied herself and then turned, reaching forward to grab the top of the frame.

'My bones aren't what they used to be,' her mother said, as if announcing the sudden dawning of a truth previously unknown. She puffed and shook her head as she began the treacherous voyage across open seas, between the back and the front of the house; away from the table that looked out onto the very small back garden, towards the larger bay window that looked out onto the unassuming street beyond their front gate. From time to time she stopped, leaning down through the frame, the strain in her shoulders ever present. Maggie hovered between the double assignment of clearing the table and watching her mother's progress towards her destination: the high-backed, adjustable chair in the living room. Only when she knew her mother was sitting once again would she turn her full attention to other household tasks.

'I see you put the box on already. Keep her quiet in front of the telly, I know…' Such habitual, muttered untruths were not worth acknowledgement.

The daughter returned to her mother's side as she began to embark upon the tricky manoeuvre of turning and reversing into the chair, like a fully laden ferryboat reaching harbour and preparing to dock.

'I can manage, stop fussing.' Her mother tried to lift her hand to dismiss her daughter's attentions but thought better of it. The daughter took a small step away in response but left one hand at the ready behind her mother, the process nearly complete. Her mother landed with a gust of triumph, though it would be a minute before she could finish a sentence.

Without waiting for any such sentence to be uttered, Maggie began her own: 'Now, then. I'll bring you some water and your glasses. There's the remote control,' she pointed to the device on the table next to the chair, 'and I'll just be in the kitchen, washing up.'

As she turned to leave, her mother caught her arm. 'I don't like that one who came this morning. I don't trust her, not a bit. She's sly.'

'Oh, Mum, Alana's lovely. She's really kind. I think it's just going to take a bit of time to get used to her as she's new, but she's very experienced.'

'Huh, experienced, I should think so...'

'Now, what on earth do you mean by that? Actually, don't tell me. As I said, I'll be in the kitchen.'

Sometimes she felt it was impossible to keep her temper and not rise to every little quip or barb. And why, she so often thought, did her mother do it? What did she gain from such sniping, from such deliberately blinkered vision? Was it that her mother had always been like it and she hadn't really noticed? Were personality traits just exaggerated with age and infirmity? Was it an unconscious response to the fear of a shrinking world and the looming shadow of inescapable, unknowable death?

The umbrella had dried for the most part and Maggie moved it into the downstairs cloakroom. She ran the hot tap into the plastic bowl in the sink with a generous squeeze of detergent and plunged her hands into the steaming, foamy water. It was a particularly good moment, she thought, to shut your eyes and feel some other sensation rather than rain on your skin, or gloopy porridge on your fingers, or sharp words in your ear.

Opening her eyes, she found herself praying, 'Oh, Lord, this is my world and You have asked me to go forth into it, but I really don't know… I do not understand how I can. Please, please show me how…'

The Canon – he was a Canon in residence – had just returned from an extra-long walk in the rain. As soon as the morning service had ended, he had made himself unavailable for any sort of communication. He had de-vested in the vestry, the small back room especially designated for the purpose, and had, as swiftly as possible and with a great sense of urgency, hurried away from the vastness of the ecclesiastical walls. He had never felt like this before, not even in his fledgling Christian days, as far as he could remember, at least. He had never been overwhelmed by such fearful doubts and anxieties, such glories and exaltations, which pummelled his mind as if it were a ripe melon, vulnerable and completely unprotected from a well-aimed blow.

On reaching home he was glad that his wife was out. It wasn't that he couldn't talk to her – he had always felt that there were good lines of communication between them – rather, it was more that he wasn't quite ready to talk about what he had experienced that morning in the service.

It dawned on him that he hadn't actually had any breakfast and had only drunk a glass of water, so he suddenly made an effort to attend to the physical. Perhaps his blood sugar was low; this was something that could soon be remedied.

With a plate of toasted raisin bread and a cup of strong coffee balanced on a tray with one hand, he opened the door to his study with the other. His shabby but comfortable office chair welcomed him with appreciation, the knowledge of all things restored.

Having now satisfied his stomach, the Canon wiped the crumbs from his fingers with a tissue from the nearby box on the desk and picked up a pen, ready to scribble in his dog-eared notepad, which was ready and waiting to be used. It meant, of course, that he had to stop and think and run the unexpected – to him, quite unsettling – scene over again in his mind. He reached for his Bible; it was an instinctive reaction, one that you might think perfectly normal for a man of the cloth, but it was something he had always done since becoming a believer, even before he had chosen this particular pathway. Opening it up to the last chapter of the Gospel of Matthew once more, he started to read aloud the words of 'The Great Commission'. The result was not the same, though it was similar enough, and this time, instead of letting any fear or loss of control overtake him, he shut his eyes. He recalled and then studied the scene before him.

He was in the pulpit, just as he had been earlier that morning. The familiar features before him were insignificant: the immense stone structure of the building; the vast, smooth Norman pillars like the trunks of mighty oaks; the intricate pattern of vaults criss-crossing up in the ceiling above his head, the dark pews lined like ruts in a frozen winter field below him; all of this was just a vague and murky nothingness. What shone out across the scene, what blazed across his vision, was the light from the souls sitting before him. There were many, many souls – countless, in fact – and he knew that that had been completely wrong for a wet and windy weekday early morning service. Where had they come from and who were they? Instead of cold stone, the huge space was warm and filled with light, as if the stars had ventured down and were now pouring their radiance in through the stained-glass windows with far greater colour and vibrancy than their humanly crafted lenses could possibly produce. As he opened his mouth, speaking the words of the final prayer, 'Go forth!', his voice was all at once inexplicably powerful and ran like water over the people gathered before him. It had not been *his* voice at all, and then it dawned on him that that was why he had been so afraid.

The Canon's eyes flickered open and he stretched the lids, screwing them up and then opening them wide several times to dispel the image. It was not that he didn't want to see that picture ever again, as he was now aware of a growing understanding; rather, he wanted to make sure that he was still himself, that he wasn't sickening for something and that he had not lost any perception or clarity. In actual fact, there had been only the usual few in attendance that morning. It was just an ordinary rainy day with no sign of any change or of the clouds lifting, and he had merely spoken the words that he had spoken many, many times before at a service, and yet... and yet something heavenly had happened. Believers – many, many believers – had been caught up together in that moment, shining with the true life and goodness of God. It was as if his eyes had been opened for the very first time to see things as they really were.

An Old Testament passage from the second book of Kings came to the forefront of his mind, where in fear for his and his master's life, a great prophet's servant found his vision suddenly filled with the true picture of the heavenly armies of God, ranged for battle. Then another thought struck him: why on earth had he been surprised? Admittedly, it was not something he had specifically prayed for, that he was aware of; it was not the usual sort of thing that happens to priests or church ministers – again, that he was aware of – but why shouldn't it be? They were servants of God, the true and living God (a fact that nowadays often seemed to be at odds with the world in which they lived), so why shouldn't it be?

'Go forth into the world...'

To have been overwhelmed with fear was something he was now all at once ashamed of. Then, a further thought, a verse from the New Testament book of Hebrews 10 popped into his mind as if to rescue him from needless guilt: 'It is a dreadful thing to fall into the hands of the living God.' Moses had seen God and lived, but that was a rare occurrence. Jesus had walked on earth and had been seen by many, but that was God taking on human form '... the very nature of a servant, being made in human likeness ... being found in appearance as a man ...' so that He could take all our faults upon Himself and know what it was to be burdened by humanity; so that we would no longer need to be scared. And, he reminded himself, he knew that God was with him right there in that moment, and that He walked with him every day. Nevertheless, he was assured that it was understandable, appropriate even, to be frightened by the sudden and unforeseen revelation of a heavenly reality.

The Canon tipped his head back to finish his coffee. Throughout the preceding moments he had hung on like a shipwrecked survivor clinging to driftwood, amid the crashing waves of many thoughts; thoughts that had finally brought him back to make sense of what he had experienced that morning. The next thing to do, and naturally for him the only thing to do, was to talk to God about it all and offer himself once again as a surrendered, faithful, expectant follower of Christ. Yes, he thought, expectant.

In Peace

It was the usual sort of row that started at about the usual sort of time, which was about eight o'clock in the evening. Maggie first heard the distant rumblings, which she knew would gradually staccato, becoming loud and clumsy, as she went outside the front door with the recycling box ready for the next morning's collection. She recognised the pattern: at first it would begin like this, with what sounded like the random throwing of small objects, followed by a lull; this would be chased away by snatches of loud, raised voices; then further crashes, snapping after the voices, going round and round about, full circle with ever-increasing momentum. It was like the onset of a great storm where heavy drops of rain would mark the pavement and the windows, and where distant clashes of thunder would race in, hot on the heels of the rain.

She winced as the clatter of her own collection of bottles and tins added to the din, and she hoped they wouldn't think she was in any way joining in or, worse, protesting against the burgeoning showdown.

These next-door neighbours were a strange couple. If you met them on the street outside the house, or at the local corner shop, or behind the houses where the garages were, there was never a problem. They were friendly and ordinarily polite; it could be said that their relationship was ordinarily normal, both between themselves and with everyone else. However, behind closed doors, things were clearly quite different.

Maggie turned to walk back into the house. The front of each property, adjacent in their mirror image, had similarities, despite displaying different finishes. Granted, her front door was probably the wooden original but it was in good condition and painted in a dark maroon red, while next door's was a modern UPVC white-fronted door. She had a few pots of lavender, a bay and two small conifers standing idly to attention on either side, while they had a small log store and their recycling box, which they had so far forgotten to put out. It looked as if it would remain forgotten at least for the remainder of the night.

The quarrelling, or, as it sometimes seemed to be, all out warfare, was not unusual, and that was why she thought they must be a strange couple. They appeared to thrive on the adrenaline created from slamming doors, from words spat out like machine-gun fire and darting shrapnel. Although, she continued to think, her scant knowledge of how couples functioned was not something she had gained from personal experience. Somehow, she had remained single, apart from an occasional friendship which had once or twice led to what could be described as a date, or even a romance, though never anything more; nothing deep or lasting. And she had long since concluded that it never really bothered her that much, so perhaps that was how it was meant to be. The desire for children or just the sharing of one's life with somebody who was always there – like the paper-patterned walls surrounding the fireplace in the living room, at which she stared every night without acknowledgement – none of this had ever been of any great importance to her. Her closest experience of how a marriage functioned had been her parents. They had never shouted at each other; well, her father at least had never raised his voice (he would never have dared), yet they had muddled along in the comfort of familiar nagging and acquiescent acceptance. At an opportune moment a good many years before, Maggie had moved out into a flat in the town, where she had lived her uneventful life, subsequently returning to care for her mother when her father passed away. Then, when this couple had moved in next door just a few years ago, the fights had been a revelation.

Her hand was on her own front door, ready to push it open as she had left it on the latch. It would not be a good situation to be in, locked out of her own house with her mother at the mercy of the television all night. Even though there was a security key-safe attached to the wall behind one of the taller plants, so that when she was out at work the carers could let themselves in to see to her mother, she was still in the habit of latching the door open.

As she began to push, a sudden, almighty thud shook the narrow strip of wall between the two houses. There was an alarming, cracking sort of sound caused by the hinges of their white front door heaving, almost splitting, as a figure crashed against it. She froze, her hand still poised on her own door; her front teeth biting her bottom lip and her heart pounding. She felt as if she daren't move, as if moving in any way would make things so much worse. For several seconds, which seemed more like minutes, there was no activity or sound or sign of life from next door. Then all at once she heard the rush of footsteps down the stairs, and a shadowy figure, blurred by the toughened glass in the panels of their front door, stirred and attempted to get up from the floor.

Letting out a breath, Maggie hovered with one foot on her doorstep, wondering whether she should gently knock and see if there was anything she could do – what could she possibly do?

Relieved, though with a little shame at such relief, the weight of next door's acute responsibility was lifted as a more manageable, chronic one took its place. Her mother called from the front room, 'Where are you? I need to go to the bathroom!'

A good hour or so later, the need for the bathroom, which had since escalated into a full-blown bedtime operation, was coming, for the most part, to a satisfactory conclusion.

The long, slow shuffle to the bathroom downstairs, because it would be too risky to wait until she got to the upstairs one, had been followed by detailed though unnecessary instructions for a bedtime hot drink, which Maggie had embarked upon while she waited for her mother to finish using the toilet. They had then travelled along the narrow pass between staircase and living room until they had reached the bottom of the stairs, where the stairlift stood ready for use, like a mountain cable car set to escort them up to the peak.

'I don't know why you don't put the arm of the stairlift down ready for me beforehand, you know. It would save so much time.' Her mother's comment was both habitual and untrue: there would be only a matter of seconds spared if this minor manoeuvre were completed in advance. However, the daughter knew better than to take the bait. Without responding, Maggie helped her mother onto the seat of the stairlift and pressed the switch; she then followed on behind. Operating the lift seemed to be a task that was beyond the capability of the rider.

Maggie resisted the temptation to say something along the lines of, 'Off we go, then!' which was what she always felt the urge to do at this point. Childlike, optimistic joviality did not seem to suit their relationship; she knew that if she did attempt to lighten the situation, her mother's rejoinder would not be harmonious.

The top of the stairs achieved, further bathroom and bedtime rituals were undertaken until, with end-of-the-day finality, her mother was sitting on the edge of her bed in her nightie. She reached out towards her bedside table for the last of the day's medication. Her bedroom was the main one at the front of the house, the house where she had lived for most of her married life and now shared with Maggie. This room was uncluttered and warm, where pools of light, in shades of muted amber and cream, were repeated in the bedclothes, lampshades and curtains. It was the most peaceful room in the house and, Maggie remembered, it was the room where her father had died. She wondered if her mother ever thought about that and then chastised herself: of course she did!

Maggie went over to the front bay window, a duplicate of the one below, to draw the curtains and to take a quick glance along the street. The thought had crossed her mind that perhaps she might see an ambulance or some other emergency vehicle parked outside next door; or instead, she might see a gap in the road where the neighbours' car had been, indicating that someone had driven off in a hurry. Everything looked as it always did; everything was still in the easy, drizzling rain. The storm that had threatened to rage all night had died away.

'I'm ready,' called her mother from across the room. Her daughter knew she was truly tired because her conversation was minimal and lacking in acerbity. Stepping back from the dark though nonetheless enticing vision of the wet street outside, lit by glistening balls of dancing light here and there from lampposts, other front windows and car headlights, the daughter moved back towards the far side of the bed nearer the bedroom door. A little framed cross-stich motif, which leaned against a wooden jewellery box on her mother's chest of drawers, caught her eye. It had been there forever and was probably some of her mother's handiwork from years ago, when she had been able to undertake more dextrous occupations. It was a verse from John 14:27: 'Peace I leave with you; my peace I give you.' The scrolling words were entwined with floral sprigs and ribbons; the bold colours had long since faded. As if like clockwork, the rest of the words that belonged to them came flooding back to Maggie's mind: '... I do not give to you as the world gives. Do not let your hearts be troubled and do not be afraid.'

Lifting her mother's feet into bed, and with them her weary bones, before covering them with the light duvet, she smiled. When her mother wasn't fighting against the world, the pain, the loss of independence and the creep of death, she was so much more at peace. In her surrender to all things beyond herself she was embraced by peace, and here in this room, this evening, it was almost tangible. Maggie rarely talked with her mother very deeply about spiritual matters. They were both aware of the other's faith and belief, of their steadfastly held traditions; yet as these things had hardly ever been discussed, which was nobody's fault in particular, their thoughts remained half-hidden in a fog, blurred by a lack of intimacy, undisclosed and untouched except in their own hearts. And it was in the heart, so the words of Jesus promised, that there would be peace.

This was a train of thought not to be ignored. She had realised this as soon as she had read the words in the frame. Echoes, so strongly imprinted in her mind, from earlier that morning could not be so easily dismissed.

'Go forth into the world in peace.'

The next morning, Maggie had to be up very early. She would bring her mother her first cup of tea and help her use the commode, as she had also had to do several times during the night. This was nothing new. Today was Wednesday, a working day, and after springing in and out of the shower and snatching a piece of toast, washed down with half a cup of tea, she would normally head straight off to work. To bolster the fragile moments between her leaving and the first carer arriving, she made sure her mother had her alarm bracelet on. She had also managed to shove a batch of laundry into the machine in the hope that one of the carers, either on the early morning visit or the lunchtime visit, might be able to hang it out; that was, of course, if the rain stopped.

With first light it had still been drizzling, but now the pale, lacy sweep of cloud, which she glimpsed from her bedroom window, held more promise than yesterday. However, what she really wanted to do that morning was somehow find a way of talking to her neighbours: either one of them, or both of them, whatever the situation afforded.

There would be some folk who would be thinking along the lines of – yes, good idea, have a talk with the neighbours and tell them that they are really beginning to disturb the peace; these shouting matches have got to stop! That would be the response of some, but that was not what Maggie was thinking, not at all. During the night, her sleep had been realised in broken portions; her own wakefulness encouraged by the need to help her mother, and in between her rationed dreams she had pondered peace. What did it truly mean to have peace? Was it the peace she had finally seen in her mother's face as her body and bones found the relief of her bed and sleep? Was it purely something akin to the scene she had watched on the street below where there was little sign of life, or at least, little sign of any activity? Was it the sudden end to the fight next door? Was it how she should feel every day as the Christian she believed herself to be? Mulling over these possibilities, she had been forced at last to leave them behind, like unnecessary baggage on a long journey. Peace described these things, but this was not the truth about the promise of peace, the promise of peace from the God she believed in: *'Go forth into the world in peace.'*

Surely, this peace was not a sense of serenity which could be summoned up or called for. It was not a guise lending one the ability to float angelically above the world's troubles, unruffled and unfazed by humanity. If it were, then you would never actually have to engage with the people you lived among; you would never feel their pain and suffering, and so would be unable to bring any comfort. From the moment the Canon had uttered that prayer in the early morning service, when his face had shone with unrestrained vision, the words that had so often meant nothing had suddenly meant everything; they had been flung out towards the small congregation as a challenge. As though from the mouth of a fellow disciple awakened to a fresh revelation of his calling, the woman had felt the call to arms and had wanted with every fibre of her being to respond. But to go in *peace*? Well, this had had her stumped.

She was not valiant – *go forth*. Her life was small – *into the world*. And she was introverted and nervous – *in peace*. How could she begin to accomplish anything? Then the other words, the ones in the nondescript, cheap plastic frame on her mother's chest of drawers, had added their voice to the mix and she had glimpsed the truth: the promised peace is a peace that is given, not manufactured. And if it is promised and given by the one, true living God – God made manifest in Jesus Christ – then it is not something incumbent upon herself. It was in trust and obedience that she would find peace. She did not need to be afraid.

Draining and then rinsing her mug under the tap, she began to feel, however, that she *was* afraid. First, there was the *how* of starting a conversation with her next-door neighbours: how should she go about it? Should she knock on the door? She was afraid that that might anger them if they were having a lie-in. If she did catch them to talk to, would they be irritated, thinking that she was really just being nosy or wanted to have a subtle jibe at them for disturbing the peace? She was afraid of what they might think. She was afraid of burning any bridges. She was afraid of what might come out of her mouth. She was afraid of her weakness. So where was the promise of peace?

'My peace I give you. I do not give to you as the world gives ...'

The world gives wanting something in return, she thought, yet God promises peace when I am surrendered, when I am just myself. The woman gathered her coat and her bag. She launched a swift prayer upwards (it seemed to be the right direction): 'Oh Lord, help me get this right!' Calling a final 'Goodbye, Mum!' up the stairs, she went out of the front door into a grey but dry morning.

There was no need to knock on any front door. With languid movements, her neighbour, a woman called Rachel, was carrying her recycling box out towards the pavement. She was in her dressing gown and slippers and her wavy hair was tied up together in a loosely scrunched band. As she had her back to Maggie, there was nothing more to be noted. Glancing at the white UPVC door, she noticed that it was open, obviously because her neighbour was about to go back inside. Was it hanging at an odd angle from the hinges, perhaps? A front door was not usually a flimsy barrier between the occupants and the outside world, so to have fallen against it so substantially, to have caused some damage, would surely indicate injury. Maggie pulled her own red front door to and the heavy sound caused her neighbour to turn her head briefly.

'Morning, Rachel.' Maggie could not remember ever having used her name before when greeting her. She took a deep breath and then added, 'I'm glad I caught you.'

Having deposited the recycling box on the pavement, Rachel straightened up, wincing a little, and turned towards Maggie. Apart from this flinching there were no other signs of trauma. On the other hand, Maggie thought, the twinges in themselves did not necessarily signify anything in particular. It could just be the early morning stiffness of a body that had once been a lot younger, or perhaps from a recently pulled muscle.

Rachel shuffled back up the short path and for a moment they were level, face to face across the low wall that separated the two properties. As if all disguises were suddenly dropped, they said nothing but looked each other in the eye. Perhaps one neighbour was searching for signs of anger or disgust or outrage in the eyes of the other. She found none.

Maggie reached out her hand and touched the purple fluffy sleeve of Rachel's dressing gown. She noted that the dressing gown was the complete opposite of anything she herself would have worn. Although it was not brand new, it was bright and rich to the touch, with pink flowers appliqued in blue thread at random points all across the front; it struck her as being a garment that might belong to someone who was carefree and quite at ease with themselves. Or maybe it was just the garment of someone who wanted to be. She wondered whether her neighbour thought of it like that.

'How are you?' Maggie asked.

Rachel's eyes filled with a thick film of tears which threatened to burst. She searched for a tissue and it was a moment or two before she could answer. After stuffing the tissue back into the pocket of her dressing gown, she mumbled, 'I'm so sorry…'

Maggie frowned. 'You don't need to apologise. I'm just really concerned, for you both, I suppose. How can I help?'

Rachel shook her head. 'You can't, and don't be — concerned, I mean. It's just that…' She had to stop again and make use of another tissue. Maggie waited. 'It's just that there's nothing anybody can do. I get so angry. We *both* get so angry. I think we're just angry people, and in some ways I suppose that makes us well suited. Who else would have us?!' She managed a little laugh at this great irony.

Maggie smiled and said, 'I need to go to work now, but…'

This interjecting revelation of circumstances overtook the neighbour and her face fell. 'Oh, look, I've held you up. There's me, blubbering to you on the doorstep, when you should be somewhere else, *and* you've got your mum to look after and all that. I'm so sorry.' She had now run out of clean tissues and Maggie pulled a fresh one out of her coat pocket to give to her.

She said, 'It's absolutely fine. I wanted to talk to you. Really. I've got some free time on Saturday morning. Do you want to have a coffee?'

Maggie was surprised that her neighbour didn't take much persuading. Although she had to leave her wringing a soggy tissue just inside her front door, she felt that something had changed. Whether for her or for Rachel or for them both, it didn't matter.

Leaving her house from the front meant that Maggie had a little further to walk to the bus stop, but what did that signify after such a conversation? Some would say that it hadn't been much of a conversation, that she had achieved very little, that she had only managed to make the poor woman cry. Yet Maggie knew that this was not true, not a bit, and she sensed a well of confidence brimming up from the depths of her soul. This was what it meant to *'Go forth into the world in peace'*. She was convinced of it.

Be of Good Courage

The cathedral spires stood out against the bright sky, which in places was blotchy with scattered cloud of every form and hue. It was a constantly shifting backdrop; altering, transforming within mere minutes as the restless currents of wind found that they could not linger over this part of the world. They headed ever onwards in an urgent search for new horizons.

During recent weeks the falcons had been busy with their mating rituals, swooping and diving, catching prey on the wing; the female even at times performing in-flight acrobatics in order to catch the hunted prey as it fell from her partner's beak. Their nest – or scrape, as it should be called – had been fashioned from the surrounding debris, bits of stone and matter deposited by the elements; it was not a bed that had been painstakingly built from foraged materials. In the world of falcons, this is not how it is done. Their usual habitats of craggy cliff faces and other remote locations have now expanded to include the rugged inaccessibility of the urban environment. These days, towering stone buildings constructed with their own peculiar architectural intricacies, such as cathedrals, provide just as robust a shelter and defence as any cliff face. Concerning this particular cathedral, the installation of webcams as well as specifically donated gravel and shale ensured that they were observed without disturbance; these slight touches of human interference proved beneficial to the birds. Regardless of its method of manufacture, the scrape was growing and filling the small, sheltered alcove hidden within the crested towers. The spires remained aloof, tolerating the formation of this falcon

45

nest, in the full knowledge that by the end of the season the wind would see to the aftermath of hatching, feeding and fledging.

As the sun moved round the tapered stone the long day through, warming every inch and allowing even the falcons a moment or two to soak it up as it paraded across the sky, a lone human figure scuttled across the cobblestones beneath. The spires, if they had noticed, might have wondered at this show of haste: it was not raining and in fact so far it was the brightest day they had experienced for a long time. Why could these human irritations, which bustled about in the streets below all day long, not stand still and erect in the sunshine, as they managed to do? Why were they not made of clean, cold stone, resilient to everything that was thrown at them? Why could they not take pleasure in the passing presence of wandering clouds?

It was late morning, and the Canon was hurrying away from a meeting at the local council. He was part of a team (a token effort) that had been set up to look into proposals concerning new social-housing projects. Now there was yet another meeting to attend, back at the cathedral with the Dean, and he was not feeling very courageous. It had nothing to do with the first meeting, which had just been ponderous, laborious and, he suspected, intrinsically ineffectual. In his opinion, it all boiled down to the fact that however revolutionary their collective ideals purported to be, the necessary finances and commitment from investors who watched and waited in the wings would never be forthcoming; as far as he was concerned, it was all just part of the game of politics.

Perhaps he was too cynical, he thought, but if he was, then in this instance at least it was with good reason, and he wasn't alone. No, the knot of growing anxiety that tightened, stretching down from his throat towards his empty stomach (the lack of any opportunity to grab lunch between meetings exacerbating the situation) was mainly owing to the fact that he was about to meet with the Dean. This was not an uncommon occurrence; for obvious reasons they met quite regularly. Nevertheless, the

Canon had never felt fully at ease in his presence. Whether it had something to do with their personalities not quite clicking; whether it was to do with their difference in rank, which he sensed was underlined more often than not; whether it had something to do with a lurking shadow in the far corner of his mind – muted doubts about the integrity and character of the man he was about to meet, he was ashamed to admit – he couldn't be sure. The only points that marked these feelings, which often rumbled through his mind like the distant murmuring of a goods train, were weak and insubstantial. It was the odd, cutting comment thrown abroad then quickly brushed away; the single swift roll of the eyes up towards the ceiling or the sky, depending on where they happened to be at the time; or the deep, exaggerated sigh blown out through puffed cheeks at an inappropriate moment.

Today, all at once these thoughts were running at full speed, rattling along the line towards him, threatening to run him down in spectacular fashion; his inability to stop them filled him with humiliation. They were, after all, brothers in Christ. They were called by the same God into this bold and weighty life of service. He stopped his chase across the cobbles, just for a moment, to collect his runaway thoughts, to halt the train in its tracks, and he offered up a little prayer to that effect. The strength of feeling was forceful today. With a sense of feebleness, he realised that because he wanted to talk about what had happened to him yesterday in the early morning service, these feelings might overwhelm him if he let them.

'Go forth into the world!' He remembered almost shouting from the pulpit over the gathered heads, the shining, glorious heads of his congregation; a congregation simultaneously many and yet few. He remembered how the call had urged him on in a way he had never experienced, as if the door of heaven had opened just for a moment, pouring out a delightful and yet fear-filled taste of another world. How often we forget, he thought, those of us who believe: we forget the truth and magnificence of what we believe.

He was anxious because his vision presented as something childlike. This was nothing academic, nothing to theologically dissect. It had just been, and he knew that it still was, the inexplicably glorious, potent, living truth. The Dean was a far more accomplished man of letters than he would ever be, so high and lifted up in his breadth of knowledge that he might not be able to look down and see clearly, and therefore understand, the earnestness in the face of his inferior brother.

'Be of good courage.'

Still halted three-quarters of the way across the cobbled square, the Canon heard the familiar words strike home. This time, although resolute, they were softly spoken. He had prayed. He had brought the matter up in his own private meeting with God as he chased across the stones between the council building and the cathedral; and although his emotions said one thing, the promise of God said another, and he knew on which of these two elements he could, beyond doubt, rely.

A sharp cry pierced the sky above his head and he twisted his neck backwards. With one hand over his eyes, he shielded the most forceful of the sun's rays which streamed out from behind a small, dark cloud, towards the topmost peaks of the building. The stark silhouette of a falcon returning to its roost was now a monochrome negative; a temporary image emblazoned upon all he saw as he turned once again towards the stone arch and open doorway. Blinking and shaking his head in a vain attempt to shift the spots of light and pattern of bird on the wing from his sight, he entered the dark cavern of the cathedral.

Sitting somewhere in the middle of the bus, on her way to work, Maggie watched the blur of folk outside rushing by. When the bus ran at good speed, she was only afforded a brief glimpse of people, just like her, hurrying to work or college or school. At other times, when the traffic stalled their progress, or when a red light halted it completely, it was the other way around. Then, the non-stop footsteps of the pedestrians, moving at pace, afforded them merely a snatched glance of the woman's face at the window of the bus, if they were of a mind to look up from the pavement. For obvious reasons it was much easier to watch passers-by and look around you when someone else was doing the driving.

At the beginning of the bus journey, Maggie had still felt the dying waves of elation at having managed a conversation with Rachel, her neighbour. She had achieved even more than that. They had arranged to meet up, and now there was the possibility of friendship, which she hoped would be helpful, perhaps to them both. And maybe, she thought, she would even be able to share some of the things she believed. It was then that the dullness of doubt had set in: who was she to think that Rachel would want to spend time with *her*? Surely the meeting would never happen. She would get home from work to find a note saying that actually something had come up and Saturday was off. And even if by some miracle they did succeed in going for a coffee, one word from her about anything religious and that would be that. Maggie felt her courage failing, and as she got up from her seat to leave the bus, the plain truth hit her: she was nothing.

The building where she worked was unprepossessing, generic and bland. The part-time post she held was of a similar nature; however, the work was steady and straightforward; on the whole, her colleagues were friendly.

Over several years working in the office, she had observed the natural formation of various groups and cliques: there were those who frequently met outside work for drinks and heavy-duty socialising; there was an informal running club, and recently a few fanatical cyclists had been trying to drum up financial support for their charity races. From time to time an unofficial book group popped up. From what she could tell, this latter endeavour tended to follow a similar pattern: read the book (although that was not a prerequisite), chat about the book (this was also not necessary) and drink wine. She had wondered if that should now be the dictionary definition of the term 'book club' – that was, of course, if it needed any explanation.

None of these groups suited her, either in taste or in time, and to her it was no loss. To the onlooker, she knew she might appear to be someone who was shy and needed drawing out of themselves, and on occasion some had made unwanted efforts in this direction, although she had not been ungrateful. Nevertheless, for Maggie it was more about being satisfied with who and where she was in life. As she took the steps up to the main door of the building, she thought about her bus journey that morning and stopped: was she satisfied?

In terms of work and social activities, she thought, yes, she was satisfied with her situation there. Nonetheless, when it came to matters of the soul, it was different. There had always been an inner turmoil created through belief. She had found the Word of God; she had met the Word of God and something fundamental had changed within her. That very Word had told her that it was no secret to keep to herself: it was something that made everything new and therefore something to be declared loudly, reliably and constantly. However, as anyone who had ever believed would know, that was never easy, and for those of an introverted disposition it was even more of a challenge. It was a battle she sensed keenly. Since the Canon had spoken only yesterday morning, she and everyone else who had been there – and if she thought about it, everyone else who had ever heard those words – had been called, once again, to *'Go forth into the world in peace…'*

Shutting her eyes for a moment she recalled the scene again, remembering the light, the burning glow that had surrounded them. The power in his voice, like a forthright commander of troops; the spirit which had flowed up from the soles of her feet. She opened her eyes as another voice spoke to her.

'Hi, you alright?'

She must have looked as if she were going to pass out. 'Oh, yes. I'm sorry, I was just thinking, just remembering something…'

The female colleague who had addressed her nodded in understanding. 'Yeah, I know what you mean. It's a pain when you forget something. As long as you're OK.' She turned away and continued up the steps towards the main door, and Maggie thought she was probably inwardly relieved that the mousy woman she had spoken to wasn't going to be ill in front of her, making her late for a meeting.

It didn't really matter to Maggie if she had been misunderstood; she was just relieved that she didn't have to explain what she could hardly explain to herself. She followed her colleague up to the main entrance; she held the door open for a group of co-workers hurrying in behind her. Vague, habitual morning greetings were murmured and exchanged, and thoughts about spiritual battles were lost.

Be of good courage.'

Where, she thought, did that courage come from, and what, most particularly, did she really need that courage for?

Several hours later, the Canon and the Dean were sitting together in a modest conference room, deep within the confines of the cathedral. It was quite cosy with plenty of light. The walls were lined with modern shelving, there to brace the body of books with which the room was filled. There was a good quality, red-patterned carpet underfoot and an oval oak table with adequate seating, around which a small group could meet.

Today, however, as planned, it was just the two of them closeted together around the table. It was not an extended meeting – it had already eaten into the lunch hour – but at least they had some coffee to stave off any distracting pangs of hunger. A few papers were out on the table between them, the contents of which they had already covered. The Dean reached out to gather together his own particular papers. He glanced at his watch, appearing eager to finish. However, when they had first sat down, the Canon had mentioned a personal matter, which as yet they had not covered.

'So, if we can safely steer these issues along the appropriate channels...' The Dean flicked the papers in his hand. Then almost as an aside, he asked, 'What was it you wanted to talk about?'

The Canon had both dreaded and longed for this moment. So far, he had failed to find the courage of expression. A constant discussion batted back and forth inside his mind – *it's not that important or unusual; it probably happened to everyone from time to time; the Dean might think it was of no importance; but he might on the other hand suspect that he was having a breakdown; was he having a breakdown? Perhaps he should just keep quiet* – all of which had worn him out.

He picked up his coffee cup and took a gulp of the tepid remains. He swallowed uncomfortably and then, trying to sound as casual as possible, he asked, 'Do you ever have visions?'

The Dean frowned, tilting his head a little further back, widening the space between them. 'Visions, eh? What sort of visions?'

'It's nothing odd or unstable, of course,' the Canon mumbled, and he tried to smile as if to dismiss the whole thing.

'So this is something you've experienced?' The Dean's expression indicated that he now began to understand what he was being told.

'Well, as I said, nothing really that untoward, but...'

'I imagine it's been a little unsettling, though, as you seem quite nervous.'

'Yes. I suppose I am rather unsettled, as you put it.' The Canon leaned his elbows on the table and rubbed his head before straightening up once more. Taking the courage now available to him by the voicing of the matter, he described to the Dean what had happened to him the previous morning, at the early service. It didn't take long. In fact, he tried to keep it as brief and as factual as possible, in an effort to dismiss any hint that he was losing his grip. 'So,' he concluded, 'that was the Blessing, and I have never experienced anything like it.'

The Dean was quiet; he looked thoughtful, and the Canon closed his eyes and was thankful that he seemed in no mood to hurry away or, worse, deride his feelings. Their subsequent exchange developed into a short series of statements and questions, as if they were naturalists embarking on a tentative examination of a strange and exotic creature on the table before them.

'Did you notice any effect on the congregation?' the Dean asked.

That was a very good question and one which the Canon hadn't really considered. A rush of guilt swept over him. He had been so wrapped up in his own experience and reactions that he had forgotten to think beyond himself.

'I didn't, I have to say. I'm sorry.'

'Well, I shouldn't worry too much about it, then. These things do occur from time to time.'

'Do you think so?' asked the Canon. 'I mean, biblically, historically, of course. People had visions, yes, but it never crossed my mind... I mean, I wasn't anticipating this.' Perhaps he had been wrong about his superior's seeming interest.

All at once the Dean stood and, pushing his papers into a plastic file, he coughed and made to leave. 'Let me know if it happens again and don't forget to pray about it, of course.' A brief, benign smile passed over his face and then disappeared. He left the door open behind him.

A new mix of emotions and questions began to bombard the Canon's mind: he was all at once angry and then ashamed. Had he been courageous or foolish? The Dean was right: he should pray some more about this; but had his parting advice been as dismissive as it sounded, lacking in any real sincerity? I feel isolated, he thought, I am surrounded by spirituality yet I am alone in this.

Standing up from the table, he picked up his thin case containing his laptop and folders, slid the remaining papers inside and zipped it shut. The Dean had left his coffee cup behind so the Canon picked both mugs up and sighed. He looked out of the narrow window, the only one in the room. Early spring foliage, emerging bold and bright from supposedly dead twigs and branches, framed the glass from the outside. Before he realised, the Canon found himself praying. It was as natural as breathing.

'Oh, Lord, if I've spoken when I shouldn't have done, if I've acted foolishly or thought falsely, then please forgive me.' Then with his eyes tight shut, he added, 'Please help me.'

Turning from the window, a new picture entered his mind. This was not a vision but purely an image suddenly revealed by well-remembered words. He saw Jesus in the Garden of Gethsemane, where He had prayed in anguish, His sweat as drops of blood; His closest friends dozing in another corner in ignorance and incomprehension. *He* had been alone and misunderstood in the face of a task unequalled in history. Shaking his head to rid himself of an unwanted thought that accused him of comparing his predicament with that of the Lord's, the Canon merely took the lesson from this momentary insight. In these battles, he thought, we are alone, no one can fight them for us. Our faith must be our own and no one else's. However, Jesus has been there before us and the pattern of crying out to God is one we can all firmly and freely grasp hold of with confidence.

'Be of good courage.'

Courage was there for the asking, a ready and open offer. Time and again, throughout the Scriptures, there were so many instances of the call to be courageous, despite our frailty and inept handling of situations.

No, he thought, the vision had been real. He was sure. He had experienced it to embolden others. As part of the cathedral chapter he had recently taken on the role of mission and outreach director; perhaps he had not fully understood until then what that signified. The call to *'Go forth'* is even more potent today than yesterday, he told himself, and I shall not be afraid.

Pondering these things, the Canon moved towards the open door. He thought about the question the Dean had posed; perhaps it was more important than he had realised. Of the folk attending the service, who else had experienced something spiritual? Who else had seen the windows of heaven open and the kingdom of God revealed?

Hold Fast That Which Is Good

It was still dry when Maggie stepped off the bus a stop earlier than usual that Wednesday afternoon. There was a brisk, businesslike clarity about the sky above the city where insignificant clouds were sent scurrying by, chased along by a busy breeze. The rain-soaked pavements had almost dried; only the gaps between each slab and crack and tarmacked join showed signs of previous precipitation. A few resistant puddles remained, encouraging wet footprints to mark their territory on either side.

Getting off at this particular bus stop fulfilled a useful purpose in her weekly routine as the route encompassed a small, independent corner shop where she could top up her groceries. As she didn't drive a car these days, the majority of their shopping was ordered online; it was one of the simplest means of tackling some of her domestic difficulties. She had learned to drive years ago, but in her current situation she found car ownership wasn't necessary or cost effective. Nevertheless, and here she was not much different from anybody else, there was always the need to pick up extras: spur-of-the-moment items and things unobtainable online. Of course, you could buy anything online these days – anything – but anything was not always everything.

She had finished work that day at 2.30pm, which was part of her fixed weekly pattern. The morning had flowed much the same as usual, without any great stress or strain, and she had had a more than normal, lengthy chat with a colleague when she had stopped to make a coffee mid-morning. This person had actually asked her about the cathedral and which services she attended. It was only on reflection that Maggie realised how significant this was and then, with a sinking heart, how little she had said; she could have said so much more! She had been bothered by doubts and her own inadequacies during the remaining hours at work; she had struggled to concentrate on her tasks.

The bus journey home (well, nearly home, as she still had to pop to the local shop) was similar to the journey out that morning: on both occasions she had been preoccupied with spiritual matters, pertinent to her own particular Christian growth. In the morning she had been bright, enthused even, with a courageous step and a positive response as a result of the conversation with her neighbour, Rachel. In the afternoon she was biting her lip, anxious that she had missed an opportunity and had not been courageous enough during the unexpected conversation with her colleague. Then all at once, out of the blue, halfway along the bus route home, it came to her.

'Hold fast that which is good.'

Like an unforeseen message popping up on her phone, the words of the Blessing caught her by surprise. Previously she had always envisaged *her* hands gripping on to goodness when she had heard this prayer, as if *she* were the one responsible for keeping hold. When in silence her own lips had formed these words, she had always pictured goodness as if it were a bundle of sheets or a string of ropes held by hands that were tight and sore from the constant straining; a battle never to be won, in this world at least. However, at that moment, a new picture filled her mind. Instead of her own hands vainly halting the slow, steady slipping away of goodness, she saw other hands aiding her in her journey of faith. Goodness was not a trail of fraying fabric, worn out and past its best, but rather a solid handrail, pinned into rock, with practical grip-holds; more than enough to climb a mountain or bridge a gap. Goodness would not fail because she did. That which was good in her life was from God. It was good that she had had those conversations today, no matter that in her own mind's eye she felt that perhaps she had not handled them correctly. In that moment of happy and relieved realisation, Maggie thanked the Lord, her God, 'Whose goodness faileth never …' The goodness of God: all at once she saw clearly that it was a gift to those who believed and trusted in Him; it was the sure lifeline to the top.

The power of the prayer she had heard, seen and felt yesterday morning had been altogether new, though not brand new. It was not as if her whole life had been changed from one state to another. No, everything was the same, yet in the revelation she had seen the light of truth pouring over them – all those gathered there – like warm showers after a heatwave in summer. The lives of those who believed had meaning and impact in this world beyond the visible. It was a lot to take in on one bus journey.

The corner shop, although not actually situated on a corner, looked welcoming, sandwiched between the rows of narrow Edwardian terraced houses. A few racks of fruit and veg boxes stood outside on a table covered with faded strips of artificial turf. Also outside, at one end of the shopfront a tall display rack containing the main national newspapers and a couple of local free papers stood before the window, which although large, was almost obliterated by a gaudy patchwork of both valid and invalid adverts, flyers and business cards. It wasn't a bustling shop, though it was well used by locals in a regular fashion. The owner and his family who staffed the small concern probably set their watches by the everyday ins and outs of their familiar customers.

Maggie thought it was a comfortable place; shabby and cluttered, but it was a good fit, like the age-old perfect cardigan you just couldn't bring yourself to get rid of. The unfamiliar and sometimes outlandish melange of items for sale would rival any shopping website, although its high prices precluded most folk from doing a serious weekly shop there; that and the impractical side of the process. She hesitated outside, scanning the eclectic parade of fruit on offer. Bypassing the more exotic items, she wondered if they had enough apples at home. The image of the half-empty fruit bowl on the kitchen worktop came into her mind. Yes, they could manage with what they had, after all. Anyway, she was really the only one who ate apples these days, unless they were cooked. Also, she remembered that they had a couple of bananas still and a few mandarin oranges.

Walking on past the fresh produce, she skirted round a skew, wire stand, the compartments of which were stuffed with shiny-packaged greetings cards, into the shadow of the shop's interior. In actual fact, although the immediate entrance to the shop was relatively dark, the aisles between the rows of shelving were well lit with fluorescent tubes which buzzed overhead. Dull and dusty cardboard boxes littered the gangways, displaying an odd stockpile of wares, and together with the pungent smell of a hundred spices, it seemed as if you were entering another time zone, in another latitude altogether. However, Maggie sensed that she had not been completely transported from her damp, Western European environment; the broad sweep of items for sale embraced a multitude of cultures. The fresh bread was particularly worth stepping in for. Bought in from a local bakery, a wide variety of delicious-smelling, attractive loaves and rolls were always on offer, even at this late stage in the day.

After nodding and smiling at the owner behind the counter, she spent five minutes wandering along the aisles, up and down, checking for anything new or anything she might have forgotten, enjoying this last stretch of time to herself before heading home. There was a little round of goat's cheese that caught her fancy in the chill cabinet and she decided it would be her treat that evening. Together with the TV magazine her mother wanted and the bottle of lemon juice she had originally come in for, she moved back towards the counter.

'Afternoon,' the owner greeted her. There was no one else in the shop.

'Yes, thank you,' she replied and then pointed to the rows of bread and rolls displayed behind him. 'Please could I have a small loaf of the soda bread?'

'Of course. One small soda bread…' The owner nodded, turned his back and, using tongs, slipped a loaf into a paper bag. 'Is that everything, madam?'

'And these, please.' Maggie pushed the cheese, the magazine and the bottle of lemon juice towards him, next to the bread, and she extracted her purse from the zip pocket of the small bag diagonally slung across her shoulders.

As she looked up again to pass over her cash, a pair of glassy-brown eyes caught her attention. A small child, a girl, had crept up towards the counter from somewhere else entirely and was peering up at her from behind the lottery ticket stand.

'Hello,' Maggie laughed. 'Where did you pop up from?'

The child's eyes crinkled as she grinned and squeaked in sudden laughter, then disappeared back into the shadows underneath the counter.

'Oh, my granddaughter, this is.' The owner shook his head in pleasurable exasperation. 'She should be at school but apparently she is too sick.' He shrugged and smiled. A further round of giggles emanated from down below.

Maggie nodded, saying loudly, 'Oh, I see. It must be an illness that makes you *very* giggly.' Packing her purchases into the larger canvas bag which she had taken with her to work, and which she used to carry files and her lunch, she smiled and added her thanks. As she left, she heard the owner reprimand the child with the sweetness only an adoring grandparent could utter.

'Now, come along, I have a shop to run. I told you to stay resting on the sofa. You have your books and your colouring things. You are supposed to be sick, very sick, so your mother says.' There were further squeals of delight as the child received a tickle for her punishment and was then ushered into the back room beyond the shop.

Maggie nearly bumped into another customer on her way out; they stepped aside, allowing her to exit the shop. It was good to see the shop would not be empty for long. Uttering another quick 'Thank you', which floated out behind her, she hurried outside and turned left, continuing along a couple of streets to complete her route home.

Maggie reached the stubborn back gate, heaving it open once again with her shoulder; the recurring thought that she really needed to get it mended or replaced flitted through her mind, only making a brief impression. It was not urgent, and furthermore it represented a whole barrage of little jobs which were too much to face that day. She was aware that one day she would wake up and feel that *that* day was exactly the *right* day to tackle them.

Once inside she called out a swift greeting and was, as always, silently relieved to receive an answer, albeit a familiarly gruff one.

'I've been waiting all afternoon for you.'

Maggie hung up her coat, put the recently purchased items on the kitchen counter and left her bag on a chair at the small dining table. Looking down the living room to where her mother sat in her chair beside the bay window, she noticed that the TV wasn't on. It was still and sunny, with warm bands of light stretching in through the glass. Her mother was not looking in her direction but instead she was staring out through the windows, almost as if she were enjoying the peaceful moments surrounding her. Without turning her head, she said, 'Well, there's something funny going on out there.'

Maggie smiled to herself. She would have been surprised to find her mother doing nothing more than basking in a rare outpouring of afternoon sunshine. She walked across the room to stand beside her mother's chair and peer over her shoulder at whatever it was that had caught her attention.

'So what *is* going on out there, then?' she wondered aloud.

'That man has been wandering up and down the street all afternoon. I don't like the look of him. He keeps staring up at the houses *and* he's been taking photographs.'

The daughter moved closer to the window, scrutinising the street, searching for a suspicious-looking man taking photographs. At first, she couldn't see anything of note. There were a few people about – a man walking a dog, a couple of chatty adults pushing buggies, walking children back from school; one lady was on her knees tidying up the front garden two houses along, the dry weather making everything just that little bit easier. Then she saw him. He had a suit on and he was clutching a clipboard; he was talking on his phone and he was leaning against a car, and the car had the logo of a local estate agent brandished all over it: pink, white and green lettering stood out from the glossy black paint of the car's bodywork.

'Ah, I see,' she nodded, satisfied that this must be the mystery man.

'Something's not right about him. I know it. We should call the police.' Her mother folded her arms, confident in her declaration.

Her daughter thought for a moment. Her instinctive reaction would be to laugh and say something along the lines of, 'It's not a strange man at all, Mother, you've got it all wrong!' However, she could also see that that sort of response would only grate on the situation, belittling her mother's interest and anxiety. Instead, she tried to shift the focus. 'There's quite a bit of activity out there today. I think the weather's brought people out. Perhaps I should get out there myself and do a bit of weeding.'

'Yes, but what about that man?' Her mother's concern would not be so easily diverted. 'Aren't you going to do something about it?'

'Well, actually, Mum,' the daughter replied, having another look down the road at the man who was still on his phone, 'I think he's OK. He's just an estate agent. That's probably why he was taking photos.'

'How on earth can you tell that? You've not even stepped outside and confronted him!'

'Mum, it's OK. I can see his car and it's got the name of the firm printed on it, like advertising. I don't think it's anything to worry about. Would you like a cup of tea?'

Her mother didn't answer. There was a skirmish being fought in her mind between her own threatening convictions and the reasonable contradictions offered by her daughter. A cup of tea was neither here nor there. Maggie could sense the conflict. She bent down, crouching at the side of her mother's chair, and examined her face. It was an old face, of course it was, and the skin hung as if emptied of all its life and vigour. But this was only to be expected; it was what awaited them all, the inescapable, waning arc of life. Despite the warmth of the sun beaming in through the window, as Maggie put her hand on her mother's she felt the chill of her paper-thin skin, all mottled and dimpled by brown spots and bulging veins. A new thought crossed her mind.

'How was your day, Mum? Who came in to see you?' she asked, wondering if the carers who had visited had perhaps been the ones her mother really didn't like and this might be the cause of her more-than-usual sharpness. For the first time since Maggie had come in, her mother shifted her gaze from the window and the strange goings-on in the outside world, back inside the house to the real world, here with her own daughter. She frowned.

'You need a haircut, my girl.'

'Yes, you're quite right. I just haven't got round to it recently. So how *was* your day?'

'Hmm.' Her mother shuffled her shoulders as if they were guards who had fallen asleep on duty and needed shaking back into order. She seemed reluctant to talk about her day. Perhaps she wanted something else to think about. However, it appeared she finally decided to answer the question. 'That new girl came in. She's local and she chews all the time. I don't know what she's chewing.'

'Was that this morning, first thing, the breakfast visit?' asked her daughter.

Ignoring this further enquiry, her mother continued, 'Then Jean came and did my lunch. But she was not in a good mood.

They're cutting things back at her work and she'll be short this month.'

It's strange, Maggie thought, Mum doesn't seem to realise that this *is* their work, coming in to see to her. Perhaps she doesn't want to see it. 'I'm glad Jean came in,' she commented. 'She's nice and friendly, and you get on with her.' She hoped her mother might agree on this point at least.

'Not today she wasn't. Grumpy as anything.'

Maggie wondered about how appropriate it was for the carers to chat about work issues in front of their clients. Maybe they just didn't realise how much they gave away and, for that matter, how much they left behind them – lingering ghosts remaining to haunt other conversations.

Maggie stayed where she was, crouched down on the floor, for a minute or so longer in case any further morsels from the day's events might fall from her mother's lips. They both stared out of the window again. Not much could be seen from that low angle, and Maggie wondered how her mother could have seen the dubious estate agent taking photos and hanging about the street, and generally appearing to be a little bit shady. She supposed that when there wasn't much else to see, a tiny glimpse of the world outside was enough to fire a still active imagination. In a way, she was also glad for her mother that the TV was sometimes not enough to fill the gap; the sinking sands of endless, empty programmes, looping continuously and purposelessly, threatened to swamp the weakened minds of those who dabbled but had not the strength to pull away.

Wincing a little as she stood upright again, her knees complaining at the prolonged compression, Maggie announced that she would be putting the kettle on and that tea would be made for anyone who wanted it.

Just as she reached the tap, kettle in hand ready to be filled, she heard her mother call from the living room, 'I think I need to use the toilet!'

Not giving elbowroom to the little tang of annoyance this created, Maggie put the half-full kettle on its stand and flicked the switch before returning to her mother's chair to be on hand to help if needed. When nobody was there, the elderly lady managed very well getting herself to the bathroom and back, but when there was somebody there, she asked for help, which naturally couldn't be refused.

'*Hold fast that which is good.*'

The words came to her softly as Maggie walked beside her mother along the short route across the room to the downstairs bathroom. Feeling a sudden compulsion to show her some affection (a feeling that was not always present), the daughter put her arm loosely around her mother's shoulder, not tightly so as to impede her journey, but gently.

'I can manage, you know,' her mother retorted. 'I manage all day on my own, when you're off out all the time.'

Closing her eyes and removing her offending limb, Maggie prayed for strength, for the power to remain calm and the ability to carry on and the firm grip of faith to hold fast. There would soon be a cup of tea, which she sorely needed. Then a little time to get on top of some of the outstanding, though ever present, household chores; and later on, after dinner, when her mother had gone to bed, a little supper of fresh soda bread and goat's cheese.

'I was thinking about that verse today, you know the one, "Whatever is true, whatever is noble, whatever is right ... pure ... lovely ... excellent or praiseworthy, etc ... think about such things."' The Canon's wife just threw this unrehearsed comment into the conversational mix as she began to unpack several small shopping bags with which she had recently returned home that Wednesday afternoon. The odd and unrelated concoction of items now being drawn from the bags were intriguing though not unusual in their form or purpose. They did not signify one particular culinary endgame but rather the result of a well-practised style of domestic management, where a hundred projects were simultaneously on the table; literally on the kitchen table.

The Canon ran his gaze over the products, as if they were rabbits pulled from a magician's hat. His understanding of such things was limited, and any culinary knowledge he had previously possessed was long since buried. As a student he had been self-sufficient to a certain degree; however, that was another era, another lifetime long since passed.

A sudden thought, disturbing in its relevance, flitted through his mind that if his wife were to become ill or, at the worst end of that scale, just not exist any more, there would be so much, so many skills, he would have to relearn. It wasn't that he thought of himself as only a mere man or that their roles had been clearly dictated or defined in that way, it had simply been how things had worked out practically.

Looking up from the consumables, he was brought back to her comment, which had almost been a question, though not quite. His mind focused on her words and the cogs started whirring, and ping! He came up with a sensible response: 'Yes, I know the one,' (of course he did, he was a priest), 'Philippians 4, verses 8 and 9.' Then he laughed, adding, 'I always worry a bit about that last bit in verse 9, "Whatever you have learned or received or heard from me, or seen in me – put it into practice ..." I'm not sure I would advocate that myself!'

She smiled because she understood what he meant; she understood him as a person. 'Well,' she continued, 'I was thinking about the first bit, as I said, when I was in the frozen food section – strange but true – anyway, there I was searching for a packet of cod steaks in breadcrumbs, when I thought, it's an ordinary day, with normal things going on all around me. I focus on these things and, if I'm honest, on these things alone, most of the time. But how do I learn to focus on the good things? And what are the good things, really?' At her own mention of frozen food, she picked up the box of fish, which was covered in tiny, wet beads of condensation, and opened the freezer, shoving it with determination into an already full drawer.

'I know,' observed the Canon. 'Yes, I do know what you mean. All the normal but necessary duties and occupations pin us to the ground. I guess the solution is to look up.'

'Yes, it's a discipline. To stop wherever we are, whatever we're doing and talk to God.' Now she had a packet of kitchen roll in one hand and a bag of sugar in the other. 'But what would you define as the "good"? Does it just mean all the goodness we see or experience around us, generally in the world, or something more?'

'*Hold fast that which is good,*' he murmured.

'Sorry?' his wife called from the far corner of the kitchen where there was an old-fashioned larder.

He raised his voice so she could hear. 'I was just thinking about that Blessing yesterday morning. Remember me telling you?'

She walked back up to the table and, placing both palms flat on the surface, her arms straight, she leaned over it with all her weight. 'Yes, of course, that was altogether... otherworldly? Not sure if that's the right word.'

'It was certainly that,' the Canon replied, nodding his head a little. He repeated the words, '*Hold fast that which is good.*'

'Ah yes.'

'In that moment I think I saw what "good" meant.' He relaxed into his words, warming to his subject and confident of his wife's faith and belief in him. 'I think that, yes, there are good things in the world – in people, in nature, in our human strivings for the welfare of others and the natural world – however, they are in and of themselves just a reflection of the true nature of God. He, the creator of all things, and despite the brokenness of the world, His imprint remains unmistakeable.'

'Unmistakeable for those with eyes to see,' she added.

'Indeed. The spiritual nature of that experience was, well, it was like a gift, I suppose. I want so much to be of service to God, all my life long. If my heart is searching, seeking after God, then maybe He just opened my eyes for a split second to see where we really are. That in truth, all the trappings of religion are of no importance.'

'And yet this is where we find ourselves.' She lifted her hands from the tabletop, stretching them wide as if she herself were declaring words of faith from a pulpit.

He smiled. 'This is where we are and this is where the work of God is carried out. So, in answer to your question, I suppose goodness is the heart of God. It is revealed here and there, in bits and pieces, in the world we inhabit, in the people we meet, but ultimately it is found in Him. Truth and goodness: that is what we must stand on.'

'Thought that's what you'd say.' This time she laughed and stood back from the table, scanning the room with the mien of one engaged in tackling household logistics.

He had been relieved to tell her the previous evening about his recent, most peculiar, spiritual experience. She had never doubted his words or belittled him or ignored his feelings of fear and excitement. She was a good friend. He had not known (he still didn't really know) how to relate to what had happened, yet the vision seemed to have ignited something within him and he didn't want to let it pass him by untouched or unexplored.

The Canon sighed; it was a heavy sigh but it lent great benefit to his soul. He turned to look for the kettle and filled it halfway before switching it on.

'Cuppa?' he asked his wife.

'Oh, most definitely!'

Hold fast that which is good.'

Render to No One Evil for Evil

Clouds like fading, fleecy remnants of unspun wool hung overhead. It was almost as if you could fly up towards them unawares and gently tug away at their edges, tearing soft pieces off in your hands; pieces that would only disappoint, dissolving in the gentle breeze. In such a guise they filled the sky, gently moving without urgency; all with the steadiness of an elderly, determined aunt on her way to perform a serious, familial duty.

Dusty cloud cover notwithstanding, it was a free and liberated sky in which the birds could swoop and roam, drifting on the delicate currents, bobbing like driftwood on an open sea. The falcons were on the hunt. With prey a-plenty in their sights, they scanned the white sky around them, fascinated by and fixated on each new winged visitor appearing on the scene.

In turn, the stone spires stood vigilant over the falcons' watching and hunting, as fierce guardians of their feathered residents. Soon there would be a more patient round of work to undertake as eggs would be laid and young would be hatched. Then, the pinnacles would prove their worth as stern gatekeepers between the birds and the elements.

In recent weeks the unwelcome activity of humans had interrupted their solitary duty. Figures had clambered up to their lofty heights to fix cameras and fiddle with wires and deposit shale among their intricate stonework, as if they had a given right to intrude. Thankfully, however, their presence had not lasted long. Dumb creatures though they be, the humans must have sensed the spires' antagonism. They had quickly finished their meddling and had left. Now the towers were confident that both birds and future young would not be interfered with again.

On Friday afternoon, walking from the bus stop beneath that protective blanket of cloud, Maggie returned from work for the final day that week. She usually worked on Mondays, Wednesdays and Fridays – part-time hours, three days a week. For her, the pattern signified a much-needed balance: she could care for her mother but had guaranteed time away, even if for the most part it proved to be only away at work. She was with her mother every evening, apart from the occasional event, when she would book a care visit well in advance. It was costly so therefore a rarity. On a Tuesday morning she had her only other regular care visit enabling her to get out to the early morning service. This was the only one she could attend without much difficulty, the rest of the day being spent with her mother. On a Thursday she was there to help her mother start the day and then they would see it through together. On the weekends she was always on duty, although her mother could be left for an hour or so at a time, if errands or appointments were on the cards. The elderly lady had an alarm button that she wore around her wrist; if pressed, it alerted a call centre with trained operatives, whose knowledge and competency so far Maggie had not had to test.

Yesterday had been Thursday and they had spent the day together. Maggie recalled that the weather had been quite different. Spring sunshine had marked the day, so in the morning they had ventured out for a wander in the park, located just a few streets away. Her mother had complained on a minor level at being forced out into the 'harsh' spring temperatures, but within a short space of time, on spying the landscape of new, green life spreading before them in the park, ready to embrace them as welcome guests, her grumblings lost their edge. Nevertheless, such murmurings were quickly replaced by a string of stringent social commentary on the comings and goings of folk around them: of shoddy floral management within the park boundaries and of the lack of respect for pedestrians by all vehicles. Her daughter had dearly wanted to observe that strictly speaking her mother herself was in a vehicle – her wheelchair – but following that train of thought could be dangerous. Her mother would probably conclude that it was a vehicle not manned by her own hands; rather, by her daughter's, and therefore she could not be held responsible for any lack of courtesy entailed.

There had been a moment (and it had been a close-run thing) when road rage could well have been said to be on the horizon. Some young lads – they looked too young to not be at school yet old enough to flout the law – had come towards them in a pack along the pavement near the entrance to the park. Bicycle wheels had blocked the way ahead, rearing threateningly like steeds on the battlefield. The youngsters seemed to be oblivious to their fellow human beings, who were at a distinct disadvantage before them. As they came closer, the daughter instinctively tightened her grip on the dual hilt of the wheelchair. Her mother's hands shot out from underneath the blanket on her lap and grasped the arms of the wheelchair. They were both steeled for a skirmish.

At the front of the rowdy gang, the first two slowed just a fraction. Perhaps they had sensed the tension and had faltered momentarily. In their almost invisible change of pace, they had not thought about their comrades behind them, and the result was an unexpected clash from the rear. In the pushing and shoving that ensued, several of the bikers stumbled against a parked car – a shiny new model with a number plate that revealed it was only six months since it had rolled off the forecourt.

The piercing pertinence of a car alarm kicked into action, alerting all to the dangers of boys and bicycles. The hazard lights flashed and the perfect paintwork was scratched. The daughter froze and, therefore, the mother in her wheelchair. At an earlier time in life, not one when she was confined to a chair at the mercy of her daughter, the mother might well have pulled herself up and tackled the raucous bunch. But today was not that day and so they remained rooted to the pavement, waiting for something else to happen.

The lads began shouting at each other. Troops caught on the back foot now turned upon each other. There was more heaving and roughness and swearing; however, the unremitting alarm caused the band to dissolve.

An angry shout followed by a deeper, louder stream of abuse came rushing out towards them from an open door across the street. In understandable fury, a man shot down the pavement towards them, but the youngsters, each of them on two wheels, swiftly dispersed. The owner of the very expensive car was outwitted.

Escaping the scene and making sure that they too could disappear without a trace was now the daughter's primary mission. She began to edge the wheelchair on past the car, towards the wide opening of the park gate, hoping that they would not be dragged into this business as witnesses. They hadn't really been involved; they were just innocent bystanders. Although, Maggie had thought, it could be argued that that was the very definition of a witness.

'That showed them.'

It was a natural remark that could have been thrown about by anyone. But it hadn't been anyone; it had been her mother.

Bending down towards her right ear, which was generally her better one, Maggie, a little nervous as well as puzzled by this statement asked, 'What do you mean, Mum?'

'What I mean is, I showed them. I saw them coming and I decided to face them head on.' Her straight-lipped expression was triumphant. The daughter decided not to mention the fact that it was she who was pushing the wheelchair, not her mother. 'I gave them a look. I glared at them. That sent them packing! Young hooligans.' Her hands were now safely cosseted back under the blanket. 'Now, let's get into that park before I freeze to death.'

The man who had been examining the scratches on the paintwork of his car didn't seem to know whether to strangle somebody or cry, raging against the injustice and unfairness of the world at large. He must have caught some of their words because, as the daughter attempted to manoeuvre the chair towards the park gate, he turned, hands on hips, to face them. Once again, another apparent adversary barred their way.

'You have anything to do with this?' He didn't shout but there was no kindness in his voice, no sense of politics or manners. Some would say that that was only to be expected; nevertheless, his tone was accusatory. He pointed at the scratches. They were in fact only minor.

Before Maggie could begin to reply, her mother, picking up the scent of blood, retorted, 'Of course not! Who do you think we are? It was those ruffians on bikes. Bikers. Hell's Angels!' As she threw down the gauntlet from underneath the blanket, her wrist flurried in the general direction in which the boys had fled.

'I saw those lads,' the man riposted, 'but I also heard *you* just now. Did you egg them on? Because if you did, then I'm holding you responsible for this damage to my car!' He had drawn closer and he was very red in the face.

'Certainly not!' her mother answered, although now she was not quite so sure of herself. This new combatant was certainly lone; however, all at once he appeared more imposing and forbidding than the previous biker platoon. With much reluctance, Maggie felt that she could not continue her preferred role of the silent servant, only waiting to fulfil her duty. Like it or not, she had a part to play. Before she opened her mouth to speak, the words from the prayer came flooding back, filling her mind as a remedy against escalating trouble.

'Render to no one evil for evil.'

Evil. This was not perhaps how one would immediately describe this man or his words and actions: not at all. He was just an ordinary guy, who, on finding himself on the receiving end of vandalism (which could be more accurately described as touching evil), was now angry and ready to lash out at the most likely, or the nearest, possible cause.

Maggie was aware that perhaps in the culture around her, in the everyday, evil was portrayed as something extraordinarily bad, deeply disturbing and serious; more precisely, something outside ourselves, as if it were something we had no control over and could therefore not be responsible for. She felt that often, it was a word set aside to delineate the man on the street from the sick criminal. But she also knew that it was just a word. Evil is something that lives in every heart on the inside, not the outside. It is seeded in the small thoughts, utterances and deeds that punctuate all of our lives, rather than a separate entity displayed in rare, sensational moments. It is subtle, clever and deceptive; it desires to draw us into its embrace, and if that can be done unnoticed, then all the better.

This blustering man before her was no more or less evil than the rest of humanity, as was she; however, she had a little insight. Through her faith in Jesus, she had the gift of God and the necessary words of love and peace with which to calm the situation, to restore some clarity and so divert further trouble.

All at once, in the brief seconds before she spoke, she found herself calling out to God for help in this, another time of need. Resting her hand for a moment on her mother's shoulder after putting on the wheelchair brakes, she walked around to the front of the chair and held out her hand.

'I'm Maggie; this is my mum.' She indicated the now demure woman in the chair at her side. 'You must be so upset about your car. We were here when it happened. I think those lads got a bit out of hand but I don't think they meant to cause any damage.'

Her hand remained as a flag of truce hanging in the air between them. Flicking his eyes from this proffered hand, then to Maggie's face and across to the old woman in the wheelchair, he eventually reached out towards the hand and shook it. It was a basic response against which he had no real need to fight.

'I was inside.' He pointed to the house from which he had come. 'I'm just visiting a friend. I saw the boys on their bikes from the window.'

'Yes, I have to say they looked a bit menacing coming towards us on the pavement. We were just going for a walk in the park.' Maggie took a step closer and lowered her voice. 'Mum sometimes gets a bit cross, a bit snappy, you know, and I think because she felt intimidated, she became defensive. She used to be a teacher so when it comes to youngsters, I suppose old habits kick in,' she smiled.

The man rolled his eyes and smirked. 'My wife's a head teacher; you don't have to tell me.' He rubbed the back of his neck; a decision was brewing. 'Look, I know it wasn't your fault. I'm sorry but I just... well, you know. The car wasn't cheap!'

'It's really smart.' Maggie nodded in agreement.

'What's going on now? What's happened to our walk in the park?' They both turned around as the old woman in the chair interjected.

'I should let you get on with your day,' the man said. The scratches on his car, calls to the insurance company and maybe reporting the incident to the police, all of this would now clearly occupy the rest of *his* day.

'If you like,' Maggie offered, 'you can take my contact details if they would be of any use, as a witness or something? I don't know what you want to do.'

The man spun his gaze away from his car and back towards the mother and daughter. He looked a bit brighter. 'Oh, yeah, that would be great, thanks. I'm not sure either, but I guess it might be useful to have them.'

They took a minute to exchange details on their phones and, after further outbursts of agitation from the elderly woman, who was not quite privy to such digital chicanery, the two parties separated. At last, they passed through the park gates, and almost all thoughts of trouble, anger and evil abated.

'You shouldn't be giving our phone number out to men like that; he could be anybody.'

'It's OK, Mum. It was my email, not the home landline or address or anything like that and I'm sure it's fine. We could be of some use, you never know.'

'Well, I don't want to get involved. I've enough on my plate without stirring up more trouble, and you should know better, my girl!' Her mother had spoken; it was the final word on the subject.

Maggie took it as such and used it for all it was worth. 'I quite agree. Now, the park looks lovely in the sunshine. Which way shall we go?'

Maggie could probably have predicted which way her mother would choose, though it always seemed fair to leave the decision to her, generally speaking. The overhead, canopied branches of birch, oak, willow and beech; the abundant beds, budding with the promise of bright tulip colour; the waving daffodils clumped at irregular intervals, in a great variety of yellows, oranges and whites, all aided their rise from the shadowy slump of confrontation and awkwardness. Disgruntlement like tattered veils slipped off their shoulders piece by piece with each new bend along the path, and with each fresh scene appearing before them.

There was a simple though welcome treat awaiting them on the far side of the park: a little café which had run for decades – open all year round – had tables both inside and out. The coffee there was good and inexpensive. To say that they were regulars would be stretching a point, but it was a frequent destination.

The daughter knew that for all her grumblings, her mother really benefited from this little excursion. Being out in the fresh air was better than being stuck inside the house all day. The stimulus of watching the activity of others was enough for a relatively sharp mind; any brief, pleasant interaction that came their way also fitted the bill.

One member of staff in the café recognised them and hurried out from behind the counter to hold the door open for them. It was not quite warm enough to sit outside, certainly not for the old woman, who was already at a disadvantage; being pushed along in a wheelchair did not class as exercise.

At the counter, the daughter ordered a cappuccino for herself and a pot of tea for her mother. They hardly ever ordered anything extra; the cakes and biscuits were not particularly special or homemade, but rather prewrapped in plastic packaging and bought in. But that was no real disappointment, as eating was not the purpose of the outing.

The windows in the café were wide and ran low to the floor, with the sun pouring through; the elderly lady shut her eyes as if basking on the beach in a deckchair. The daughter studied her face, not speaking, not wanting to disturb her enjoyment. The many furrowed lines melted somewhat and a modest smile emerged; a confirmation for Maggie that perhaps she was, for most of the time at least, doing the right thing.

For a weekday morning, the park was relatively busy. It seemed that after several long, wet days, which had felt as if they would never end – where the drains had clogged with winter debris and people had murmured that there could never possibly be a drought ever again as there had been so much water – the skies had lifted and spring was truly on its way. People were out with their dogs, some of them with a whole pack together at one time: she thought that they must be professional dog walkers who were probably getting far more exercise and fresh air than most. Other people were pushing buggies, some of them with a whole gaggle of youngsters bouncing around, running from bush to bush and waving sticks. What appeared to be a nursery group out for the afternoon toddled past the café window; they were all holding hands in twos and wearing fluorescent tabards on top of their coats. They were guarded front, back and at the side with easy-going yet vigilant staff. A few more boys on bikes sped past the window, shouting to each other as they slalomed through the pedestrians; too quick to be recognised as perhaps the ones who had caused the earlier ruckus. In a spilt second, they were gone.

With the teaspoon provided, Maggie was now skimming off the chocolate-speckled foam from the top of her coffee, which had just been served but was as yet too hot to drink. She let her eyes drift between the animated scene outside and the almost inanimate frame of her mother soaking up the sun. There were so many people in the world; so many with busy lives, with full lives, living the dream; perhaps, but more than likely not. Did they ever stop and think like she did about God and His Word, and the manner of their spiritual existence? Did they manage perfectly well without? Often this appeared to be the case. It was not that she envied the lives of others; she had never had any great ambition or desires that had not yet been met. She felt content most of the time, even on a day when it was impossible to escape her mother's truculent mood. It was all down to the fact that she was never alone; in her innermost being, in her soul, all was well. The battles were constant but ultimately the war was won.

She prayed for her mother as she dozed. She prayed for her neighbour, Rachel, whom she hoped to meet on Saturday. She prayed for the colleague who had asked her about her church life yesterday at work and then she recalled the most recent service she had attended. She thought of the Canon who had led the service and whose words at the end had burst into life and light. And she prayed, hoping that for him, for the others who had been there – herself included – that their faith would continue to hold.

'Your tea's here, Mum.' Her mother had woken with a start as the café door had banged shut in the wind. She wiped her mouth and blinked a few times, shuffling in her chair. The daughter made sure her mother was close enough to reach the small teapot, milk jug and cup, with its saucer and spoon. She watched as her wrinkled, blue-veined hands carried out the tricky operation of pouring herself a cup of tea; if possible, this was still something she liked to perform herself.

'The sunshine's lovely, isn't it, Mum?'

There was no reply to this observation, except that of her mother putting down the milk jug and looking out of the window. Eventually she muttered, 'I don't like the look of those clouds.'

Maggie craned her neck to search for the ominous threat in the sky, which was mostly hidden behind the trees. 'I can't see any clouds, Mum. I think it's just the trees blocking your view, perhaps.'

There was no answer, and then the daughter realised that of course none was really required. She pointed out the colourful coats of some small children running by: vivid reds and oranges standing out perfectly against the surrounding green backdrop.

'Why aren't they at school? They should be, you know. It's not a holiday,' her mother observed.

'I imagine they're not old enough, Mum.' Maggie was surprised to find that her mother was so keenly aware of what time of year it was. Maybe once ingrained, the school calendar never failed. She had finished her coffee and watched while her mother lifted the shaking teacup up to her mouth with both hands. She was thankful that she didn't seem to notice, and therefore didn't mention, the mediocre temperature of the tea, as it had been stewing in the pot for longer than was preferable.

Out of nowhere a folded newspaper was slammed down on the tabletop between them. 'Look at that! Pure evil! It's disgusting. They should be shot!'

After she had recovered from the initial shock, Maggie stared wide-eyed at the man who had spoken. He was already on their level because he too was in a wheelchair, although after an initial glance the daughter realised that his was more of an electric scooter. Presuming that he must have been sitting at another table when they came in and that he was now on his way out, it seemed that he had decided to share his thoughts on the tabloid headlines before he left.

'There you are, you can have a paper to read with your coffee. I'm done with it. Waste of money.' His demeanour was that of someone who had made up his mind about the world and life in general, yet needed the confidence and endorsement of others to back up his thoughts. Although it looked like he was leaving, he didn't move away from their table.

Not wanting to accept the bargain and own the paper, the daughter swivelled it around with her fingertips just so that she could read the headlines. She presumed that these were what he was referring to. She mouthed the words splashed in red and black, defiant in the largest possible print across the front: EVIL PREDATORS GET LIFE! Underneath were two slightly blurred mugshots.

It was not an unusual headline; sensationalism was now everyday.

'Thank you, but I don't think we want to read it today.' She twisted the paper back round, pushing it slightly forwards so that it faced its original owner.

'No, you keep it, love. As I said, it's all rubbish.' Nonetheless he picked up the paper; he couldn't resist. 'Look here.' He jabbed at the headline with a vicious fat finger. 'These…' He swore and then said, ''Scuse my language, ladies, but…' He struggled to find the right word to fully convey the strength of his wrath without causing offence. Eventually he dredged a word from the dusty back shelf of his mind. 'These *villains!* They ought to be executed. Don't you think?'

The dreaded question – the challenge – had been slammed down on the tabletop just like the paper. Maggie could either turn it around and examine it as she had with the headlines, without committing, or she could push it away and leave it unanswered, or she could pick it up and own it.

'Render to no one evil for evil.' The thought came quickly to mind.

'I haven't read the story so I don't really want to comment, but I think we all have the potential for evil and that there is always the chance for forgiveness.' She wasn't sure whether this would shut him up or lead to a sensible discussion. Naturally, it didn't achieve either.

The man just stared at her for a moment and snatched the paper, *his* paper, from the tabletop, clutching it to his side as if she had wounded it. 'I think that's out of order, I do!' His voice was raised and now they all felt the embarrassment. 'Chance for forgiveness?' he yelled, astounded. 'You tell that to the parents! Go on! See how that goes down. Evil people like that deserve evil in return. They deserve everything they get, and more!'

He stuffed the, all of a sudden, precious paper into the front basket on his scooter, squashing it down beside a collection of thin, cheap, plastic shopping bags. Without another word, he pressed a button to kickstart his vehicle and headed for the door. It looked as if he wasn't going to stop when he reached the exit; however, a sharp-eyed member of staff had been watching and he nipped across to open the door just in time, raising his eyes to the ceiling behind the rolling scooter as it trundled outside, around the corner of the café. Walking over to the table where the man had been sitting, the assistant cleared the empty mug and crumby plate, smiling over at Maggie and her mother at the table by the window.

'Sorry about that,' the assistant said when they came past again with a cloth to wipe the vacant table.

'Oh, it's fine, not a problem,' Maggie replied.

'He's in most days and he usually gives us a bit of aggro,' the assistant laughed and shrugged.

'I expect he's just angry when he reads about all the trouble in the world and doesn't know what to do about it,' reasoned Maggie. 'Maybe he feels vulnerable?'

The assistant finished wiping the table and stood still, a slight frown puckering his face. 'I'd never thought of it like that.' Yet after limited consideration, the brief thought was dismissed; an unwieldy idea to put back in its box. Once again, he flashed a smile before returning to the safety of the small but busy kitchen behind the counter.

Maggie's mother had been silent throughout the whole episode, which was surprising but welcome; she had maintained her focus on the all-important task of drinking her tea. After a minute, she placed her cup back down on its saucer, then, speaking like a child, she asked, 'Has that person gone now?'

Laying her hand on her mother's, Maggie answered, 'Yes, he has. Have you finished your tea? Shall we head home?'

Bundling up in readiness to face the breeze, with tentative movements Maggie reversed the wheelchair out of its position at the table. Her mother waved a regal hand as she thanked another member of staff who was holding the door open for them once more and they left the café.

'I think I might need the toilet soon,' said the mother.

'Home we go, then,' said the daughter.

That had been Thursday, and the rest of their day – the journey back through the park, continuing the circular route around until they had reached the gates – had been uneventful.

Strengthen the Fainthearted

The Canon had a call from one of the priests who was responsible for an outlying parish. They chatted briefly about some minor issues, satellites of both a practical and a religious nature which from time to time affected them both. Though their conversation was casual, the Canon sensed instability. He recognised the overtones of anxiety and doubt as they talked. It was with relief for the priest at the other end of the line that the Canon agreed an appointment for them to meet and discuss what was really at the heart of the problem; the Canon understood the importance of supporting his fellow ministers. He knew that it was about more than just sharing good advice, as if there were a tidy little leaflet he could hand out on spiritual weakness; on putting wrong thoughts right; on superiority of title or position. He knew this because he knew himself, and when it came down to it, he knew who he was before God, and therefore, who he was – no more, no less – before any other human being.

After putting the phone down, he stopped for a moment to pray for the priest.

'Oh, Lord,' he whispered in heartfelt compassion, 'let this dear one of Yours who is trying to draw others closer to You, let him be refreshed today. Give him clarity of mind and a generous dose of grace to help him with the burden of service in this dark and heavy world...' As his words drifted into silence, he shut his eyes even tighter against the tireless forces that strived to hinder the kingdom of God and its servants; the good work of bringing light into darkness, peace into pain and life into death.

His office was a calm place to be that morning. Although the phone had rung on and off with unfailing frequency, and the list of emails never seemed to shrink, in the face of these mundane battles the Canon felt at peace within himself. This was not how he always felt but he was mindful and grateful when this was the case; and he reminded himself to use times such as these, rather than waste them.

He thought about Heaven's Gate — that was how he referred now to that strange spiritual experience — and all that had gone with it, earlier that week. Finding his pen and notebook, he began to scribble down the words again, not that he didn't know them, or that they weren't already written down; of course they were. They could be found in prayer books all over the country and, he supposed, the whole world, in one form or another. However, he sensed the urgency of writing them down again just for himself that morning, in that moment.

Almost as if his eyes were still closed, his pen ran along the lines of the page. He saw the vaulted cathedral ceiling above them — magnificent but imperfect in its finitude — break open and the eternal armies of heaven ranged across the sky in shining power. He saw the seated, mute congregation, enclosed in the dark wooden pews, all at once brilliant, numerous and alive in glorious splendour. It had been his vision, perhaps their vision too, and it would not be forgotten in a hurry.

'Go forth into the world in peace; be of good courage; hold fast that which is good; render to no one evil for evil; strengthen the fainthearted...'

His pen stopped at this point and the most recent conversation he had had with his fellow minister came flooding back with overwhelming force. They had not mentioned details, and he really didn't have much of an idea about the nature of his brother's disquietude; nevertheless, the priest had been faltering, truly fainthearted in his brief but soulful expression. In one sense the Canon was aware that the vision made no difference to what he could achieve, or to who he was; however, perhaps it had been a gift. It lent strength to his own faintheartedness and colour to his dull faith, and like the marking of all questions, mysteries and happenings, it called him back to God.

'*Strengthen the fainthearted.*'

As the Canon looked up from the page where he had been writing, he turned to watch the small patch of sky that could be seen from his study window. Fresh words from Psalm 27 came to mind:

> Do not hide your face from me,
> do not turn your servant away in anger;
> you have been my helper.
> Do not reject me or forsake me,
> God my Saviour.

Maggie woke up on Saturday morning with anxious thoughts bombarding her mind. She could hear the steady breathing from the adjoining bedroom; her mother was still asleep, and in thankfulness she wrapped her dressing gown around her, tightened the belt and headed on down the stairs to the kitchen.

It was still early, yet the dawn had nearly completed its principal task of sweeping away the debris of the night. Outside, through the kitchen window, she could see the remnants of a hoary frost. A delicate hand had spent the night gilding every single leaf and every blade of grass with a crystal halo. From a human perspective you could be forgiven for thinking it a wasted effort; so much meticulous work, to be noticed by a few and praised by even fewer, before it vanished with the banishing warmth of a new day.

She thought of the verse from Psalm 27 which she had read last night: 'Teach me your way, LORD; lead me in a straight path.' She thought of the hours ahead and doubted her ability to carry out the main mission of the day, something she herself had set in place.

The previous evening, long after she had returned from work and re-established herself as her mother's carer, after she had prepared a meal and sorted some laundry, she had watched and waited for signs of her next-door neighbour's return from work. A car door had slammed and she had heard their front door being unlocked, opened and pushed shut again. It had been difficult to tell which member of the household had been first to arrive home, Rachel or her partner. Maggie had never really paid much attention to the dusty-red car often parked outside or, for that matter, to whom it actually belonged. Maybe they had a car each and she just hadn't noticed; there were so many regularly parked along the street, a correlation to which she had never given much thought.

After half an hour or so, she guessed that a reasonable, neighbourly length of time had elapsed which would allow her to knock on their door and see if Rachel, whom she planned to meet the following morning, was in. Leaning over the low wall from her own front doorstep, with a lump in her throat, she had reached across and had lifted the knocker, rapping it several times against the door. They hadn't made any proper arrangements regarding meeting up for coffee when they had spoken just a few days before, and now Maggie was worried about so many things. First, who would actually come to the door, and second, if she managed to talk to Rachel, would there be tell-tale signs that she would really prefer not to meet after all? It had been a spur-of-the-moment thing. Maggie imagined that Rachel had far better things to be doing with her time on a Saturday morning than having coffee with her bland, unexciting next-door neighbour who stayed in to look after her elderly mother when she wasn't catching the bus to work or going to church. And who did Maggie think she was, anyway? What qualifications did she presume to have that would enable her to be of use to Rachel, a person who wore her bold, fluffy dressing gown outside without a care to what anybody else might think?

Before she had had too long to ponder these things, noises from behind the door, inside the house, told her that someone was coming. Because the door, as well as the occupants of the house perhaps, had had a bashing just a few days before, it proved hard to open. However, it served to remind Maggie of the reason she had offered to meet with Rachel in the first place.

It was Rachel's partner who pulled the front door open, and Maggie realised that she didn't know his name. His blank expression didn't alter on seeing her there and she wondered if he even knew that she lived next door. It seemed as if she would have to speak first.

'Hello, sorry to bother you.' She paused with her hands clasped together in front of her. 'Is Rachel in, please?'

The man raised his eyebrows at the specific mention of the name Rachel, as if this stranger on their doorstep, who knew his partner's name, were a complete enigma. His only response was to turn away from the door, calling the name in question while he slouched back inside. He had left the door half-open. It had caught on the mat just inside the threshold, yet from where she stood it was difficult for Maggie to see any further into the house.

Sounds, shuffling and banging came from the kitchen at the back; she presumed their property was a mirror image of her own. Snippets of a partial conversation reached the doorway:

'What?'

'The door...'

'Who is it?'

'No idea... for you!'

'What?... Can't you?'

'It's for you!'

The dilemma felt like a sinking ship and it began to drag Maggie down. It was clearly a bad time to be calling round. She should just go. But she couldn't go now, not after she had set things in motion. This really was not going to work out at all.

'Go forth... be of good courage... strengthen the fainthearted...' The words were swift to come to the forefront of her mind. 'Oh, Lord, I'm the fainthearted one at the moment!' she prayed under her breath.

Through the frosted glass Maggie could see a figure returning. It was Rachel, who now attempted to yank the front door open a little bit more. As soon as she saw Maggie, her face brightened. She was wiping her hands on a tea towel.

'Oh, hi!' She leaned back and called over her shoulder, 'It's Maggie, from next door!'

'Sorry to bother you,' Maggie began.

'No, it's fine, really. Are we still on for tomorrow, or is it a bit tricky with your mum and all that?'

And so, the mountain of an impossible mission had disappeared into mist; suddenly it was gone. After a lot of indecision, mostly on Maggie's side, as to time and place, the two neighbours had pinned down the details and all that was needed was for Saturday morning to dawn, which it had.

The kettle finished boiling and Maggie made a pot of tea. She carried a tray with two mugs upstairs and hoped that she would have some time to enjoy this first cup undisturbed. There was a strange irony brooding when she thought about the whole meeting for coffee situation. She could not imagine, not for a moment, that Rachel was feeling the same apprehension that she was. On the doorstep, yesterday evening, she had been all bubbly and bright, wearing slim-cut jeans, a yellow designer T-shirt and large, gold, hooped earrings, her wild hair escaping in a fountain from a topknot. She had looked as if she could conquer the world. And yet, and yet there had been the fight – the most recent in a long series of battles – only a few nights ago, *and* there had been the pain she had seen in Rachel's eyes the following morning.

Having taken one of the mugs of tea to her still dozing mother, leaving it on the bedside table, she now propped herself up against the pillows in her own bed. With the comfort of a hot mug of tea in her hands, she closed her eyes; such small but necessary moments of goodness were to be treasured and she was so grateful. To let the doubt and anxiety fly around her mind in an ever-increasing flurry would not achieve anything, she knew that much, so she prayed and talked to God about the day ahead: how unprepared she felt, how odd that Rachel would want to talk to someone like her and how little experience, and therefore advice, she would be able to give.

'Be of good courage ... strengthen the fainthearted.'

Maggie opened her eyes and sipped her tea. Perhaps, just perhaps, Rachel was the sort of person who was very good at putting on a good show for the outside world, while hiding her problems and pain. It was not a fault – it was a solid and often necessary defence mechanism employed by most people at one time or another. Perhaps Rachel was still keen to meet (there hadn't been any hint of an excuse that might point to the contrary) because she, Maggie, had glimpsed beyond the show. She had seen behind the curtain, backstage where the struggle, the blood, sweat and tears of humanity, was played out.

She checked her bedside clock. There were still no signs of stirring from the neighbouring bedroom. Putting down her mug, she reached for her Bible and the daily reading notes tucked inside. The words she read that morning referred to the preparations for the building of the temple in Jerusalem, in the time of King David – ancient times, ancient words – yet the spirit behind them was still relevant for today, for that very day, her day.

> The LORD be with you, and may you have success ...
> May the LORD give you discretion and understanding ...
> Be strong and courageous. Do not be afraid or discouraged ... Now begin the work, and the LORD be with you ... Now devote your heart and soul to seeking the LORD your God. Begin to build ...

The words came from a passage in 1 Chronicles 22 where David is charging his son Solomon with the outstanding task of building a temple for the Lord in Jerusalem. 'Begin to build' was a key heading in the Bible-reading notes which charged her, as well as other readers, with the building of the kingdom of God. As there had been for the construction of the physical temple so many centuries before, like precious gems, stone and wood, so there were still materials available; elements spiritual in nature; an ample provision to build a kingdom. Unfit for and unequal to the assignment, in and of herself, Maggie knew that all that was asked of her was a willingness to undertake the work. Everything else, all that she would need, had already been promised and set aside for the morning ahead, like an already chosen set of clothes – the perfect outfit.

In the soporific sunshine that streamed in through the bay window later on that same Saturday afternoon, Maggie was sitting with her mother. Between them a small table was decked with a Scrabble board; their racks arsenaled with letters and the board itself a petty skirmish. The game was in its early stages, still lacking a probable victor. Maggie had suggested the game, as she felt a measure of guilt at having been out for an hour or so that morning. She recognised that such self-condemnation was needless; nevertheless, it was not easily outwitted. They had set the board up and had begun their game, her mother taking charge as best she could; however, after only a short way in, her concentration had waned; her eyelids had drooped and play had stagnated. Maggie left the letters on the board untouched and went to the kitchen to make some tea. Creeping back to her chair she sat down at the table once more with her mug. She was relaxed but primed, ready for when her mother's snatch of sleep would come to an end. She thought about earlier that morning and her coffee with Rachel.

They had driven in Rachel's car, the dull red one (now she knew to whom it belonged, though it was in fact used by them both) to a coffee shop along a row of local high street shops. It wasn't in the centre of town, rather just a few streets away, near a supermarket where parking was free. Rachel said she would pop in and buy something afterwards to justify using the car park, and Maggie thought of one or two things she could get for herself that would make the trip seem more worthwhile.

The two of them had chatted away like good friends, although Rachel did most of the chatting. Maggie had wondered why they had never done this before. Of course, she knew why they hadn't: she had never felt brave enough to approach her neighbour on these terms, and now, suddenly all her concerns seemed silly, soft excuses blown away in the wind. Rachel had also kept up a constant chatter while she drove, as if that was something she always did. Again, Maggie had wondered: perhaps it was immaterial to Rachel whether there were any passengers in the car or not.

The coffee shop had been busy. Maggie thought, this is what people do; on a Saturday they go and do their shopping and then have a coffee, or the other way around, whichever comes first.

The décor was rather dated; the tables and chairs were homogenous, standard and functional, all chrome, plastic and glass. There was nothing to hint at a more contemporary style – no cosy leather sofas or refurbished mismatched furniture. Nevertheless, the enticing, rich smell of roasted coffee was the same everywhere.

The shrill, industrial sound of the coffee machine – steaming shots of milk, the rattle of grinding beans, clanging stainless-steel pots, frenzied spouts of boiling water – bolstered the busyness of customer chatter and the scraping of chair legs on the vinyl floor. It was not going to be a quiet place to sit and talk; maybe this was why Rachel had suggested it. An environment such as this would easily mask any overspill of emotion or tears, whereas in a more comfy, tranquil corner café, such displays would be far more noticeable. Then again, maybe she had suggested it simply because she liked it and it was familiar.

At the counter they had ordered creamy coffee in tall glass mugs, which were brought over to them with a delicate, cellophane-wrapped Italian biscuit balanced on the saucer. Maggie had been wondering how they might begin, but she needn't have worried.

Running her teaspoon through the chocolate-sprinkled foam on top of her frothy coffee, scooping up mounds of sweet fluffiness and repositioning them on the far side of her cup, as if she were searching for the treasure of darker coffee beneath, Rachel said, 'Thank you for thinking of this. It means a lot to me.'

Maggie was surprised by her statement; she felt the invitation had been one-sided. Now she knew that Rachel had been equally keen.

'To be honest,' Maggie responded, 'I thought you might have forgotten; well, I mean that you might have far more important things to do.' Then Maggie had been surprised further by the tears that came thick and fast, running down Rachel's cheeks. 'I'm sorry,' she murmured.

Rachel shook her head. 'No, don't be,' she sniffed, and wiped her face. 'It's just that I haven't told anyone about this. Not my family, my sister, my mum, anyone.'

Maggie had waited for her to continue.

'Everyone thinks I'm all fun and outgoing and anything for a laugh, but...' she struggled to hold back the overwhelming urge to wail, 'but I'm just trying to hide everything, and...'

'And that's exhausting?' suggested Maggie.

Rachel had nodded and covered her eyes with her tissue. She had motioned with her hand towards Maggie's coffee which, like her own, was losing its heat. Maggie had understood and while Rachel blew her nose, she had taken the tall mug in both hands and sipped her drink. She was glad they had chosen a table tucked away at the back of the café. No one had seemed to notice either the conversation or the crying.

Maggie remembered that she had mostly listened, mainly because she didn't really know what to say, though she had sensed that that was exactly what she should have done. Her companion's long-held emotions had finally broken through the sturdy floodgates protecting her heart, and at that point in time nothing more was required than to let the words, and the feelings they expressed, pour out, pooling between them.

All the while Rachel had been speaking, from time to time Maggie had been praying; praying for understanding, for compassion, for light in a dark situation and for a way forward. Rachel's domestic situation was not clearcut. There were, she had confessed, deficiencies on both sides but it was reaching a point of being intolerable. Maggie knew there were ways to help in these sorts of situations, although it was an area in which she had no experience. Nonetheless she could listen, and over the days ahead, she could think.

Outside the coffee shop they had been aware that it was drizzling and so they had hurried back towards the supermarket car park. They walked straight on past Rachel's rain-spotted red car, directly into the supermarket. In the hit and miss of the public arena, Rachel switched back to her regular persona; she was the lively one. Maggie supposed this to be default behaviour owing to years of ingrained habit, yet she also wondered if a burden had been lifted; perhaps Rachel was feeling a touch lighter than before. They had scurried up and down the aisles, grabbing what few items they could carry in their hands; they had paid at the self-checkout points and, clutching their shopping bags, which they had remembered to bring from home, they headed back to the car.

As they had pulled up outside their respective homes, where they had been thankful to find the same vacant parking place, just as they had left it earlier, Rachel had spoken again. She had reiterated her thanks for the company, a listening ear and friendship. With the engine turned off, the street was quiet, as if expectant for renewed conversation on matters of the human condition.

'I never thought about you much before, it's awful! And with your mum to look after and everything! I never noticed, and yet here you are thinking about *me*. I'm so grateful, really.'

Maggie smiled. 'I get so worried when I hear everything blowing up, you know. But I never felt I could push myself forward and ask. It's not really my business.'

'But I'm so glad you did make it your business, to ask... I mean, to show concern. It's more than most.' Rachel hesitated before adding, 'I know you go to church and all that, but I wondered if... well, you'll think this is silly, but will you pray for me, for us?'

Maggie had found that she could not reply straight away. She had swallowed and nodded, before saying, 'Of course, it's the least I can do.' Then, correcting her statement, she had said, 'No, actually, it's the best thing I can do. Shall we pray now?'

It was Rachel's turn to be dumbstruck, as if her coffee-companion had just offered her £1,000.

'I can't do that! What – now?'

'*You* don't have to, it's OK, but if you want, I will. Don't worry; it'll only take a minute.'

Before she had said anything aloud, Maggie thought of the words from the prayer that had imprinted itself on her mind so very recently.

'*Strengthen the fainthearted.*'

Then she had opened her mouth and prayed.

In the sun-filled living room later that afternoon, Maggie felt a whole concoction of thoughts and emotions. She was elated that they had managed to have a coffee together, that their plans had not come to nothing, and she was proud of herself for not giving up. However, she was daunted by the depth of sadness and pain which her neighbour was dealing with; she was moved by her courageous disclosure.

Additionally, she was excited that something of her faith, of her belief that God could change things, had so quickly been established between them, and she was renewed in her hopefulness that God could even work through her.

Her mother twitched in her chair, jerking one eye open and then the other, yawning and grimacing as the discomfort of waking and then moving her frail bones caught her off guard. Her brightening eyes moved across the Scrabble board on the table, taking in the state of play.

'I must have nodded off. Whose turn is it?'

Support the Weak

An unexpected cold snap brought with it an even more unexpected blast of ice and snow from the north-east. In the early morning light, heavy clouds, weighed down by their belated wintery burden, lent a dusky pink glow across the landscape from the top of the cathedral.

The spires were a bit put out. It seemed to them that they had not been informed of such an event and were therefore quite unprepared. Nevertheless, they had resisted over centuries; they had stood firm through all weathers and there was no reason for that to change now. At least they would be providing shelter for the falcons who would very soon have offspring of their own to shelter. Although the pinnacles were solid structures, stone rectified with lead as a counterbalance, they were intricately ornamental, filled with patterns and spaces and alcoves where wind-blown snowflakes could collect; even mounding high enough in places to alter their outline against the sky. The falcons, however, were tucked away, hidden from the worst of the weather inside the footings of the spires. It was winter's last gasp before finally releasing its grip on the coming year; spring warmth would inevitably force its hand and melt the cold, hard heart of a dying season.

From the front bedroom window, Maggie watched the snow fall in breezy batches, gusting along the road in front of their house. Downstairs she had ready her winter coat and boots, which had not yet been stored away. Not because she had anticipated such weather, but because it was one more thing on the weighty list of uncompleted tasks. It was darker than usual for the season owing to the blanket of snow cloud, and the dense air around the streetlights glowed like rose quartz. From what she could see, the roads were not clogged with snow, although she judged that it would probably be icy underfoot. She supposed that the buses would be running, and anyway, she thought, the main roads would have been gritted. It was not the prospect of the buses not running that worried her but more the fact that the carers might not be able – or might think it unsafe – to reach the house and see to her mum. If she were to go to work only to find that her mum had been left high and dry, it would not be a great state of affairs. However, they had had far worse weather than this to deal with over the years and she had never been let down yet, so she would carry on with her normal Monday routine.

'Is it Monday?' her mother's thin voice called over from the bed to where her daughter was peering through the curtains.

Maggie turned back, drawing the curtains once again. She had been about to reply that it was indeed the beginning of another working week when her mother was distracted by a new annoyance.

'Don't draw the curtains; leave them open. I want to see the sunshine!'

The daughter couldn't help but smile. 'Mum, there isn't any sunshine today. Not this morning, at least. It's snowing.'

'Don't be ridiculous. It's...' Her mother stopped, and her daughter could see she was feeling sure she should know which month it was, and that it certainly wasn't a month with snow in it.

'It's March,' Maggie completed the unfinished statement. 'And we do sometimes get the odd late snow shower now and again. Anyway,' she crossed along the bottom of the bed and turned towards the door, 'you've got your tea, you've been to the toilet, your clothes are out ready...' Counting off the list on her fingers, she scanned the room for anything else that might have been missed. 'I need to go to work now. You can call me if you need to, remember?' She leaned down to kiss her mother on the cheek, thinking that she better not add, 'If the carers don't turn up.'

With a swift glance at her mother's bedside table to check that her alarm bracelet was there, and that the phone was to hand on its charging stand and was displaying a full battery, she left the room and hurried downstairs to prepare herself for the elements.

Hoping she had allowed enough time to navigate the slippery pavements and roads, she pulled the front door shut and tested the short path down to the gate and the street beyond. Behind her she heard the next-door neighbour's front door grate open. It had only been just this Saturday when she had met and talked with Rachel. They hadn't made any further plans to meet. The footsteps joining her on the parallel path were not Rachel's but her partner's. Maggie wanted to appear friendly. She doubted much, if any, information about their conversation had passed between the couple.

As they drew level, each of them with a hand on their respective gates, Maggie ventured, 'Bit of a surprise all this, isn't it?' She smiled but didn't look up to see how he reacted.

'Too right,' he grunted, and that was the sum total of his response – but, she thought with buoyed conviction, it was nonetheless a response. They headed off on their separate routes to work: he towards the old red car, which was already topped by an inch of snow, and she down the street in search of her bus stop.

The traffic was understandably congested; visibility seemed to be the main issue as dense, falling snow swirled through the streets in unpredictable bursts, catching both driver and pedestrian unawares. At least as a passenger she did not have the burden of dodging through the junctions or grinding along at a snail's pace to reach traffic lights; she sensed a benign contentment from being at the mercy of the bus driver, although she realised that not many felt as she did.

The salted path, which led up to the main door of the building where she worked, crunched underfoot; it was reassuring; she was not the last one to hurry inside and leave trailing puddles of grit and melted snow along the corridors.

Because of her part-time status, she did not get a full lunch hour; however, thirty minutes was plenty of time to make a cup of tea and eat whatever she had brought in that day. Where several corridors met, there was a small seating area with low chairs and tables arranged in a horseshoe. This opened out onto a wide landing, up on the first floor. From here you could look out through huge full-length panes of glass across to the dingy, city-stained buildings opposite and down upon the cluttered street below. The scene varied slightly according to the weather. Sometimes in the middle of the day the sun would reach down between the buildings, a benefactor of warmth and light. More often than not, the gorge between the buildings became a ravine where the wind and rain would gust, teasing the industry and fortitude of those on the ground. Whatever the scene, it was always a rest for tired eyes after a morning focused on a screen. Today it was a far more exhilarating sight than usual as a cabaret of snow showers provided perfect entertainment. After setting down her steaming mug of tea, she found herself lost in the unchoreographed display.

'Pretty amazing, isn't it?' said a voice behind her. She looked around and saw the colleague she had spoken to, so very briefly, just last week about the fact that she went to church.

'It's wonderful. I might just forget to eat my lunch!' she replied.

'OK if I sit here?' he asked.

She thought this a strange request as it was a communal seating area for the express purpose of taking one's break, but of course he was just being polite. They were the only two office staff there, so from that point of view it made sense. 'Of course,' she replied, and shuffled her lunchbox unnecessarily along the table just to seal the agreement.

Together they became the perfect audience; their eyes each following a different flake until it fell out of sight, only to be superseded by another. It was not usually the case that she sat here alone, although of course she now had a companion. When there was a group of them, however, she was always the quiet one on the outer edges of the conversation; it was where she was most comfortable. As she opened up her box of salad, which seemed suddenly a bit cold and disappointing on a day like today, she wondered if her colleague might reintroduce the subject of church once more.

'Support the weak.'

The words from the prayer popped into her mind and burst like a bubble. Why, she had no idea, as this person sitting next to her did not seem in the least bit weak; rather, the other way around.

After a minute or two of silent snow-contemplation and unhurried munching, the colleague spoke: not about the weather or the traffic or whether they would all be able to get home that night, but rather about his fear and his faith. It was obvious that he was nervous, and she was surprised.

'You don't meet many people these days who go to church, who believe things, you know?' His question was rhetorical but also a desperate grasp for conversation.

Maggie nodded. 'Yes, you're right. But there are still a lot of Christians out there, although there aren't many that go to the service I go to, but then I don't go on a Sunday, so maybe there are lots more...' She stopped and let her voice trail off, suspecting that in her effort to explain she had gabbled on too much, which wasn't like her at all. She wanted to apologise. Maybe, she thought, that would only make things worse, so instead she waited and picked up her mug of tea, which had cooled enough to drink.

After a minute, the colleague – his name was Mike – took the reins. 'I used to go myself, as a kid, a teenager, you know, and then for quite a few years after that... but not for a long time now.'

Outside, above the row of buildings facing them, a break in the clouds, which promised a cessation in wintry weather, briefly illuminated the spires of the cathedral. The four white peaks suddenly capped in glorious sunshine appeared to be rising above the world.

'Oh, look at that! That's beautiful,' Maggie remarked, breathless. They both stared until the clouds won again and the sight was snatched away. 'So where did you go to church?' she asked, turning for the first time to face her colleague.

'It wasn't here. I didn't live here then. We moved here, my wife and I, about fifteen years ago. We went to a Baptist church up north where we lived.'

Maggie nodded; it was a conversation she couldn't believe she was having, and all at once she decided to say so. 'I don't ever really talk about my faith, you know. I suppose I'm just quiet and it's not the sort of thing that comes up very often.'

'I've seen you and heard a few things about you, and so I knew you believed. Don't worry,' he added, laughing, and she realised her face must have portrayed the horrific realisation that she was being talked about at work. 'It's not the latest office gossip or anything. It's probably just who you are, the sort of stuff that comes across without you realising.' Mike opened up the wrapper on a chocolate biscuit bar which represented the end of his lunch. He continued, 'I wanted to talk to you because I want to start going to church again and I don't know how. I do believe, but my faith is very weak, almost non-existent. I guess it's like the proverbial mustard seed...'

'Lord, I believe, help my unbelief.' She spoke the words aloud without really intending to, but it seemed to help.

'Yes, exactly! I'm glad you understand.'

Maggie checked her watch. 'I need to go, sorry, but perhaps we can talk again?' Gathering her now empty lunchbox, fork and half-finished cup of tea, she stood to leave. 'What about your wife?' she asked. 'How does she feel about it all?'

He stared in silence back out towards the snow, which looked as if it might be easing. Eventually the sunshine would win through for sure. 'I'm a widower. My wife died a few years ago.'

The early morning, dream-like, fairytale landscape had completely vanished by the afternoon. After only a few hours since the snow had stopped falling, the warmth of triumphant spring temperatures had been victorious; most of the snow had been reduced to piles of slush and spreading puddles, which blocked the drains in the gutters, or stood in mounds like white flags of surrender. The traffic now rushed through the disappearing snow, with wheels spraying those picking their way on foot along the slippery, obstacle-ridden pavements.

Maggie reached her bus stop just in time to catch the earlier bus; it seemed that everyone on board was sodden and complaining, despite the sunshine. Squashing herself into a double seat next to the window she thought about the extraordinary lunchtime conversation. It had felt just like the snowfall: out of the blue. Although that wasn't quite the case if she really thought about it. There had been a cursory moment the previous week when they had exchanged words on the subject. As a conversation, it had hardly registered on any scale, and yet that was how things started. And there had been the prayer in last week's service – now *that* had registered indeed!

She had always thought of herself and her faith alike as something very paltry and weak; something that floundered, intermittent in strength, always struggling to hold on. In one way the prayer – the vision – had changed things, and in another way nothing had changed. She had seen with fresh eyes and heard with keen hearing the call of God on those who believed; and despite her opinion of her own faith, she still counted herself among them. She knew this was not because of her own ability to persevere; rather, because ultimately she knew it was God who held on to her, not the other way around. Ever since the Canon had spoken those words, which had flowed like living streams, powerful and potent, ever since the vision of the glory of God had burst upon that scene, things had started to happen.

Some might say they were very small, insignificant things; however, for her, they were anything but. This was where she had seen the change.

Nevertheless, she realised that actually nothing had changed: she was still the middle-aged woman who lived with her mother, who went to work three days a week, who went to church once a week, who had a meagre social life, who rarely spoke to others, who always travelled on the bus, yet who still believed, after many quiet years, in the reality of Jesus Christ as Saviour to all. Perhaps it was just that she had seen it so clearly for the first time in a very long time. Perhaps she had just needed rescuing from a pit of despondence, or perhaps this was just the right time for God to use her.

As she had heard nothing from the care company to say otherwise, she presumed that the morning's weather had not impeded their planned visits for the day. She began to think about what she and her mother might have for their supper that evening. In her mind she opened each freezer drawer and each cupboard and rooted through the fridge, recalling what was in stock; what her mother would enjoy and whether she should pick anything up from the small shop on the way home.

Tomorrow was the day she would go to church once again; another Tuesday seemed to have come round far quicker than usual. There were a small group of regulars who, like her, attended the early morning service once a week, though it often struck her that they were not a group who were obviously joined together. This had never bothered her before. She wondered whether, after last week, there would be a change, and whether or not anybody else had had the same experience. And if so, then perhaps someone might even say something about it.

'Support the weak.'

Heaving her way through the old back gate, as was her habit on returning from the bus stop, she carried a cheap plastic bag containing some semi-skimmed milk, a tube of tomato puree and a packet of bacon. All of these items she had thought of on the journey home. After all, even if she didn't need them, as she hadn't been too sure, they were essentials which would never be wasted. Calling out a greeting through the kitchen door, she plonked the bag on the counter top and started to pull off her coat. The next thing would be to fill and switch on the kettle.

'Mum, do you want a cup of tea?' She hoped her voice would reach all the way through to the front of the living room, to the chair where her mother would be sitting by the bay window. The television was loud and its invasive, penetrating presence grated her insides. She could hear that clearly enough and she guessed her mother must have fallen asleep.

Walking through from the kitchen she found that her mother was not asleep and was not in her chair. She was lying awkwardly on the floor with her head almost under the small dining table where she ate her porridge in the mornings. Her legs were wrapped around her walking frame.

'Mum!'

Her mother's hands were chilled as she touched them and she grabbed a blanket from the sofa to cover her immediately.

'Mum, can you hear me?' With a gentle hand Maggie shook her mother's shoulder and the elderly woman opened her eyes.

'Yes, of course, I'm not deaf.' Her voice was cracked and dry.

'What happened, Mum?'

It took her mother several minutes to reply. 'Well, I've been here for a while now...'

'Yes, I can tell, you're cold.'

'It's very dirty underneath this table, you know. You should clean it up.' Her mother licked her lips.

Maggie closed her eyes. 'Yes, Mum, I will. But what about *you*, how did you get down here?'

'Well, I don't know really.'

'I guess you had a tumble.' The daughter tried to step back from the looming panic. She must keep a clear head and think through what needed to be done. Where was the alarm bracelet? She noticed it wasn't on her wrist. That could wait. 'Does it hurt anywhere when you move, Mum?'

'When I move? I can't move, you silly girl.' Her mother's face contorted as unconsciously she did try to move her legs. They were lying at a strange angle and although the daughter had minimal medical knowledge, she understood that something was seriously wrong.

She sighed, puffing out her cheeks. 'Mum, I need to call for some help. Because I can't move you.' Resisting the urge to add, 'Stay there,' she found the phone and called for an ambulance.

'I hope you're not calling an ambulance or anything ridiculous like that,' her mother groaned, although still with an air of command.

After a few minutes of conversation, in which details and information were exchanged across the line, Maggie, still holding the phone as she had been requested to do, began searching for the wristband with the alarm button. Had the carers not given it to her when they had left after lunch? Or had her mother taken it off? That was what she suspected. She found it on the side of the small washbasin in the downstairs toilet. Her mother must have taken it off to wash her hands, even though it wasn't necessary to do so, and had forgotten to replace it.

Back on the floor, kneeling beside her mother, the daughter noticed the difference between their breathing rates. Her mother's, for all her predicament, was steady though weak. Her own was rapidly increasing as she felt the creep of fear and panic take hold. Her mouth was dry, as was her mother's.

Together they waited on the carpet, looking at the crumbs under the table, wondering how long it would be until someone came to save them. The voice on the phone had told her to stay on the line. They were unable to tell Maggie when they might be rescued.

Every so often the daughter would hurry to the front door, which she had now left open on the latch, to see if there was an ambulance searching for an emergency. After checking the street in both directions, she would hasten back to her mother and talk to her. So far, she had managed to avoid the mention of the word 'ambulance', instead saying that help was on its way. She did not want to disturb her mother any further.

Every so often her mother would attempt to push with her left arm, which was draped over her body as she lay on her right side, in an effort to get up. Every time she squeaked with pain.

'Don't try to move, Mum, somebody will be here soon to help.' Maggie tried to sound calm but she found that reassurance was difficult to project. She had managed to squeeze a thin cushion under her mother's head.

'*Support the weak.*'

Nearly an hour had gone by. The silence (she had switched the television off before she had picked up the phone) was occasionally broken by the normal sounds of human activity from the street beyond – kids running along the road, finding fun in the last of the snow or chasing their friends on bikes; dog walkers meeting other dog walkers; cars starting up or pulling in to park; doors slamming. Maggie remembered the words from the prayer and so she prayed, out loud, so that her mother could hear. She brushed the hair on her mother's forehead as she whispered words of faith and peace and love, and they waited some more.

As if slicing through a dense, fibrous web of time, which seemed to hold them fast, a voice reached them from the hallway, piercing the nightmare.

'Maggie? It's Rachel. There's an ambulance outside. Are you OK?'

Help the Afflicted

Swirls and crowns of frost patterned the windows of parked cars. The lines and forms of fenceposts, gates and pavements were sharpened, caught in the dual beams of streetlamp and moonlight. Maggie noticed every detail as the taxi stole between the silent rows of stationary vehicles. However, although her senses were heightened, an acute reflection of her agitated state of mind, it was only a certain part of her consciousness that recognised the minutiae of these temporarily iced features; a part that was closed off from the recent onslaught of domestic trauma and hospital drama. It was a safety loop which allowed her racing thoughts to rest after the adrenaline-soaked rush of the last few hours; a pitstop where facets of normality could be ordered, reorganised and brought to the fore. She had some idea of the time but it was almost irrelevant in the light of her troubles.

The taxi halted in the middle of the road before her house. They were in no danger of holding up any other traffic in the early hours of the morning. Maggie paid her fare, thanked the driver and, clutching her keys, turned into the short pathway that led up to the front door of the house. She was breaking the neighbourhood silence as her footsteps bit the brisk frost, as her key turned in the lock and as her front door unlatched; everything resounded with surprising discord around her.

It was an awkward hour, neither night nor morning, and the decision about what would be her next best move, on a practical level, wrong-footed her. Whether to make a cup of tea (she had already drunk something that passed for tea at the hospital) and something to eat or whether to go straight to bed and recoup her strength was suddenly a difficult decision to make. In the end she achieved a compromise by taking a small mug of tea to bed. Despite the catastrophic intrusions of the last twelve hours, sleep found her swiftly and carried her off into a restful oblivion.

The Canon stood with his hand shielding his eyes as he gazed upwards towards the spires. He could hear the falcons squawking in the light breeze – such a difference from the previous day's weather – and he strained to catch a glimpse of them from his momentary pitch on the cobbled stones outside the cathedral entrance. Every now and then he saw a dark-winged silhouette darting against the light swathe of cloud which allowed a gracious measure of sunlight to fall upon the scene. The keen figures slip-sliding across the sky, in and out of the pinnacles and decorated balustrades high above, appeared jet-black as if forged in iron; though, he imagined, their feathers were probably as soft as velvet. From the faint knowledge he had acquired when a well-known wildlife expert had visited the cathedral some years previously, after growing interest in the nesting falcons had demanded some such event, he had learned that the falcons were in actual fact not solid black at all but a mixture of tawny brown, white and black, with yellow feet and beaks. From their lofty command they had the proverbial bird's-eye view of the goings-on beneath their wings and were able to pinpoint myriad details with superb vision. Mere humans on the ground without the talent for looking upwards against the sunlight were, at first glance, much more easily deceived. However, the advent of the digital age and the installation of tiny cameras had struck a blow against the nesting falcon's private companionship, daily catching them unawares.

The early morning service had passed without event and in one way, a very strange way, he found himself disappointed. He had prayed vigorously, hours before the service, with some degree of trepidation. On the one hand, he had wanted everything to go ahead as normal without any heavenly intervention; for the words to be spoken, the responses to be heard, the prayers to be uttered and the people to be encouraged as they left the pews and returned to live their lives. Yet on the other hand, how would that equate with the revelation of the true and living God, who longed – he truly believed – and desired above all, to have a deep and personal relationship with every one of them? The tussle between the sudden vision the week before, which in his mind had seemed to clothe him in a fine, bright cloud of dust ever since, lifting him above ordinariness, and the knowledge that God was just as much alive in the small, the mundane and the everyday was, he felt, too much for him to grasp.

After a while he turned his eyes from the sky and the birds, and continued his way across the rounded stones. He followed the path around the side of the cathedral, where the flying buttresses jutted out like firm hands to steady the bows, towards the small chapter meeting house.

All at once, not a vision but a recollection entered his mind, as he thought of the familiar Bible passage he had brought to the gathered few, just that morning from the Gospel of Luke, chapter 9, verses 37 to 43; a father bringing his son to Jesus, calling Him 'Teacher' and pleading for Him to look at the boy who was possessed by an evil spirit which was gradually destroying him. Jesus had reacted with emotion at the shadow of human unbelief, with authority in the face of the spiritual onslaught, and with compassion and complete healing for the boy and his father.

'Help the afflicted.'

These were the words from the prayer: Jesus the Son of God, the firstborn of all creation, had walked the earth; He had seen the affliction of humanity – evil, blindness and suffering – and had brought restoration, by His life, His death and His resurrection. This was the supernatural interruption into everyday lives by the power of the living God.

These are the sorts of lives we live, the Canon thought, just ordinary lives but through faith they are touched by the extraordinary power of God, and that is not down to us but down to Him. With momentary insight, the Canon saw that what had happened the week before was inexplicable; nothing whatsoever to do with him. But as a believer in Jesus, it confirmed him and all others in the task of building the kingdom of God.

His thoughts continued; they were constant, rolling eternally like unfinished business; they spilled over and over in his mind. There is affliction in this world, he thought, which we all experience to some degree or another; however, there is also healing, compassion and restoration.

"'And they were all amazed at the greatness of God.'" He repeated the last verse aloud as he walked.

It seemed that for some of them, some of the time, the strength of belief and faith wavered under the dull, insidious campaign of doubt and despair. All those who chose to respond and believe in the complete saving power of God in Jesus would be targeted, because otherwise what would be the point? The Canon understood all this. If it was just a choice of one set of ideals as opposed to another of equal value, then doubt would be unnecessary; the paths would be different but would achieve a similar end, and therefore one way could not be judged better than another. He had always known that to falter in the face of uncertainty and misgiving indicated that there must be a great and all-important truth at stake. All the spiritual forces of evil must be ranged against those who set their faces towards that truth. It was perhaps the most common affliction of those who believed.

The priest whom, as a result of the previous week's phone call, he had arranged to meet the day before, had been burdened with just such cavernous thoughts of confusion and hesitant faith. It was an especially heavy and significant weight to carry for a person in such a position. Responsibility and leadership could not be easily laid aside. It was not the first time for such afflictions, and it would not be the last. Faith works best when it is blind, the Canon thought; when there is a greater call for courage.

They had talked together about doubts; about what triggered them; about where they might lead and the process of facing them. They had talked about the ultimate source of all doubt and faithlessness. Then they had finally talked about the all-important fact on which everything else hung: one might feel blind in one's faith, but not deaf. Heeding the Word of God was the only sure foundation on which to build, and the promises of God, though often intangible, were nonetheless sure. In their weakness they could bring it all to Him, laying it at His feet as a precious sacrifice. The Canon had not spoken with his fellow priest from a position of infallibility but with an all-too-present awareness of his own similar struggles.

'When it comes down to it, the only role we are ever called to fulfil is that of a servant: no more, no less,' he had answered as the other confessed a sense of failure. On this they had agreed; and the Canon had continued, 'We only have one example, thankfully. I imagine all the rage and subtle deception of hell is unleashed on believers, especially those who commit to serving others in the name of our Lord. We can be sure of affliction in this life. Though again – another thing for which I am thankful – in the light of eternity, that isn't very long!'

Maggie woke and for a moment found it difficult to grasp her situation. She reached for her glasses and looked at the small clock beside her bed. It was so late! In a scramble she sat on the edge of the bed and then stopped. She had been to the hospital last night and had only returned in the early morning hours. Her mother had been admitted and they were planning to operate on her broken hip tomorrow, or did that now mean today? She did not have to cancel work because it was a Tuesday, but she would be missing church, which was something she did not have to cancel. She wondered if anybody would notice that she wasn't there?

Then she heard the key in the lock. *The carers!* she thought.

Fighting with her dressing gown sleeves as she hurried down the stairs bare-footed, Maggie was in time to catch the arrival of the first carer of the day before they had a chance to call up the stairs to her mother, who wasn't there.

'Oh, hello…' It was Alana again, one of the newer faces. She smiled but was obviously confused. 'It is Tuesday, isn't it? Is everything alright?'

'Oh, I'm so sorry that you've had to come all this way, but well, Mum is in hospital. It all happened last night and I've only just realised now that I'd completely forgotten to let your manager know.' Maggie was aware of how thoughtless she had been. Shaking her head she added again, 'I'm so sorry…'

'Ah, I see. I am sorry to hear that, about your mother, I mean. What happened?'

Maggie described how she had found her mother on her return from work yesterday, and how the paramedics had bundled her up into the ambulance. How the hospital staff had suspected a hip fracture, and how the X-ray had confirmed this, and how that would mean an operation.

'So it's all been rather a muddle.' Maggie had wandered into the kitchen as she recounted the events, which somehow helped to stabilise them in her own mind. She had filled up the kettle and switched it on.

'I'm making a drink – do you want one, or maybe you can't stay? I suppose I need to call your manager…'

Alana seemed a sensible and confident young woman. She had taken off her coat already and had slipped her hand across to the container where the teabags lived and now had the other hand on the door of the fridge.

'I'll make *you* a cup of tea and you can make the phone call. Go and sit down.'

Without hesitation, Maggie did as she was told. A few minutes later Alana brought through a fresh mug of tea and put it on the dining table in front of her. Maggie nodded her thanks, as she was in the middle of a call with the care manager. Alana sat at the table opposite her and waited.

After a few more minutes, Maggie had completed the business and she put the handset down on the table. Taking her glasses off, she rubbed her eyes before replacing them and picked up her mug of tea.

'Thank you so much, this is lovely.' She took a sip. 'What about you?'

'Oh, no, I'm fine, thank you. So did you manage to explain everything?'

'Yes, your manager said that a lot of people forget to call in when this sort of thing happens. It's the stress of it all, I suppose. You'd think, though, with all that waiting around in hospital, the hours and hours of waiting, I would have remembered to let you know.' She shrugged. 'Anyway, it's all sorted for the moment. I have no idea how or when she will be back home, of course.'

'Have you rung the hospital today?' Alana asked.

'Not yet. I just woke up before you arrived, so when I've had this tea, I shall try the hospital. You never know how long it might take to get through.'

'Is there anything else I can do for you?' Alana was exactly the right carer to have turned up that morning, and Maggie felt she could face the day with more confidence than she had previously imagined.

'No, thank you, you've been really helpful. As soon as I'm a bit more awake I shall get on to the hospital and I'll let your office know of any changes.'

Alana stood up. 'OK, then, well I still need to record the visit this morning, so…'

'Yes, of course.'

The carer sat for several minutes writing notes in the file on the change of plans for this particular visit. She snapped it shut and returned it to its usual nook on a shelf in the living room bookcase.

'Let me know how she is and how it all goes. You have my number?' Alana asked.

Maggie frowned. 'I don't...' Then she smiled, 'Yes, I think I do. You called me a few weeks ago at work, do you remember, when Mum had a cold? I put the number in my mobile.'

'Yes, yes, of course. Perfect. I had better go now.' The carer began putting on her coat and found her car keys. 'I will be early for my next lady, for a change!' she laughed.

Maggie understood that this visit, much curtailed, would give Alana a boost for the rest of the day. However, it underlined to her the time constraints the carers were under, and perhaps how much care had to be squashed into a service with limited capacity. Alana was obviously a person of good nature and character, even though Maggie's mother had expressed her doubts. When she opened her mouth to speak, her rich, eastern European accent lent her colour and warmth. Again, Maggie was thankful that she had been the one to turn up that morning.

'Oh, I nearly forgot.' Alana handed Maggie a key. It was from the secure coded key-safe at the front of the house.

'Yes, no problem. I can put that back. Thank you.'

'Also,' Alana turned back from the open front door. Usually so sure and bright, her expression revealed concern. 'I want to say that I will pray for your mother, that God will protect her during her operation.'

Maggie wondered if Alana was hesitant in saying this because she had said such things before and had only been met with scepticism or a cold shoulder. Maybe it was because in doing so she was in danger of crossing a line and might put her job at risk.

Maggie stepped up to her and took her hand. 'Thank you so much, and yes, we will *both* be praying. God is good. He is always good.'

Alana looked surprised but she smiled nonetheless and waved goodbye as she climbed into her car to drive away.

'I can come any time, as soon as you like. It's just a bus ride away. What can I bring in for her?' Maggie was on the phone to the hospital.

It had not been straightforward getting through to the right ward, but eventually she had located her mother. Initially, the elderly woman had been shifted onto an emergency admissions ward, the only one with a bed at the time, though she had since been promised a place on the orthopaedic unit later that day. There had been some chasing around between doctors and the consultant, and a few misplaced forms and test results; however, those issues had mostly been resolved by mid-morning. There was a question over the timing of her mother's proposed operation because a raised temperature, possibly signalling a small infection, had been noted. Whether this had been brewing all the while, since before the fall – maybe even causing it – or had come on afterwards was difficult to say. As the staff member on the end of the phone had explained, especially with the elderly, these things could be rumbling along in the background, needing only a change in routine or an accident like this to exacerbate things.

Maggie sensed the tightening creep of anxiety as the call had ended, and she resolved to get to the hospital as soon as she could. A compilation of several nightdresses, fresh underwear, a pack of small incontinence pads, a new tube of toothpaste, the recently started crossword book together with her favourite pen, her watch, another cardigan (she had already taken one in with her the previous night) and a small box of apple juice were packed into the two largest shopping bags she could find. It would be a load to carry to the bus stop and then to the hospital, but Maggie had no leisure in which to be bothered by such impracticalities. She had just stopped at the door to reconsider the items she had packed (perhaps taking in something valuable like her mother's gold watch was not so sensible, even though she knew she would be asking for it) when the phone rang. It would be foolish and also impossible not to answer it. It could be the hospital. Catching her breath, she grabbed the handset.

'Hello?'

'Hello, is that Maggie?'

'Yes, is this the hospital?'

'No. Oh dear, I'm sorry, were you expecting them to ring?'

'No, well, not really. I might have been, I suppose.'

'Oh, I see. Well, so sorry to bother you, but this is Canon Davis, from the cathedral.'

'Oh, I see. From the cathedral,' Maggie slapped her hand to her forehead. 'I'm so sorry I didn't manage to get there this morning.'

'No, not at all, please don't apologise. I was just calling because, well, I knew you were missing from this morning's service and you're such a regular part of our congregation that... well, we missed you.'

The sudden silence at the end of the phone, as if the rapid flow had been cruelly cut short, broke through the barrier of politeness between them. Maggie was speechless that she had been missed and, without intention, quiet tears spilled over.

The Canon had not been struck immediately by the human hole Maggie had left in the service that morning, but something odd about the configuration of the congregation had niggled away at him. Together with his ranging thoughts on supernatural visions, faith and doubt, and the struggling priest, he had not really been able to concentrate sufficiently on the gentle plod through the agenda of the chapter house business meeting. It had only been when they had stopped early for coffee and another member of the cathedral staff, who often attended that particular service, brought the subject up, that the penny had dropped.

He had recalled the unassuming, middle-aged woman with heavy glasses, who always sat two rows back from the front, on the left. Once or twice he had chatted with her – he knew a little of her situation – and the scene of that morning's service came to mind. He realised that she had not been there.

'Yes, you were not in your usual spot; in fact, you weren't there at all and I just wondered if everything was alright?' He sensed she was crying, which confirmed to him that although he had taken a risk (perhaps it could be judged intrusive), he of all people had the time, the licence even, and at the very least the calling, to ask. He hesitated before adding, 'What can we do to help?'

Honour Everyone

'Hello there.'

The elderly woman's eyes flickered open and the first thing she saw was her daughter's face. Maggie was bending down, smiling at her mother, her head tilted at an angle. At first her mother hadn't realised who was looking at her, as the bright lights in the ceiling above were bouncing off the broad lenses of her daughter's glasses, for a moment, blanking the identity of the wearer. But then she recognised the voice and the smile. She slowly shut her eyes again, thinking that it must be early and her daughter had brought her tea and was now heading off to work. She didn't understand why her daughter felt the need to go to work. Enough money could be found to keep the two of them quite happily; they never seemed to spend a lot.

'What time will you be back?' The mother's voice was dry and cracked. It surprised even herself and she tried to cough to clear her throat, yet somehow when she did, everything hurt. A frown crinkled her brow with a hundred more wrinkles than were there before.

'I've only just got here,' her daughter chuckled. 'Well, actually, I've been here for a while, but I've just being talking with the nurses and I didn't want to wake you.'

Maggie watched as her mother widened her eyes; she betrayed fear and incomprehension. Then, shuffling her shoulders, her mother put one hand flat on the pillow by her cheek as if she wanted to sit up. She struggled for a few seconds but Maggie could see that it was a wasted effort. Instead, her mother focused in on her hand where a thin plastic tube looped out from underneath a white gauze bandage, and frowned once more.

'Do you want to sit up, Mum?' Maggie stood, glad at last that she could do something practical. With careful, deliberate easing and rolling and encouragement, the elderly, exhausted woman achieved a sitting position against the pillows. Every so often, as if surveying a foreign harbour bobbing with boats from the lofty rigging of her own, she would look out upon a sea of other beds, patients, curtains, staff and visitors, and appeared to wonder at this sudden and inexplicable change in her environment.

'Do you remember having a fall, Mum, and the ambulance bringing you to hospital? Do you remember that very nice paramedic who made you laugh? He was good at his job.'

'Ambulance?' The mother, her eyes wide with horror, had picked up on the one word she dreaded. 'I don't need an ambulance. Don't you dare…'

The daughter wanted to say that it was a bit late for that; instead she explained, 'Mum, you broke your hip and you're in hospital. You need an operation.'

With her head resting back against the pillow, the elderly woman shook it slightly from side to side; it was unclear as to whether this signified refusal or resignation. Then, after a few minutes she asked, 'Why haven't they done the operation yet? It feels as if they have. It's so painful…'

'Oh, Mum.' Maggie took her mother's hand in both of her own. 'I think you feel awful because you've got an infection which they're trying to deal with and because you're on strong painkillers, which make you feel woozy.' She leaned over to kiss her cheek. 'As soon as the infection is gone, they can sort your hip out and you'll be home again.' As she spoke the words, all too reassuring and confident, Maggie reminded herself that in actual fact they couldn't really predict the outcome that precisely. First, this indefinable infection, which had somehow been lurking in the background, like a wild cat frozen in steely eyed intent, needed to loosen its grip on her mother's body. Second, although it was considered to be a routine procedure, the operation needed to be successful. And third: well, third, the staff had told her that although her mother's mind was relatively sharp, her general state of health was far more fragile than anyone had realised. There was a lot of ground to cover before her future could be talked about with any kind of certainty.

Across the small six-bedded bay where her mother's bed was the middle one of three, the occupant in the opposite bed was calling incessantly. It could quite easily be deduced that she was in some kind of distress, though whether the source was physical or psychological was perhaps only something that an experienced eye could confirm. From time to time, various staff would approach the bed, drawing the curtains as they did so. From this shielded seclusion a concoction of shouting and swearing bubbled up like steam from a cauldron, interlaced every so often with firm responses and sensible reassurances. The curtains would then be swished back once more and the patient in the bed appeared to be none the worse for her private ordeal, although her continuing remonstrations told another story. It was clear that the staff had the situation under control, at least from a medical point of view; however, the eternal disturbance could be heard throughout the ward.

'Why is that woman calling out all the time?' her mother groaned, after a particularly invigorating round of swearing, which this time included the hurling of a water jug and plastic beaker across the shiny hospital floor. Inwardly, her daughter also found herself groaning in fear that this may never let up, and that her mother, and everyone else subjected to the voluble display, would struggle to get any rest.

Maggie suggested, 'I think she's really not very well, Mum.'

'Well, *I'm* not very well, but I don't sound like that.'

For a woman of fragile health, her mother could certainly come up with the goods.

'I think I had better find someone to clear up the spill before there's an accident.' Maggie got up and, stepping around the puddle in the middle of the floor, went in search of somebody with a mop, at the same time thinking the bizarre thought that if anyone did slip on the wet floor and injure themselves then at least they would be in the right place.

On returning from alerting the staff to the hazard, Maggie walked over to the patient in the bed who was shouting while in the process of flinging off her bedsheets. As she approached, the woman stopped pulling at the tangled bed linen and looked up. Maggie could see fear and anger in her eyes; her whole body heaving with breathlessness as if she had just crossed the finish line of a marathon.

Maggie smiled and stepped closer, resting her hand on hers with a dubious anxiety that the staff may not view this as a wise move. It was a risk and she wasn't sure what to expect: the woman could have lashed out or spat at her or even thrown herself at Maggie, but she didn't. Speaking kind words seemed to ease the situation and the patient remained still, her gaze fixed on Maggie who nodded and smiled and held her hand. All at once the patient, whose trembling body she could feel through the hand she held, lay back upon the pillows and her fierce stare began to subside. Behind her Maggie could hear somebody clattering in with a mop and bucket and probably, she thought, some of those folding yellow plastic warning signs designed to identify a pitfall.

'Look at all this!' exclaimed the voice of a cleaner. With unconcealed venom, she added, 'They're trouble! How is anyone supposed to get any peace around here?'

The mopping-up operation began, punctuated by strident repetitions of discontent and ill will. Maggie did not turn her back on the patient in the bed, who for the first time since she had arrived was relatively calm.

Within five minutes, for the most part, the pool of water had been sponged and transferred from the tiled floor to a plastic bucket, and it looked as if order had been restored. The patient had closed her eyes and Maggie wondered whether she dared slip her hand away and cross back over to her mother's bedside.

However, before she could make that decision, the grumbling soul behind her with the mop and bucket made one of their own. Stamping around to the foot of the bed she stood astride, with her cleaning implements lifted high like weaponry. She was poised for attack.

'You have been making so much noise!' she shouted, her words booming towards the patient down the length of the bed like cannon fire. 'You have not stopped since you came in last night, and this,' she rattled the mop and bucket, 'is the last straw! Enough!' With red cheeks and spitting lips, the cleaner turned and stomped away, to all intents and purposes as if she were the nurse in charge.

The woman in the bed began to shake again. Maggie could sense it. Tremors were swiftly followed by a fresh repetition of the earlier disturbance. The patient would not be quiet this time; with screwed-up eyes she refused to heed Maggie and be pacified.

'Are you a relative?' Another abrupt voice, this time a nurse, at Maggie's shoulder enquired. 'Because if not, we would appreciate it if you didn't interfere, you're only making things worse.'

'Actually,' Maggie felt the sudden injustice of her position, 'this lady had managed to calm down a bit just now, before the cleaner came and started…'

'The cleaner was just doing her job,' interrupted the nurse. 'Now please leave this situation to the staff.'

It was obvious that any further remonstrance would not be welcome.

'*Honour everyone.*'

The words of the prayer slipped into Maggie's mind as her hand slipped away from the distressed patient. Sometimes, she thought, just sometimes I wish I could have the last word. Although she didn't feel like it, she smiled at the member of staff, apologised and crossed the ward; she took care over the still damp tiles. Behind her, she heard how the team had decided to tackle the situation: 'Right, then. We are going to move you

121

to a nice side room. So at least the other folk can get some rest.'
A scurry of determined feet kicked aside the yellow folded
warning sign. It was all hands on deck and the bed was
surrounded. The brakes on each wheel were disengaged and the
now unmoored vessel was tugged across the bay, out into open
water. Some crew stayed behind to gather any freight that had
been tossed overboard. Soon, the only sign that a patient had
once been there was a wake of dispersing profanity.

'Oh dear...' Maggie sat back down beside her mother once
more. She knew that the staff had to do something but she also
knew that *she* had done something, which unfortunately had not
been recognised as anything worthwhile. She could have been
angry with the staff who were annoyed by her actions; she could
have been annoyed by the patient who would not shut up
(although it seemed far more likely to her that this was not
something she could help). Nevertheless, she supposed that the
staff were right: it was not her job to interfere. However, she
thought, it was always her place to honour everyone, as far as it
was within her power to do so. But it is not my own power
which I have to rely on, she thought.

Glancing across at her mother, she saw that her eyes were
closed; the almost translucent lids appeared soft and without
tension. Her breathing was steady and her face held the peace
of all things restored. Her mother was asleep, and Maggie was
glad.

The Dean and the Canon were not quite in tune with each other.
What seemed like an ever-deepening gulf stretched out between
them. At the earlier meeting that day when the usual chapter
business had been unfolded like a pile of fresh laundry, shaken
out and refolded with slightly fewer creases, the Canon had felt
a clash of spirits. There had been several of them gathered there
– Catherine, a fellow resident canon; John and Brian, two lay
chapter members; Paul, the treasurer and Marilyn, the chapter
steward – yet he had not been able to pin down the exact source
of this threatening tide which, with dull regularity, seemed to

wash over him when he was in the presence of the Dean. Perhaps it was just how he was. Perhaps his own insecurities and deep personality flaws were the sole reason for his sensibility; his *over*-sensibility to supposed undercurrents that put him on alert.

If he was going to be honest – and everything in him wanted to be honest – and if integrity was a thing to be prized, then he would have to admit that the invisible threads connecting him with the Dean were stretched to breaking point. If they had been plucked like harp strings, the sound produced would be no melody. He constantly examined himself after any meeting with the Dean, by chance or otherwise, to see if he could discover the trigger; as if either one of them, like silent stalking soldiers, had unwittingly stepped on a tripwire buried beneath the rough surface of an unrecognisable no-man's-land.

At the meeting they had discussed, among other things, the partnership between diocese and cathedral, the latest updates from the proposed refectory extension project and the revised business plan for the coming year. The subjects closest to the Canon's heart – the promotion of discipleship within the various congregations; his proposed addition to the Sunday service of an add-to lunch, followed by further Bible discussion, with a more informal session of worship – was again rebuffed. It was not completely thrown out, that would have been too obvious a strike against the whole existence of the cathedral ministry, but once again it was pushed to the back of the queue: more time and research was apparently required to bring the idea fully fledged to the table. No one could say that his proposal was spontaneous or off the cuff, and having discussed it with others, he knew that in principle he had support; however, it was not something that excited the Dean. That much was clear. It was also clear that it had something to do with him – the Canon himself – as a person, and he felt powerless to respond. Frustration and irritation began to shake his solid, calm soul and an inability to fight back haunted him.

After the meeting he had chatted with another attendee about the quiet lady with glasses, Maggie, and her conspicuous absence at the Tuesday morning service.

There had been the subsequent phone call and offer of help and he had arranged to join her at the hospital himself and give her a lift home later that day. It was not often that he made personal hospital visits, as the in-house chaplaincy team was very well served; nevertheless, he had asked what it was that her particular part of God's great global family, could do to help and she had requested his visit. The lift had been his suggestion after hearing her mention catching the bus home. That had been settled and he therefore had a couple of hours for preparation and study before he took the trip.

In their kitchen at home, he sat on a stool at the breakfast bar and ate a cheese and pickle sandwich. With a large mug of decaffeinated coffee (he was trying to cut down on caffeine) and a faraway expression, he stared down the length of the old stone floor towards the front door. There was a ripple-effect glazed panel to the side of the door and although the view was never sharp, he could tell if a car pulled up to the house or if anyone was coming to the door. He was not watching with any specific sense of purpose; rather, it was purely somewhere to look, and there was always the thought in the back of his mind that if his wife returned soon, he could talk things through with her.

Always was indeed the correct word because that was how their relationship worked: they talked, always, back and forth, exchanging the common, and the not-so-common, thoughts that trickled through each day, colouring, flavouring and sometimes sparking into life what he feared would otherwise be a monochrome, tasteless, mundane existence. When something was eating away at him, then she would be his first port of call.

The sandwich was down to its last crust when he saw shifting, broken shapes in the glass turn into dark blotches, which swiftly filled the panel. He heard the key scrape in the lock and then the front door opened, and his wife in her long grey coat appeared, and all was clear in the glass panel once more. He frowned at the sight of her coat just for a moment; it was not the everyday sort of coat she normally wore. Then he remembered that she had been attending a funeral in a local village that morning. She had been representing them both.

'Well, that was a sorry affair.' She spoke with a light-hearted kind of exasperation, and threw her coat onto the chair in the hallway and kicked off her shoes, before padding through to the kitchen in stockinged feet. 'Is there another sandwich?' she asked, looking at the remains on her husband's plate.

'No, but I can make you one, no problem. Cheese?' The Canon slid down from the stool and opened the fridge, retrieving a block of cheese and the pickle jar. His wife scrutinised the level on the kettle to check that there was enough water for another cup, and flicked the switch.

'So, no fun at the funeral, then?' he asked as he buttered two slices of wholegrain bread which he had laid out across the wooden board on the counter.

'Thanksgiving service, remember? Not quite a funeral.' She wagged a mock finger of admonishment at him and pulled herself a mug out from the cupboard above the kettle. 'No, but then I wasn't expecting any fun, surprisingly enough. I meant that there was a poor turnout.'

'Oh dear, that's a shame. Thank you for going, at any rate.' The Canon felt a twinge of guilt at his lack of effort, but of course he could always qualify that by telling himself that they – she and he, him and her – worked as a team and that he couldn't possibly be expected to attend every call of duty; he couldn't be in two places at once. Nevertheless, he hadn't gone and that was that. If he was being honest, which, he reminded himself, he strived to be, then he really hoped she wouldn't expect him to recall who the service had actually been for. His guilt was mounting.

'That person,' she continued pouring hot water into her chosen mug, into which she had already put a teabag, 'that person who, as it turns out, very few people actually seemed to want to be thankful for, was the person who, for the most part, single-handedly ran the children's and youth work in that village for more than forty years! Even when she was elderly, she made sure there was something going on for the local children even if she didn't actually run it herself. Who knows what lives she influenced along the way, or how many young people she steered in the right direction.' His wife took the plastic bottle of milk offered to her by her husband to finish off making her drink, and added, 'I know that I didn't go there knowing a lot about her, but I'm so glad I did. She sounded like a force for good rather than a force of nature, if you know what I mean.'

The Canon nodded; he understood exactly what she meant and was glad that his wife was exhibiting such vehement passion on this person's behalf. Although unable to escape the sense of guilt for his own part, he was proud of her.

'You didn't stay afterwards?' he asked.

'I did for a while, actually,' she glanced at her watch as if to verify how long she had been. 'I chatted with the few family members and friends who had turned up. I was sort of expecting the usual bun fight in the church hall. Though, as I said, it was poorly attended and there was just some very weak tea and a sorry plate of biscuits wheeled in on a trolley, you know the sort of thing.'

Squeezing the teabag in her mug, ensuring that this cup at least would be anything but weak, she deposited it on the counter with its spoon.

'Now, this is more like it,' she added, referring to the dark shade of brown in her mug. She sat up at the breakfast bar on the opposite stool from the Canon, where he had resumed his perch and where the freshly made sandwich was now waiting for her. 'Thank you, darling. I'm so sorry, I've been rabbiting on about my morning and I haven't let you get a word in.' Taking a large bite of the welcome lunch offering, she waited for her husband to respond.

'Well, my morning…' He folded his arms and leaned forward on top of the bar. 'I led the early service this morning as usual, though in actual fact it wasn't usual.' Noticing her widening eyes, he added, 'No, it wasn't like last week, nothing like that. No more visions!' He tried to laugh it off but they both knew it had meant more to him than that. 'No, what I meant was that we were one down on the usual crowd.' His wife nodded and smiled although her mouth was full. She sipped her tea, which was hot, but she clearly needed something to wet the half-chewed sandwich in her mouth.

'There's a woman who is always there, and I mean *always* there,' the Canon continued. 'She's sort of middle-aged, I guess, with thick glasses, and she seems very shy, or maybe she's just quiet. I wasn't even sure of her name till today. Well, anyway, she wasn't there in her usual pew. It was only later, after the meeting – chapter business – that Brian mentioned it.'

His wife nodded again. Everyone was aware of that man's canny ability to put names to faces and remember them both.

'I found that we had some contact details for her from those feedback forms we gave out last year. And so I called her.' After filling her in with the details of the conversation and how he would need to be off to the hospital later, he suddenly changed the subject. He wanted to talk about something else that was bothering him. 'I don't know how to feel, how to be...'

His wife looked puzzled. 'How to be, in relation to what, exactly – this hospital visit you mean?'

He shook his head. 'No, no, I wasn't thinking about that. That, I feel, is quite straightforward, my regular line of business; the sort of thing I *should* be doing. No, what I mean is... what is really troubling me is the Dean.'

She rolled her eyes; this was not a new area of difficulty. 'What's he done now?'

'It's not what he's done so much as...'

'What he hasn't done?'

'I suppose so. Maybe it's just me...' His voice trailed off. He wanted to say more, to explain fully. It was like tackling a huge, sticky cobweb, trying to talk about something intangible yet tenacious.

His wife shook her head. 'No, it's not just you. You know that. Everybody finds him, shall we say, awkward from time to time.'

'If we were at school, I mean if all this,' he threw his arms wide indicating their surroundings in general, 'were the playground, I would say that it feels like he's got it in for me! But that's daft.' It wasn't daft; it was how the situation made him feel. His wife put down her mug and reached out across the counter between them to hold his hand. 'It's ridiculous, he's the Dean, my boss, my brother in the Lord, my mentor, my...' They waited in the silence while he found some more words. 'I just want to respect him, but it's so hard and it really shouldn't be!'

'No, you're right, it really shouldn't be. But I can absolutely see why it is. And, I suppose, the frustrating thing is that it's something we have no power to do anything about.'

'It's as if he's deliberately setting himself above us all, keeping himself out of reach, out of contact, the sort that matters, at any rate, especially in this job. The worst of it is, my imagination runs riot and I start thinking about why he behaves like this: what is he trying to hide? Or am I just being dramatic and he is simply just a very different person from me? How can I, how dare I, question his integrity?' He felt his hand squeezed in fellow feeling.

His wife said, 'I don't think we should go down that road, not yet at least.'

'Yes, I'm sorry. It's a bit messy. But all I can do is keep my head together, do my job, walk along the road and...'

'Honour everyone?' she interjected. 'That's what it says in the prayer, isn't it? And,' she added, her eyes brightening with sudden recollection, 'I've been reading in Philippians 2 where it says, "Rather, in humility value others above yourselves."'

'And,' he grinned back at her, 'there is always something we *can* do, always. We can pray.'

In the dim light of the low stone building, where age-old heavy beams straddled the ceiling, black on white, a rectangular box punctured by deep-set windows on either side, the husband

and wife held hands together over a plateful of crumbs and the dregs of tea and coffee.

They thanked God for all He provided; for each other, for the security that brought; and then they laid before Him the difficulty of the Dean. And once they had started, they found themselves praying for the village where the service had been that morning; for all the young lives touched by the care and thoughtfulness of a devout lady; for the proposed hospital visit later that day where an elderly mother and her daughter were caught up in the uneasy landscape of ill health. Moreover, the privilege and rarity of such a situation, in a hollow and broken world, where two people could sit together and talk to God because that was the most natural and established response, did not completely escape their attention.

'And,' the Canon said, finishing his prayer, 'above all, we pray that we will have the strength and the courage, in Your name, Lord Jesus, to honour everyone. Amen.'

Love and Serve the Lord

For those keen observers of the natural world, the live camera footage from the very top of the cathedral was a regular online draw, especially during the bona fide months of spring, when many living things were looking for love and, inevitably, reproduction. There were some viewers whose excitement in the activity of the falcons, or more precisely, the noticeable inactivity of the female in particular, was renewed. She was spending more time resting in the scrape now than before, as if preparing and warming the nest for the eggs that seemed likely to follow. For the moment it appeared that the male was doing most of the hunting, returning with prey – pigeon, starling and even the odd bat – in his bloody talons.

There was a generous portion of sunshine bathing the spires this morning. The perfect blue above their heads was spanned by a criss-cross of jet engine trails and thin, striped cloud; routes both manmade and natural, travelling off in every possible direction. If this were a map meant to guide the journeying pilgrim through the atmosphere, then it would be hard to tell the true path from the false.

The gothic cathedral spires had nowhere they needed to be. Centuries ago, they had arrived and were as content with their location as any architectural feature could be: guardians of nesting birds and tributes to the majesty of human achievement and, although a thought often overshadowed, signposts to the heavens and the glory of God.

The previous afternoon, just before the rush hour had descended in full, Maggie had been given a lift home in the Canon's car as arranged. To have the Canon visit her mother in hospital had produced a whole host of emotions. She was almost embarrassed at having such a religious dignitary appear at the bedside, although nothing about him conveyed the fact; he was not wearing a name badge, just his dog collar, and so apart from that he looked like any other grass-roots vicar. She was overwhelmed by gratefulness at the interest shown in her, and her mother's, situation. Moreover, she was concerned that he might have taken time out of an important meeting or event simply at her request. She had expressed these worries in a silent prayer as the time approached for his visit.

The situation hadn't changed much for her mother, who remained unwell and not yet fit for surgery, and whose wandering mind flitted in and out of reality. Maggie and the Canon had chatted about their home life, about her work and her faith and how her mother felt about these things. During the course of this conversation, taken slowly in drip-feed portions between the wakefulness of the patient, the rattling around of the staff and the constant ringing of numerous telephones and call-bells, Maggie realised that it all seemed to boil down to certain basics. Her faith, and probably that of her fellow believer sitting next to her beside her dozing mother, rested only on two things: love and service.

Just before a trolley came round with what looked like an evening meal for those who could manage it, they had left her mother with a prayer and, for the daughter's part, a promise to be there the following day. The walk through the ward and the corridors, and finally through the main entrance, exiting the hospital, had left her overly conscious of the fact that she was with somebody else. What had just appeared to be the natural movement of two people walking together through a building, for her had been utterly out of the ordinary. It had given her the sense of being outlined in sharp strokes against an otherwise dull backdrop.

Journeying inside the car through traffic had also been a novelty. Nevertheless, she was glad to say goodbye and wave her thanks as she had turned towards her own front door, after what had suddenly become a very long and exhausting day.

It had been impossible to organise her feelings into anything she could recognise as the door closed behind her. Finding herself alone, greeted only by silence, she had leaned back against the door with her eyes shut, just breathing – in and out, in and out. Like errant children, she allowed the day's events to slip away.

'Love and serve the Lord.'

Somehow, these words became the one element of thought she was able to fix her mind on with any clarity; to love God, Father, Son and Spirit, was all she could ever do, and to serve God was the only natural outcome of such decided devotion. And therefore, whatever happened in life to disturb, alter, distort, challenge and devastate, these twin foundation stones would never be moved. The only thing which might change that state of affairs would be her decision to walk away.

But where would I go? 'You have the words of eternal life.'

In the normal run of things, on a Wednesday morning Maggie could be found in the office at work. However, during a conversation with her line manager, she had explained her altered circumstances. Her request for time off to deal with the immediate and as yet undecided outcome had been given without hesitation; they had arranged to discuss any possible further leave as each day unfolded. So she was at home instead.

Light in speckled shafts extending through the window was like the kindly, comforting hand of friendship resting and spreading its warmth across her shoulders. Maggie was sitting listening to the news on the radio, with tea and toast on the small table before her. She could almost imagine, just for a moment, that this was her life; that there were no cares or worries or difficulties to be faced, and that this would be where she always sat to eat her breakfast in sole contentment. Guilt pierced the fragile bubble in an instant. She picked up the telephone once more to try to contact the hospital for news of her mother. Although she understood that the basis of communication between herself and the hospital would be that *no news was good news* – if her mother's situation deteriorated, they would inform her whatever the hour – she still felt compelled to check in and confirm the lack of change in her condition, at least change for the worse. The lines were, of course, still busy and she had decided that she would go in later that morning whether she received any news or not.

A few more minutes basking in the embrace of sunlight, another refill of tea and she would be ready for the day. Just a few minutes more…

There was a knock at the door and her reverie was broken. For a split second she was tempted not to get to her feet and answer it. Every tenet of social necessity won through, however, and she put down her mug and left the table.

It was Rachel.

'Hi,' she called as Maggie opened the door, a brief smile of friendly concern flashed across her face. 'Just thought I'd see how things are. How's your mum?' She looked awkward, almost grimacing in her asking, as if fearing her enquiries might be painful or unwelcome.

Maggie beamed, not because things were fine but because she so appreciated such kind thoughts from a neighbour who she had only recently begun to call a friend.

'Oh, thank you, that's really kind of you,' she replied, then, hesitating for a moment, she explained the situation. It turned out that Rachel also had the morning off work and if she, Maggie, wouldn't mind fitting in with her trip to the supermarket, she could easily give her a lift to the hospital. A time was arranged for the lift and with further expressions of thanks, they both departed from the doorstep conference.

Maggie cleared the breakfast things away. She washed up the pile of dishes and pans and cups that had grown over the last few days. She was aware of a lurking, uncomfortable thought, which lay like an unpredictable, unfriendly – possibly sleeping, possibly not – cat across a doorway; a thought that could suddenly lash out and take a swipe, destabilising her inner control. Rachel, even though she had been ordinarily dressed for an everyday kind of day catching up on jobs, had still looked, in her stonewashed jeans and pink-hooded top, perky and young, without appearing childish; even her trainers had glitter on them. In comparison, Maggie felt drab.

Deciding to ignore the potential threat this petty thought conveyed, and step over the sleeping cat, she tidied the kitchen and made the beds. She took the opportunity to change the sheets on her mother's bed ready for when she came back from hospital. Just as she finished, a tsunami of unforeseen questions slammed her down upon the freshly smoothed quilt of her mother's double bed as if she were paralysed.

What if her mother never recovered enough, even to have the operation? Would she remain immobile for the rest of her days? How would they cope at home if that were the case? What if she did have the operation but never fully regained her current level of mobility? What if the infection took a deeper hold and she lost the fight before or during or after the operation? What then?

Lying on the bed in the warm glow of the bedroom, Maggie felt alone. A handful of knick-knacks decorated the room: a porcelain figurine or two; several prints of squally ocean scenes; lace-edged cream linen cloths adorning the tops of the dressing table and chest of drawers; a few framed photographs and efforts at cross-stich pinning them down, just in case the stormy sea prints on the walls threatened to spill over into the room and disrupt its equanimity. Her emotional reactions to the rush of imagined outcomes frightened her. What sort of daughter was she? What sort of human being was she if the overwhelming feeling to the worst possible outcome was that of relief?

The telephone rang and she jumped. Thankfully she was still lying on the bed and there was a handset in its charging stand on her mother's bedside table. She sat up and reached across for it.

'Hello?'

'Hello, am I speaking to Maggie?'

'Yes.'

'It's the hospital, Macarthy ward. We just wanted to let you know that the medical team have decided your mum is well enough for her operation. She'll be going down to theatre this afternoon.'

'Oh… thank you.' While trying to find her way back to shore, Maggie was all at sea. 'I was planning on coming in later this morning. Would that still be a good idea?'

'Yes, of course. I can see that all the necessary consent forms and everything have been completed so that's all OK. You can see your mum before she goes down to theatre.'

'Yes, of course, thank you very much.'

As arranged, just after ten o'clock, Maggie knocked on her neighbour's door and waited for her as she bustled about finding her shopping bags and her jacket and her purse. Rachel then thought that she had lost her mobile phone so the subsequent search held them up for another five minutes. Then she found it under a sofa cushion and they were on their way. Rachel was clearly feeling bubbly but trying not to be obviously so; under the circumstances she was probably aware it would have seemed crass. But sensing this, Maggie tried to reassure her. She *wanted* her to talk about her life, how everything was going along between herself and her partner; she wanted to hear about real life rather than her own situation; anything other than hospitals, operations and outcomes.

'He's agreed to go to counselling,' Rachel beamed. 'It's the first time he's really opened up about our problems and he's accepted that it can't go on like this. You don't mind me telling you, do you, today, with your mum and everything?'

'No, of course not, I'm really pleased for you. That's a great step forward. I can see why you're excited.'

'Oh, I know it's silly but I really am! Whatever's happened, I do still love him and there must be a way to change things for the better.'

'There always is, I think… a way to change things, I mean, if you decide to, if you love each other.' Maggie was surprised at her own conviction on a subject she could hardly claim to know anything about.

'Absolutely. I know it's not the same for everyone, I understand that, but we have a chance here.'

They were both in agreement. As the enormous sprawl of buildings that comprised the hospital complex came into view, they concluded their conversation.

Rachel said, 'I hope your mum's OK and that the operation goes well. I'll be thinking of you.'

The car pulled up outside the main entrance where there was a drop-off point and Maggie gathered her things ready to climb out of the car. 'When are you going for counselling?' she asked.

'Next week, Wednesday evening.'

'OK, I will pray for you both. Thanks for the lift again. It's been really helpful.'

'Thanks for listening to me prattle on. Are you sure about not wanting a lift back?'

'Yes, it'll be easier if I make my own way, you know. Not sure how things will work out this afternoon, so…' Maggie shrugged but smiled.

'Yeah, I understand. But you've got my number just in case.'

'Thanks, you've been brilliant. Have fun shopping.'

They parted like friends of longstanding and Maggie was so grateful. Despite the roughness of the road, there were new and happy discoveries along the way. Nevertheless, an annoying buzz of yet more uncertainties swarmed above her head: had she been bold enough in her faith with this newfound friendship? Had it been just a throwaway comment that she would pray for Rachel? How was she, Maggie, any different from any other neighbour? She tried to swat them away as she walked through into the hospital reception area. All she could be was herself. All she would ever be was the person God made her to be, and all that was required of her was to adhere to the basics: *To love and serve the Lord.*

'*To love and serve the Lord*: what does that look like?'

The Canon pronounced these words before the warm and cosy atmosphere of his small study. The books lined up on the shelves stared back at him, utterly unmoved by the question. Of course, each of them, within the secrecy of its pages, would have its own point of view on this particular subject, depending on whether it was of interest. Some of the books were naturally very interested indeed, as they might be full of words expounding on the details of the Christian life: its calling, its trials, its highs and lows; the life of the early Church and the biographical insights of great people of faith. In contrast, others were quite stoic, hard-backed in their resolve to ignore such a question; the fine gold lettering on their haughty spines declaring that they were above such trivialities, and preferred to deal with more meaty matters like ancient Greek, Hebrew and a host of various theologies and doctrines. What was the Canon to do?

He had, of course, consulted the relevant passages and commentaries over the last few days in preparation for this particular sermon. Nonetheless, as a regular consumer of reading matter and an avid student, he was fully acquainted with the wild and capricious ways of books. Needless to say, if the volumes in his study had shown any actual sign of anthropomorphism he would have been stunned into silence.

It was a thought, among others, which had been chasing around his mind ever since the morning service last week, the morning of the vision, the prayer; the day he now referred to (purely to himself, of course, because he was sure that nobody else would think it amusing) as Heaven's Gate. On a trivial level, he was quite pleased with this little attempt on word play. There were so many – *so many* – points to be raised and to focus on in that prayer, but this was the one in particular that he wanted to unpack. (That was the new phrase, wasn't it, he thought, when you wanted to examine something and try to understand it?)

Despite the numerous possibilities, he already had a view in mind. He had been reading from several of the Gospels – Matthew 10 in particular – the accounts of how Jesus sent out the new, fresh-faced disciples on their first missionary trip. He had called them to follow Him; they had witnessed His miracles and listened to His words; they had watched His life play out in public ministry and private prayer. That was all the training they had had. Comparatively uneducated and unprepossessing, and definitely without connections, He had trusted them with the first phase of kingdom building.

'Love and serve the Lord.'

They loved Him indeed, although as yet without a full understanding of His earthly purpose, and to a point they recognised Him as the promised Messiah. But what had struck the Canon as noteworthy was that they had been utterly *prepared* to go and serve as He had called them to go and serve: taking nothing with them – virtually nothing – to preach the kingdom and perform miracles; they appeared to have gone without hesitation. They had not debated doctrine or argued over tricky passages of Scripture; they had not packed a suitcase or booked ahead for accommodation. Their love for Jesus carried them forward, and their service was simply working with whatever lay before them. And they had returned full of it! Both love and service relied on a total trust in His provision.

'That's the key!' he announced once more. Still the stiff, starched bookshelves stood silent. He took up his pen and, with markings legible only to himself, he scribbled in the margin of his already full page of notes, which he would later type up: *It's not that we should never plan or be wise in taking precautions but that we should always trust…*

From the corner of his eye, he caught sight of the regular, flashing, tiny green light on his mobile phone: a message awaited. Although he had set his phone on silent, which was his normal habit when preparing or studying, and although he had a personal rule of not checking his messages until he had finished, or until he stood away from his desk to take a break, something prompted him to check this one.

'I see…' He spoke aloud, although this time he was in no way addressing the tight-lipped tomes. The message had been from Maggie, alerting him to the change in her mother's situation, as he had requested she should do: 'Let me know how everything's going,' he had clearly said by the hospital bedside, and she had taken him at his word. Of course she had. If *he* couldn't be trusted to say what he meant, then who could? On the message she had asked for prayer and so he prayed at his desk. After a few minutes, or maybe more, he had found that his errant thoughts were wandering off track, picking through the wayside rubble of irrelevant matter as if sifting for treasure. He grabbed them by the collar and dragged them back to the highway.

'And Lord, please comfort and keep Maggie strong in her faith because she is Your disciple, she is one who loves and serves…'

His eyes opened with sudden revelation and he picked up his pen and began scribbling once more. Skimming through the tenth chapter of Matthew's Gospel with his finger, he reached verse 16 and read onwards. Several things caught his eye and his imagination: 'I am sending you out as sheep among wolves … but the one who stands firm to the end will be saved … So don't be afraid; you are worth more than many sparrows … Whoever finds their life will lose it, and whoever loses their life for my sake will find it.'

What words, the Canon thought, what words are these? Naturally, they were not words that he had never heard or read before, but as anyone who reads the Bible as a believer would understand, he knew it was often the case that certain words at certain times shone out like never before. They would strike a sudden and harmonious chord within the soul, calling for a response or providing an answer or shedding light in the shadows.

Addressing the books ranged along the shelves once more, he continued, 'To love and serve the Lord is glorious: not glamorous, or easy, or simple, or always pleasurable, but truly glorious. Our Father in heaven showed His glory to us in sending Jesus, and that glory was perfected in His death for us. To love and to serve means suffering and pain, not always and certainly not forever, but in this life...' He halted and stood, looking out of the window. 'In this life God is glorified in the mundane and in the difficult, and often it is there that we find Him.'

Maggie, he thought, was a quiet person who would never be noticed by the sea of people who clamoured and roared for their piece of this world's glory. She was not experiencing anything more unusual than most of us go through at certain times in life; her current difficulties were not out of the ordinary, by any means. Undoubtedly, she loved and served the Lord. Although she appeared as nothing in this life, she would always be something in the eyes of God.

He glanced at his watch and decided it was time to put the kettle on.

Rejoicing in the Power of the Holy Spirit

Maggie had been surprised at how quickly the tables had turned. Her mother was now ready for the operation. She supposed that the medical team would not attempt to carry it out if they had deemed her unfit. Also, she was aware of the importance of getting her up and mobile again; the longer she stayed in bed, the harder it would be. These clinical decisions were a delicate and challenging balancing act, akin to being atop a high-wire with a pole in your hands and your bare feet curled around a rope. It felt risky enough watching from the ground as a bystander, although, she thought, I'm more than that. Perhaps if she were to continue the metaphor, she was an agent with a vested interest in the act. But this was no sideshow: this was mother and daughter.

Waiting at her mother's bedside while together they watched the constant back-and-forth activity that shaped the life of the ward (occasionally involving her mother, though mostly not), Maggie tried to occupy her mother and keep her distracted. She was clearly better in herself because her character, which had been dampened by infection, pain and drugs, was now displaying more familiar signs of tetchiness and irritability. She was making up for lost time. It was quite a relief when a bright and cheery member of staff came to collect her as if it were the most joyous part of her day.

'Now then, my dear!' the young nurse began, sparking with an almost manufactured enthusiasm. Maggie could sense her mother bristling instantly. 'We're off to theatre at last, my darling. We've been waiting for such a long time, haven't we!'

Maggie bit her lip as her mother replied, 'Have we, indeed?'

Thankfully the nurse did not seem to pick up on the sarcasm; her functional mode was programmed to display warm and encouraging condescension. Therefore, she beamed with efficiency, wiggling her head so that her high ponytail flicked side to side with each brisk phrase.

Once the cumbersome process of transferring the patient from the bed to the trolley had been completed, her mother, Maggie walking alongside, made her exit from the ward.

'Why don't they wear smart white caps any more? That would keep them in order, I should think,' the mother asked the daughter in a loud stage whisper as they journeyed through the hospital. Considering the dry, raspy condition of her mother's mouth, it was surprising what vocal force she could achieve, for nothing had crossed her lips since very early that morning.

'Oh, we haven't worn caps for years, my dear. They're *very* out of date,' the nurse chipped in, quite clearly missing the point.

Maggie saw a chance to pour oil on troubled waters. 'That just shows how well you've been, Mum. You haven't been a patient in hospital since...'

'Since I had you!' Her mother looked smug, relishing the sharpness of her own retort.

Maggie nodded. 'You're probably right, Mum.'

There was a point at which she could go no further. Maggie gave her mother a kiss and a brief wave goodbye. The hospital treadmill continued its process and its control over the fate of the elderly woman. A treadmill it was indeed because this was no extraordinary procedure. The method of mending a broken hip was calmly brutal in its normality and Maggie was thankful that at this point she could walk away.

After discussion with the staff on the ward, who informed her that although the operation would not be lengthy her mother would be under the effects of the anaesthetic for a good while afterwards, she thought it best to make that the end of her visit for the day, unless of course the situation threatened to stray outside the boundaries of routine. She would walk into town and pick up a few things, perhaps; she would try not to extract too much enjoyment from the unexpected leisure before catching the bus home.

Her step was light as she exited the hospital's main entrance and she supposed that it was down to the handing over, albeit temporarily, of responsibility. However novel and strange it felt, she was determined not to allow the lure of lurking guilt to engulf her; she was also aware that such a decision was not something she could maintain alone. Dark spirits waited in the wings for a chink in her armour, but the promise of God was the filling, the protection and the power of His Holy Spirit. She had read about it, about the promise and the fulfilment of that promise; and lately she felt that she had truly experienced it for herself in a way she never quite had before. She recalled the end of the service the previous week; it was as if heaven's gate had opened and the power of God had been revealed.

The hospital was fairly central, and choosing to walk into town rather than catch the bus outside, it only took her ten minutes to reach the main pedestrianised shopping area. Both the cathedral and her place of work were quite nearby. Maggie realised she was hungry; the hours of lunchtime and afternoon were overlapping. She walked along the row of high street shops looking for an appealing place to stop and eat. This was something she hardly ever did, and yet it was difficult to shake off the unfamiliar sense of being on holiday, because she *did* want to shake it off, in the face of her mother's trials.

The door to the café opened easily and she entered a steamy haven smelling of soup, toasted cheese, coffee and bacon. There was space at a single table at the front, and although the windows were partially misted over, she could still peer through and watch the world pass by. Leaving her coat on the chair, after a moment's deliberation – there was no queue at the counter so she wouldn't be taking the space of anyone who had come in before her – Maggie stood and read the chalkboard where the lunchtime menu was written. The original bold black of the board was now dulled to patchy grey where remnants of previous menus and prices had never been completely wiped away. The words from today's list of items on offer sloped down to the right, losing height and width along the way, as if travelling into the distance only to fall off a cliff. Nevertheless, she managed to work out that she could have a toasted sandwich and a cup of tea for £6.50, which seemed quite reasonable under the circumstances. She placed her order and waited to collect a large mug of tea; she carried it over to the table, securing it finally as her own.

Cupping her hands around the mug and taking her time in occasional sipping, while waiting for the sandwich to be ready, she watched the folk passing backwards and forwards along the pavement outside. Inside the café, comforting smells and warm vapours were the order of the day. As well as the large windows suffering in the humidity, Maggie had to remove her glasses several times and wipe them as the heat from the tea rose to meet her. It was pleasant and soothing to observe her surroundings without feeling any need to be involved.

Her thoughts circled back around, again and again, to her mother and the situation she had left her in at the hospital. She reminded herself that to sit there, to drink tea and eat a sandwich was by no means a dereliction of duty. Then she remembered that she could do more than just be firm in her thinking: wherever she was; she could pray. Prayer, she so often imagined, was like sudden shafts of light, strong and vital, which shot upwards from the person praying, connecting with and breaking into the other great world beyond the visible. The very act of praying linked her own situation with that of another, immediately and without hesitation; in sitting and waiting, in drinking tea and watching, she was not powerless.

The door of the café gusted open with a welcome exchange of steamy air for fresh. Maggie looked up and saw with surprise the face and figure of her colleague, Mike. It was natural, of course it was, that people should pop out from work at lunchtime to grab something different to eat. Maybe they hadn't had time to prepare something for the day; maybe this was what most people did anyway, although, she thought, it would be an expensive way to feed yourself on a day-to-day basis. As she only qualified for a relatively short lunch break, it was never something she'd considered.

He had obviously hurried out for lunch as his jacket was half-slung over his shoulders and she noticed that he was actually carrying a lunchbox, but it did not appear to be a coincidence that he had walked into the very same café. He looked straight over at her and waved. Until that moment it had not occurred to her that in claiming a day off because of her mother's illness she would now appear to have deceived them all and was instead wallowing in tea and toasted sandwiches on an illicit holiday. But then, she thought, why would I take an extra day's holiday when I only work part-time, and why would I then place myself in prime position just down the street?

Maggie lifted a hand from around her mug and gave a little wave in return; she smiled, though she wasn't sure why.

There was a small queue at the counter now but Mike came over to her table and asked if he could join her. Maggie shrugged and said that of course he could, and in a moment he had removed his jacket and put it over another chair which was turned towards the neighbouring table, which he then swung around to face hers. Hiding his lunchbox beneath his jacket on the seat, he joined the end of the queue at the counter.

With his back towards her, he perused the chalky menu. He tilted his head to the side, following the words as they disappeared off to the right. It suddenly seemed like the most natural thing in the world that he should be there, and the woman with steamed-up glasses, at the table by the window – the daughter whose mother was at that very moment under the knife; who believed in prayer and in so much more – was strangely at ease.

'I saw you come in here from across the road.' He grinned as he put his own mug of tea on the table together with a fresh bacon roll. He scanned the table, which was devoid of crumbs or an already used plate. 'You not eating?'

'No, I'm still waiting for a toasted sandwich. I suppose they take a bit longer to prepare... Oh, here we are.' Maggie's bemused expression lifted as a girl carrying a tray with her toasted sandwich on it stopped beside them.

'Sorry for the wait,' she explained. 'We forgot to add the cheese. It's not much of a ham and cheese toastie without the cheese, is it?!' They laughed a little in agreement.

'That's fine, thank you,' Maggie answered.

'Anything else I can get for you?' the girl queried, half-turning away, though obviously hoping that her task had been successfully accomplished.

'No, it's all OK, thanks.'

The girl whizzed away to help with the crowd that was now growing at the counter, leaving the couple to their lunch. The piping-hot sandwich was still sizzling on the plate, too hot to sink her teeth into immediately. Maggie was intrigued and not a little unnerved to hear that Mike had seen her and followed her into the café. Not that she suspected anything untoward from him; more that her earlier concerns about being seen outside work, supposedly enjoying a relaxing time, had perhaps proved possible after all.

'You saw me come in here?' She needed to prod and probe the subject before it became an issue.

'Yes. I had just left work to get some fresh air and I thought I might eat my lunch in the square up the road, you know.'

She did know. There was a large space, a wide alcove between two buildings, with benches and spring bulb planters, and one small beech tree in the middle, surrounded by a circle of rocks.

'I didn't think you were in work today,' he added.

'Well, I know it looks odd that I'm here, but I'm not – in work, I mean. How did you know I wasn't in work?' she asked, cutting the halves of her toasted sandwich into quarters; the savoury aroma of cheese and ham seeped out.

'Your manager told me. I asked because I was looking for you, just before lunch...' His voice trailed off and he bit into his bacon roll. Then, with his mouth half-full, it seemed he needed to explain the purchase of the roll. 'I brought my own lunch as usual but I thought I shouldn't really attempt to eat it in here and I was hungry. The smell got to me as soon as I opened the door.' He took another bite.

It was her turn to talk. She imagined a cloak of collusion and duplicity wrapping itself in tentative folds around them: he had bought a bacon roll and had hidden his lunchbox; she had called off work but was eating out in a café just down the road. She suspected he wondered why she was smiling.

'So, the thing is,' she said, taking her turn to clarify matters, 'it's my mum.' He nodded for her to continue. 'Well, I look after her; we live together and she had a fall the other day. On Monday, when I got back from work, I found her on the floor. So she ended up in hospital and then we had to wait for them to operate...' She took a deep breath, aware that from within a swell of emotion had suddenly surged up out of nowhere, threatening to breach the walls of flood prevention. Although, if she stopped to think about it, a storm such as this did not just appear out of the blue. Deep changes in atmospheric pressure, highs and lows, unexpected currents, these were the elements required to birth a storm.

Picking up a quarter of her sandwich, she went to bite into it, then changed her mind and finished her story. 'So I was all set to go and visit her this morning, which I did anyway. Then they called to say she was going to be operated on today after all, to repair her hip fracture. So she's not long gone down to theatre. I wanted to walk and get something to eat and I ended up here.' Finally taking a bite of her toastie, she looked around her. 'I've not been in here before.'

Her colleague had finished his roll and he followed her gaze. 'Me neither.'

Maggie had been thinking about a plan. She was not usually one for plans, but sometimes she realised that they were necessary. Although the problem with plans, she thought, was that they didn't always go according to plan. So what *was* the best way to plan for the breakdown of a plan? However uncertain, she was going to have to make provision for their future, for both herself and her mother. As with any good arrangement there needed to be a contingency – yes, she decided, that was how you planned for the failed plan.

At this moment in time, it all depended on her mother's recovery and how well she could claw her way back to her previous level of mobility. The other thing to consider was the fact that even if she did achieve the standard of independence she had had before, would her risk of falling again increase? Would she slide further down the slope of infirmity? Would they regain and yet be unable to hold on to their current pattern of life? These were all questions that could not be answered with any certainty. For the moment, whatever plans she made for the future could only be based on well-informed guesswork.

After lunch, where she had shared an unexpectedly pleasant hour with her colleague, instead of picking up some shopping and heading home as she had originally intended, and despite advice to the contrary, she had walked back to the hospital to see if her mother had come out of surgery.

She felt inexplicably buoyant and relaxed. Perhaps it had been the fact that she had taken an hour or so for herself – completely for herself – but then again, she mused, as she tripped along the pavement back towards the hospital, she had not been by herself; she had had company. Perhaps it had been the company...

The staff on the ward had told her earlier not to worry, instead to go home and they would call her. Surprised to see her, they informed her that her mother was not back from theatre yet, and when she was, she would be more than groggy. They advised her again in the kindest of terms to leave the patient management to them, to go home and be ready to visit the following day. Maggie felt awkward and realised that she should have stuck to the original plan after all. Although plans had flaws, she reminded herself that for the most part they were worth sticking to.

This was only another hiccup in an already unusual day, and Maggie muttered a quick 'I'm sorry and thank you' to the now otherwise preoccupied staff. She supposed that they were used to far stranger and frequently more dramatic reactions on a daily basis; this particular incident, if it could even be called that, would disappear off their radar in seconds. Maggie left the hospital once again. Preferring to walk, she headed back into the centre of town to catch the bus home.

It had remained dry all day and the warmth of spring was undeniably upon them. Budding trees and plants, papery-thin blossom and late-flowering daffodils, robust and forthright like royal standards, marked the slipping back of winter into shadow.

'Rejoicing...'

She recalled the word from the prayer and felt that her heart was light. It shouldn't have been, not really, not under the circumstances. Nevertheless, it was, and she decided that the best way to deal with that was to be thankful. It occurred to her on the journey home, through the early afternoon traffic, that in actual fact her state of mind was not perhaps surprising. Had she not asked for prayer? If she sensed indefinable comfort like a warm blanket, then that was only to be expected, and should then be returned in decided and grateful praise. Every situation in life did not work out with quite so much ease, she knew that; however, she had to acknowledge goodness and blessing when it did arrive at her door. To react with cynicism and negativity, though it might feel justified for a moment, should never be conclusive. Their current upheaval was not over and done with. This was just the beginning for them – for her and her mother – as they climbed out of the hole into which they had fallen, as they dusted themselves down and looked ahead once more. She would not always feel this bright but she would always strive to rejoice.

'... in the power of the Holy Spirit.'

These were the words that followed and they held the key. Humanity blighted her belief and without the living power of God inside her she would never be raised or changed or renewed. She wondered at her own thoughts on this subject: where had they come from? How had she understood these things? And why were they so important to her?

The bus rounded a corner a few streets away and she suddenly realised that they were near the park. Pressing the bell on the floor-to-ceiling pole beside her, she stood. It was the perfect day to walk home through the park.

It was good to see people out and about, making full use of this amenity. There were dog walkers and walkers without dogs; walkers with toddlers and buggies, and couples, arm in arm. Most of the people, she noticed, who like herself were walking alone, were also plugged into headphones, and she wondered if that gave them a sense of security. The tables outside the park café were full and buzzing with business. As she passed the entrance to the children's play area she saw a familiar face, or rather two familiar faces, crossing over towards the gate as they headed for the swings. It was the owner of the corner shop with his grandchild once again, the little girl who had been off sick from school. They must have spotted each other at the same time and they waved together. The grandfather stopped to say hello.

'What a lovely afternoon,' he said as he tried to stand still despite his granddaughter's eager tugging on his coat sleeve to get to the swings.

'Yes, it's perfect,' Maggie answered with a smile, adding, 'Off school again?'

'Yes, but only because it's a teacher-training day,' he laughed. 'This little monkey's quite fine, as you can see!' Addressing the girl he said, 'Now you can go to the swings; I'll be there in a minute. Off you go.' They watched as she dashed through the gate making a joyous, vocal charge for the one remaining, unoccupied swing.

'How is your mother?' he asked politely.

The question caught Maggie off guard. She didn't think he knew anything about her. 'Oh, well, that's kind of you to ask. She's not well, actually. She's in hospital, I've just come from there.' Maggie waved a flimsy hand behind her in the direction of town.

In turn, the shopkeeper appeared to be caught off guard. He responded, 'Oh, I'm very sorry to hear that; yes, very sorry indeed. I've seen you pushing her in the wheelchair. What's wrong with her?'

'Well, she had a fall. I look after her at home, though I still work part-time.' It felt like she had had to explain herself a lot recently. 'Her hip was broken and so, well you know, they're trying to fix it now.' She shrugged because there was nothing further to say.

'Oh, I think they should make a good job of that at the hospital; they're very good, you know.'

'Yes, I think so, I hope so.' Maggie looked across at the little girl, playing. She was draped over the swing seat with her legs dangling, occasionally propelling herself backwards and forwards while she sang. 'It's difficult to tell, with Mum's age and health, you know,' she said.

'I'll be thinking of you. Be sure to let me know, when you come into the shop.'

'Thank you, that's very kind. Yes, I will. Who's minding your shop at the moment, then?'

'My wife is in charge today. She sent me off to the park with this one, for peace and quiet, I think!' They both nodded in complete understanding. 'I had better go and do my duty. Goodbye for now.' The grandfather's face had shown reluctance to leave but she felt it was all for show; he clearly relished the time with his little live wire.

Maggie wandered back through the park following the circular route, which took her to the gate nearest their street. In the midst of their little catastrophe, grace abounded.

As she approached her house, harsh sounds, shouting and screaming, reached her ears. There was nothing to be seen but she could immediately tell where they were coming from. Like a bull rattling to be free of its cage, the neighbouring front door opened with a shudder. Almost wrenching it from its fixed hinges, Rachel's partner stormed out in a rage. He threw several luggage-sized bags out onto the path, letting them slide towards the car, and turned back to grab another. She didn't want to look but Maggie thought that if she were to see his face it would be very red and his nostrils would be blowing out steam.

At her gate, she hesitated. This was not something you could politely ignore and march up to your own front door as if normality reigned supreme. On the other hand, it was not a situation in which you would want to intervene.

Partly hidden by a short panel of hedging, Maggie kept her eyes down. She could hear Rachel's voice – one moment crying, the next moment yelling. The jarring sound of Rachel's front door being kicked shut from the inside followed by the thud of car doors slamming, then the grating of tyres on tarmac as the car tore away down the road brought the final clashing cacophony to a close.

The street was quiet, hushed into fearful silence, and Maggie let out a breath. She already had her key in her hand. She stared at it. It could so easily be accomplished: just a few steps up to her house, the key in the lock, the door would be opened and she would be safe inside. But she couldn't do it. Brushing aside the nagging voice which told her not to disturb her friend (she could call her that now, couldn't she?), Maggie retraced her steps and turned up the short path that led to Rachel's front door.

Her dim figure approaching could probably be seen through the mottled glass, she thought, but that was neither here nor there. Maggie – the woman, the daughter; the neighbour, the friend – took a moment to pray. Before knocking on the door, she asked God to fill her with His Holy Spirit and to help her, right then and there, to be the best person she could be.

And...

As open and exposed as they are, the cathedral spires are not overcome by any sense of vulnerability. They are raised high, above the insignificant creatures scuttling around on the earth beneath; both majestic and proud and all at once magnificent in the glancing rays of sunlight, which waltz between the steady revolutions of cloud.

If you were to climb one of the nearby hills that curve up from the broad river valley, where the city splays across flat fields, you might find a squat, stone beacon, upon which would be marked the location and distance of a variety of landmarks. One of these points of interest would be the cathedral, its ancient architecture appearing at odds with surrounding modern construction – utilitarian buildings, suburbs and industrial estates – that make up the bulk of the city.

If you were to read the inscription on the flat top of the stone beacon – an inlaid weathered-metal disc mimicking a compass design – you might follow the directions, your eyes searching the cluttered landscape for the celebrated cathedral, distinctive both by its height and its age.

But what if it couldn't be seen? What if it had, as if in mystical legend, been whisked away before the morning sun appeared above the horizon? What if the beacon had lured you under false pretences to its very top, only to disappoint?

Ah, but no; this is not the case. It is merely a shadowy illusion created by dark, drifting cloud. All of a sudden, with the drama of a magician's revelation, the velvet cloth is pulled back and the cathedral spires stand out golden and sharp against the purple backdrop of distant hills as the sun breaks through.

From the ground the cathedral is a colossus, though compared to the infinite canopy above it is merely the dried husk of an insect among fallen leaves. Thin layers of ancient sculpted stone have been gradually – fleck by fleck – blown away into dust and only God in heaven knows if its end will come before the whole of creation itself dissolves into eternity.

Falcons – hovering, gliding, swooping and diving at breakneck speeds – are like snapping, rattling flags in the breeze, almost as if they are tethered to this portion of the sky. Here is where they belong in perfect companionship, existing within their chosen boundaries. With hardly a sound, eggs have been laid and are now cocooned in the constant care of warm feathers, each parent taking its turn to perform this secluded duty. Total privacy, however much assumed, is not theirs to claim. The sly intrusion of an enthusiastic host of humans far below has them trapped within the confines of a camera lens; their daily activities are scrutinised, leaving them pedestalled as unwitting celebrities.

There is prey a-plenty for them to hunt within the expanse of the untidy, urban territory beneath: an ever-increasing flock of fat pigeons and a variety of smaller birds lured by the rapid spread of new, budget-built housing, with their gardens and hedged alleyways. The alternating interplay of rain, wind and sunshine delivered by the arrival of spring creates diversity and burgeoning interest in the secret, little-known world of all things wild.

The Dean is a man of energetic thought and process; he relishes the structure of meetings and committees; the strong hand of human intervention, planning and innovation. Over the years, what had once been a calling has somehow been remoulded into a career. Where once a passionate heart was drawn by the indefinability of everything spiritual, prompting him into divine service, there is now a dull and deadly cast of a priest tied to institution. Dehydrated and brittle, it carries out its duties with a diminishing sense of sight.

This, of course, is not what is seen at first glance, or even on closer human inspection, because his involvement in the life of the cathedral is very much in evidence. However, inwardly, when the heart is inspected, it seems to be a pouring out of mere human labour and knowledge, and any search for the hand of God upon his life is rather a dwindling dream.

What promise had been visible in his early years! How far from that road, which points towards a golden vista, he has wandered! So far it is hard to measure. He is reliant on his own judgement; he is following his own map. The voice of rite and incantation sings loud; the whispers of God go unheeded. What he may not have realised is quite how much distance he has allowed to come between them. He is far from the original pathway.

The Canon, on the other hand, has pondered the pathway all too often. Each day the trials of discipline, the journey's fatigue and inner self-doubt bother him like a cloud of midges nipping away at the flesh of his faith. He senses the attrition of spiritual battle, ever lurking in the shadowy undergrowth. Enemies bristle and rustle on either side of the pathway. They are waiting to catch him unawares, to trip him up with an awkward, protruding root or distract him with a desirable, exotic sideshow. He is increasingly aware of his inability to ward off the darts of evil; he knows that without the protection of armour he would be caught out, tripped up or drawn away into faithlessness.

And now, because of his recent vision – his Heaven's Gate experience – pride, that long-forgotten enemy, has been resurrected and is solemnly marching alongside him. In creaking strides, it looms beside the road, ominous in blank expression. Although the Canon has been unnerved by the vision and puzzled about its whys and wherefores, he now hears whispers that tell him he is special and deserving and honoured, and that it should all be about him. However, although it took him a while to comprehend this, he has come to understand that the Dean's dismissive attitude is something to be grateful for: it compels him to keep this peculiar experience between himself and God. His wife knows, but that is almost like knowing it himself; the strength of their partnership, through an unbroken age of trust, has fostered a keen and comfortable absence of reserve.

Spiritual onslaughts, old and new alike, have driven him to prayer. As though he could view his very soul through a transparent, fragile membrane of skin, his weakness and failings grow increasingly apparent with each passing day. Perhaps it is the same with the vision: as he prayed in that morning service and truly meant each spoken word, he glimpsed through the wispy layer of this world. In that moment, the vast splendour of the heavenly one had been visible and knowable; and perhaps in that brief attainment, others who had been gathered there had seen it too. Nevertheless, as he ponders it all, he understands that it is not in his character or his remit to ask.

Rachel is a woman torn between thrashing emotions. One minute she is relieved that the burden of a troublesome, fiery relationship has been lifted, and the next she can almost feel the gaping hole inside her. Every time she stands and looks in her full-length bedroom mirror, she is convinced she will see a perfect, cartoon-like circle cut right through her, revealing the white-painted pine wardrobe parked against the opposite wall. And anyway, if she looks in the mirror at all these days, all she sees is an unruly disguise of unkempt hair with dry straw ends, and cheeks blotched from the frequent taint of tears.

Has she lost weight? Well, that would be likely. She tugs at the unfamiliar loose waist of her jeans, pulling it out to reveal what could almost be called a spare inch. On the other hand, she supposes, if she were to take a pragmatic view, this is an unexpected bonus.

There had been another, and she now understands, final, blast-force argument which had shaken the walls, and her partner had left, driving off in *her* car. The storm had blown up out of nowhere, as they often appear to do, but now, only on reflection, can she see that there had never been a nowhere. In the far-off distance, over the horizon, a boiling sea had already been bubbling and their twin boats, with masts and sails entwined, could only ever have struggled endlessly in the rise and fall of foam.

She does not understand what has happened to her life. It has not gone according to plan, although the forecast had been set fair. She does not know what to do about her absentee partner and the counselling appointments; he has not made any contact or answered any of her calls or messages. She does not know how to go about fixing her front door, which badly needs replacing, though it is likely to be expensive. She does not know how to move forward with the recent discovery of a neighbour who has become like a sister; who has held and comforted her in her immediate grief, despite having trials of her own; and who has even prayed with her and promised to continue praying. She does not know how to manage the introduction of God into the equation.

Then there is Mike, the colleague from Maggie's place of work. Now here is an interesting character who also seems to have blown up from nowhere. Unlike the storms, though, his presence is not in any way foreboding, and the only threat he poses is perhaps to usher in a sweep of fresh air: new currents merging and new pathways melding.

He had been so alone since the death of his wife, and in that loneliness, all has been laid bare. The state of his soul, for so long frozen in time, has begun to thaw; he can feel how cold he had grown. From his perspective, the steps he would have to take to turn around and head for home stretch before him, an illusion of gigantic ravines, where precarious rope-bridges dangle in the air. He wants to talk to God again but the way back looks too hard.

Nevertheless, ever since he met Maggie, or rather noticed her in the office, he has been drawn by something intangible, something invisible. She is not beautiful, or dazzling; she is not a figure to catch the eye, but he has nonetheless been caught; moreover, he has realised that it is not mere romance. In her, he sees (he often wonders why nobody else does) a person of grace, of rich spirituality, of glory, even.

It is hard for him to describe, as he turns the matter over in his mind, which is something he finds himself doing more often than not these days. In no way is it any kind of haughty grandeur or superiority that she evokes, not in the least; rather, a depth and richness of soul and character.

One day, as he was standing gazing at the lawn which needed mowing, words that encapsulated her so perfectly came to him. It seemed as if they had flown in through his living room window. They were old words, buried far back behind the splintered beams and cobwebbed boxes in the attic of his mind: 'The fruit of the Spirit is love, joy, peace, forbearance, kindness, goodness, faithfulness, gentleness and self-control. Against such things there is no law.'

The elderly woman, who has had an operation to repair a fractured hip, a procedure all too common in a person of her age and well within the boundaries of routine for the surgeon, is hardly aware of her surroundings. There is a part of her that understands the facts: she is in hospital and she is in some pain if she moves, but they keep bringing her 'something for the pain, my dear'.

Another sort of person stands beside her bed and talks to her about 'getting up and about' and then pulls and heaves at her until she sits up and then stands.

Oh, the shock of her feet against a cold, solid floor! Why don't they help her put her slippers on?

Then there is another one of them, and together they stand on either side of her shaking frame (this frame being her actual body, rather than the walking frame, which is metal and which she is holding on to for dear life) and they *encourage* her to take some steps: pain, fear, panic, and again pain!

When will she leave this awful place? What is her daughter playing at? Why isn't she in her own home, in her own chair, with her own window to look through? Where have the days – no, she means years – where have they gone? If this is now her life, then it is a strange and alien thing and she cannot see how she fits in.

Maggie – the woman, the daughter, the neighbour, the friend, the colleague, the believer – has been coming to terms with many things of late. The daily, weekly, schedule, which had been set in stone for an age and a half, has come to an end. Maybe it is just a pause, a slight diversion, like the propped-up yellow council signs you see on the roads when there are traffic works: *road ahead closed – follow diversion*. That's it, she is just following the black arrows to skirt around the problem. Soon she will round a corner and reconnect with her old route. But that is all a 'maybe'. The thought crosses her mind that in fact the diversion could be far more permanent.

Her mother is not making a good recovery, and her mobility as well as her cognitive ability remain poor. That's how they word it at the hospital: poor.

So, does *poor* equate with *hopeless*?

Her mother seems to be lost in a fog that at first had been put down to the anaesthetic. As yet it hasn't lifted and now other causes are being discussed. Maggie finds herself alone at home; she has the place to herself. There are no carers popping in and out; there is no one else to make a cup of tea for or to walk to the bathroom with, or to help onto the stairlift, or to dress and undress, or to kiss goodnight.

Sometimes she finds herself just staring into the mirror. It is not because she is looking *at* her image exactly – whether her hair is messy, or her fringe is straight, or her eyebrows need attention – but rather because she is looking *for* herself, as if the Maggie of old has gone missing and maybe she is hiding on the other side of life.

To counteract these unhelpful and unproductive moments she has returned to work, just her normal hours as before. There has been no reason not to, as she can still easily visit her mother in the afternoons and on her days off. More than ever before she is grateful for the structure and distraction it provides. And more than ever before she is – oh, so thankful – for a God who is faithful and who stands by her, of that she has no enduring doubt. Of course, she cries and pleads with her heavenly Father for the pathway to be cleared ahead as the current obstructions dominate her horizon. Yet in moments of clarity, she understands that it is not the restoration of normality she craves, rather a resolution: a way in which she and her mother can move forward. She doesn't really have any notion as to what another pathway might look like; however, she is prepared and ready for change, but she is not unafraid.

Nevertheless, there are already two new elements in her current circumstances which, all at once, like bold and beautiful sculptures, are slowly forming in front of her: her friendship with Rachel, who is suffering the after-effects of frontline relational warfare, and her friendship with Mike from work. He has suggested that they go to the Sunday morning service together because, he said, it would be so much easier to go with someone than to go on his own.

To go to the cathedral on a Sunday morning would certainly now be possible if the situation with her mother didn't change. She explains as much to him, without wanting to feel the pressure of anything that might pull her in either direction. An odd sense of disloyalty ripples through her mind: is it to her mother? Or to her usual Tuesday morning service? Or to her old life?

The words of the prayer from the other week, before everything changed, sometimes stand before her, golden and dazzling, full of divine wonder. The image helps her to pray because, although it was nothing she could explain or describe to anyone, it was as real and as concrete and as true as everything she believes in.

'And the blessing of God Almighty...'

God is almighty and He has a heart that longs to bless.

The Blessing of God Almighty

On Thursday morning, the Canon and his wife were having a conversation.

'Have you seen any of the footage yet?' she asked.

'No, I haven't, not yet,' he replied. 'Is it any good?'

'Well, pretty much like last year so far, except the picture quality is much better. I think they've adjusted the cameras or upgraded them or something.'

'Yes, a few weeks ago a wildlife team went up and fiddled about with the equipment. I meant to go up and see what was what. They invited any of the cathedral staff who wanted to but something came up, I can't remember what exactly…'

The Canon paused by the breakfast bar in the kitchen, a collection of papers in hand. His wife had her laptop out and was checking the live falcon feed from the spires. Once bitten by the bug she tended to get engrossed in the daily drama from the top of the cathedral, a soap opera which managed, without clever scripting, dramatic pauses or devastating twists, to keep its fans gripped.

'You should've told me; I would've loved to have gone and seen what they were doing.' Her disappointment sounded only mild.

The Canon knew that this wasn't quite true, as she hated heights, and if she had really known about it beforehand nothing would have tempted her any further than the walkway which ran around the lofty inside of the main building. It was his wife who subtly changed the subject.

'Do you think they might do a TV episode on our falcons again like last year?'

'I have no idea, though unlikely, I should imagine. Not heard any rumours circulating but I will keep my ears open.' Holding his papers vertically on the counter, he tapped them to straighten any waywardness, then he picked up his recently refilled mug of coffee. 'I'm back in the office now till this afternoon. That OK with you?'

'Of course.' His wife flicked him away with a few dismissive hand motions. 'Go and study; blood, sweat and tears; prepare to enlighten us all.'

The Canon couldn't think of an appropriate response to this rhetoric; she was always sharper than he was when it came to spontaneous wit and banter, so he just shrugged and murmured, 'If only...' and wandered back towards his study.

A shout of 'I'll bring you a sandwich in for lunch' wafted along behind him.

Over his shoulder he called his thanks and then closed the door on the kitchen, the falcon-feed, the house, the drizzle outside and the rest of the world. Some would say he closed the door on his wife but that would never be the case; she just happened to be among all the other things he was closing the door on, and if he so wanted, he knew that he would only have to ask and she would be there.

Over recent weeks he had been thinking about discipleship. He had been turning the thought around and around in his head that people had made it all so complicated when in actual fact it was perfectly simple. But that's what human beings like to do, he thought. Where something is straightforward, we like to question and say, 'What if?' or, 'Why that?' or, 'How can I?'

To study discipleship he had been studying those first disciples and how Jesus had directly interacted with them. How He had sent them on mission; how He had explained in pictures; how He had taught from the Scriptures which they already knew; how He had warned them of His coming suffering and sacrifice; how He had promised the Holy Spirit;

and how all the powers of hell could not overcome them. These were some of the fundamental matters that were dissected and examined behind the Canon's closed door; matters he wanted to bring to his congregation so that they too could see what it meant to be a follower, a disciple of Jesus Christ. The pattern of the world was there to be turned upside down, or rather put the right way up, and Almighty God had chosen those who would believe to be the instruments of such a revolution.

Earlier that morning, the Canon had been reading two passages from the Gospels – the first from Mark 10 and the second from Matthew 20 – both of which described a small incident, a seemingly uneventful conversation, where the disciples had been all too evidently human. The disciples had taken the teaching on board that Jesus was the Messiah, the promised one, and that subsequently, ultimately, they would see Him raised in glory, His true nature revealed to the world, and a request had been voiced – a favour. As they had been so closely involved from the beginning – *they* were the specially chosen ones who had witnessed everything, all the miracles and the teaching – couldn't they be guaranteed a place of honour at the end of everything? Surely that was not too much to ask?

This request had started a quarrel, which threatened to hoist overboard all that had been gained so far. Jesus had called them together (the Canon imagined Him using His arms spread wide to bring them in, beckoning them to huddle up shoulder to shoulder) and said, 'You know that the rulers of the Gentiles lord it over them, and their high officials exercise authority over them. Not so with you. Instead, whoever wants to become great among you must be your servant, and whoever wants to be first must be your slave.'

As he had read these words, although not at all for the first time, they had jarred on his ears like the squeaking brakes on his car (which he needed to take to the garage). It wasn't because the words were wrong, or like the brakes they required replacement and repair. It was rather because he felt it was his own soul that was out of order, so much so that what was wrong sounded right and vice versa. Nobody would have thought the Canon a proud man or somebody who liked to throw his weight about, not at all; instead he himself knew what was in his heart and what grand temptations lured him in. He read on in Matthew's Gospel: 'just as the Son of Man did not come to be served, but to serve, and to give his life as a ransom for many.'

'To understand the greatness of God is to see Him nailed to a cross...' the Canon said aloud, and then with a nodding head comprehending the truth, he wrote it down.

An endlessly dank morning had been followed by an afternoon of the same. The air had been still; no mad, gusting April showers, but instead incipient, deep-set dampness. It was more like autumn then spring. It was Thursday and Maggie had been to the hospital. She had spent a few hours with her mother, who had dozed on and off. It seemed to Maggie that this soporific state was not just owing to her physical condition but was also a shutting off from the unpleasant world she now found herself in. Perhaps her mother had decided to take on the true form of a helpless, hopeless patient, languishing in fictitious ill health. Whatever the daughter said or did, however much she cajoled or encouraged, her mother remained aloof and unheeding.

Maggie had been there when the physiotherapists had come along to engage their patient in yet another round of exercise; a sparring match in the fight against immobility. She had watched how they approached the task and thought how gentle but assertive they were with her mother, a method she tried to emulate. She had attempted to get her mother to eat some lunch, almost having to feed her each long, ponderous mouthful, which before all this would most certainly not have been tolerated.

She had talked with the staff about the difficulties of 'getting mother moving', and now as she walked out through the main entrance of the hospital, in her mind she went over the discussion once more. The upshot was that her mother was taking up a valuable bed in an acute orthopaedic ward, and that without any rapid improvement, her recovery would prove to be a long haul. One possibility was that she should be moved to a smaller outlying rehabilitation unit where her recalcitrant presence in a bed would not be so begrudged; where concentrated therapeutic efforts could be made to get her back on track. The thought of bringing her back home in her current condition seemed impossible, and yet, Maggie thought, perhaps she should have anticipated such a situation. Perhaps she had ignored the inevitable, thinking that everything would just tick along as it had been, forever and ever, amen...

How foolish she had been.

A sturdy waterproof jacket, long enough to be called a coat, warded off the drizzle, and she was even tempted to walk into the centre of town rather than catch the bus directly outside the hospital. She wanted to discharge some energy, to be alone with her thoughts, to wrestle with the possibility – the definite possibility – of unforeseen future developments concerning her mother. She wished she had a car. Then she would take the road out of town and into the country. Maybe she would drive up through the hills and then park somewhere and climb until she got completely out of breath. That would feel good, she thought. Maggie supposed that she could also take a bus out of town, but that wouldn't be quite the same.

Her usual bus was there, waiting at the stop, so it seemed sensible to catch it; she would resign herself to just thinking about hiking in the hills. The journey would take her through the centre of town and then onwards along her normal route home. Maggie decided she would get off early again and walk through the park despite the now unrelenting rain. It was early enough in the afternoon for the bus to be devoid of school children, not that she minded children at all; nevertheless, a ratty tide of scruffy youngsters always created in her an inexplicable sense of depression. Perhaps she felt drenched by a wave of how they all seemed to feel: the day was over; they only had energy left for frivolities and trouble and home.

Lifting her hood back over her head, Maggie stepped off the bus to walk towards the park and thought about what she might cook for tea. She had forgotten to get something out of the freezer but there was always an egg or some pasta which she could do something with. Although the urge to expend some frustration had dissipated somewhat, she strode out, walking quickly through the gates, feeling her leg muscles tighten at the sudden call to action. If she walked around the park several times, she thought, no one would notice or care, so that was what she did. Soon half an hour had disappeared and Maggie felt the benefit.

However, what she really wanted to do was to talk to somebody about her growing apprehension for both her mother and herself; how their future would unfold. Would she make the right decisions? Would she be left alone to make those decisions or would they be made for her? A myriad of implications stood jagged along the horizon like the dark, ramshackle silhouettes of enemy soldiers. Yet who would fight for her?

God Almighty: that was who.

Stopped at the gate between the park and the street, with her hand on the railings, Maggie closed her eyes and prayed, lifting all these tumultuous thoughts and questions heavenward.

'And the blessing of God Almighty...'

The scene in the cathedral, as the words of the prayer had been spoken, materialised before her once again; a scene she could never escape (why would she want to?). It was a taste of a far greater future, far more assured, far above any trouble she could possibly have in this life.

'Are you alright?' queried a voice at her side.

Maggie opened her eyes and smiled, realising how she must have appeared.

'Yes, I'm fine, thank you. I was just praying.' There, she had said it, and now the local shopkeeper, the one with the granddaughter, whom she probably spoke to about once a week when she popped in to buy the odd item, would begin to suspect, if he hadn't done before, that she was really not quite normal.

He tilted his head to one side and looked a little puzzled. He nodded his head as if he was seeing something more than a regular customer and murmured, 'Oh, I see…'

She was not sure that he did.

With weak laughter he added, 'I was just walking this way and I thought you were going to faint. You had your eyes closed and you were holding on to that post for dear life!'

Maggie lifted her hand from the end of the railing that formed part of the gate and saw that she had been pressing so hard the pointed finial had made its impression on her palm. 'No, I'm OK, really I am. But thank you for stopping.'

'Well, OK, then.' The man seemed as if he would prefer to move on.

Light rain was still falling around them, almost like mist, which hung in patches over the trees, their interlocking branches shielding the ground beneath.

The shopkeeper dug his hands in his pockets and nodded goodbye, saying, 'I must get along now. We'll leave it to the gods, I suppose. You never know…'

It was clear that he was making a reference to the fact that she prayed; it was also clear that he had more faith in fate than prayer. Meeting somebody who didn't probably made him feel uncomfortable.

Maggie watched him hurry down the street, crossing between the parked cars as he headed back to the safety of his corner shop. Readjusting her hood and pulling it further forward, she followed along the same street herself and crossed the same road. Then she turned away, heading off in another direction, one that would lead her home. Even that small amount of exercise had elevated her mood and she approached her own front door with a lighter tread, thinking about which domestic tasks she would attend to first.

Glancing across at her neighbour's door, she hesitated, and a sombre shadow of thoughtfulness descended on her again.

Stepping over the low wall that marked the boundary between the two properties, she knocked on Rachel's door. She had no idea if she would be in or not; more than likely she would be at work. There was no sign that anyone was in, although it dawned on Maggie that Rachel's red car was parked on the road outside once more. Maybe it had been there for a while and she hadn't noticed; maybe her partner had dropped it back; maybe he himself was back; even so the house remained quiet.

There was no response. Maggie crossed back over to her own doorstep, turned her key in the lock and went in.

Shaking the spring droplets from her coat, she hung it on the hooks in the hallway, spreading it over several at once to speed up the drying-out process. Finding her slippers, she changed out of her wet boots, thinking that soon the season for boots would be over, although she had noticed that these days people dressed more in line with the dictates of fashion than seasons. As this thought occurred to her, another followed swiftly behind: she sounded like her mother, uttering sweeping judgements on the perversities of the current age. This made her smile and she marched through to the kitchen to put the kettle on.

The house felt surprisingly cosy. She hadn't left the heating on, although it was still set to the timer – morning and evening – so she wondered if the warmth of spring was in fact prevailing. While the kettle boiled, she went into the living room and crossed over to her mother's chair. Standing beside it for a moment, she was not sure what she felt. Reaching out a hand, she stroked the well-worn arm and sighed.

Then stirring once more into action, she gathered up the cushions, unzipping the covers. Together with the shawl, which lay across the back of the chair as a head rest, she returned to the kitchen and shoved everything in the washing machine. None of these items had been cleaned for ages. Just before she switched it on, another idea struck her: she might as well wash as much as she could while the opportunity was there. In a few minutes she had stripped the seat cover from the chair and had added it to the pile in the machine. Rummaging about in the cupboard under the sink she found a plastic spray bottle of upholstery cleaner. Before long she had employed it on the rest of the chair's fixed covers, scrubbing them with sudden energy. The room began to smell of synthetic floral sweetness. Cracking open a window, she was all at once annoyed with herself for not waiting instead for a bright sunny morning to embark on this process, when she could have opened all the windows wide and let daylight and fresh air flood the room. She shrugged; the heating would come on soon and she had plenty to do elsewhere in the house, so the rather overpowering smell could be avoided.

Later, as she sipped her tea, standing at the kitchen sink, staring out across the small back garden, over the old fence, where ivy stretched upwards unabashed towards a slate sky criss-crossed by drooping cables, she wondered if she ought to send Rachel a text message, just to say she had called round. It was difficult to know how much was too much and how much was enough. Their friendship had grown rapidly, swooping them up in great leaps over the usual milestones that configured comradeship, yet she still sensed that she was new to all of this; awkward both in action and inaction.

It should be instinctive, she thought, following the rules of human interaction. Though perhaps, she concluded, some found it easier than others, thanks to either an innate ability or just practice. She suspected that she had not had much of either. It was like the spontaneous process of cleaning the chair: she sent the text and tried not to think about whether or not it was appropriate.

Maggie had the vacuum cleaner roaring at full pelt before she realised somebody was ringing the doorbell. She switched it off and, avoiding the curling cable, which she had plugged in at the bottom of the stairs, she opened the door. It was already getting dark outside; the late afternoon did not need much help establishing itself against a blanket of grey sky. Rachel stood there, hands in the pockets of her jeans, looking much more like her old self: bright and bubbly with gold earrings bobbing among wisps of wavy hair.

'Got your text. Sorry I wasn't in, I just got back from work.'

'Oh, that's fine,' Maggie smiled. 'I was just wondering how things were?' She wanted to add that it wasn't important, but that was just a turn of phrase because, of course, it was important.

Rachel's smile dropped and she shrugged. 'Oh well, you know, just the same, although I'm beginning to think that the situation is a bit more permanent than I'd realised...' she reflected.

All at once it dawned on Maggie that she was letting her neighbour stand there on the doorstep in the dusk; although the rain had stopped it was nevertheless chilly. 'I'm sorry, come on in.' She pulled the door wider and stood aside.

'No, it's OK. I've got some stuff to get on with but I was wondering if you wanted to come round for a takeaway tonight, later on?' Rachel looked as if this request made her uncomfortable. 'I expect you've something planned; it was just a thought, you know.'

Maggie rarely had takeaways. They were not something her mother enjoyed, apart from the occasional fish and chips; for herself, she never bothered. She couldn't remember the last time she had done anything like that. It was the kind of lifestyle that was spur-of-the-moment and sociable; these were not words that described her situation. Why would her neighbour want to include her?

Rachel seemed to sense that Maggie was wavering and appeared to conclude that she had better things to do than spend an evening with her melancholy neighbour.

'It was just an idea, but you're probably doing other things. No worries...' Rachel stepped back as if to leave.

'No!' Maggie laughed, looking round at the dormant vacuum cleaner. 'I've stupidly embarked on a crazy lot of cleaning jobs and the house stinks of chemicals, so actually it would be really great if I didn't have to sit in it all evening.'

Rachel beamed. 'Brilliant. How about seven-ish?'

'Lovely. Thanks, that's perfect.'

As she moved to cross over the wall back to her own property, Rachel added, 'Curry OK for you, or do you prefer sweet 'n' sour?'

'Either's fine, I really don't mind. I'll eat anything.'

'OK, well, in that case I'll order in a meal for two. They'll deliver. Bye for now.'

The deal was settled and that left them both with a couple of hours to tick the boxes on their respective lists. Maggie remembered that she hadn't asked her neighbour about the reappearance of her car, but that was something they could discuss later. Later, when they would enjoy some company and some tasty food, which neither of them had had to prepare; later, when they could talk about their situations and share worries and hopes for the future, and even, if Rachel was willing, Maggie could bring something more than good food and good company to the table.

From what she could tell so far, her neighbour had not been put off by any talk of prayer or belief or ideas about God, which Maggie had introduced to their recent friendship. However, she worried that if she pushed too hard that might change. How could she approach the subject in the best way? A subject that was more than a conversation starter, more than just another aspect of human interest, more than a preferred lifestyle choice. It was the answer to life itself, and although the visible world around tried to persuade her otherwise, Maggie knew and was determined to hold to the truth, even though it might cost her the friendship.

With a few swift movements she finished off the vacuuming and tidied away the cord. Everything else, she left as it was. Because she was still trying to air the living room, she went upstairs to escape the cold and the smell, and she shut her bedroom door so that she could pray.

When she thought about it, there was so much to pray for, and she wondered at her general lack of urgency. Surely as a believer, it was the one thing she should be doing more than any other. But it was so hard, so difficult to concentrate, to stay focused and to feel that you were achieving anything of any substance.

And that is why I *must* pray, she thought, because if I don't then everything falls apart. Then evil will have the upper hand and I will be weak, even weaker than I feel at the moment. Because prayer is so important, because it makes such a difference, it is one of the hardest things to do. Oh, Father, she said, teach me how to pray.

'And the blessing of God Almighty...'

The Father

As soon as she walked round the corner into the six-bedded hospital bay, Maggie could tell that something had changed. It was Saturday morning and she was exactly on time for the visiting hours between 10.00 and 11.30. She had not gone the day before after work as she sometimes did. That end-of-the-week feeling had completely overwhelmed her, and slipping away from the crowds to the quiet haven of her home had been her only goal.

It was the way her mother was sitting beside the bed. This was the first thing to catch her attention. Instead of half-slumping, half-slouching, limp as a dying damsel, oblivious to her environment, as if longing for the dream to carry her away, she was upright in the chair next to her bed. Her elbows were resting on the padded arms and her hands were neatly folded before her. She had her glasses on straight and her hair had been brushed, and both feet rested on the floor with her knees drawn up tightly together. Pushed under the tidy bed was the base of the wheeled table, the top of which jutted out at a practical angle between her mother and the pillows. It had the appearance of being arranged just so rather than having been left in a careless muddle, and an empty cup and saucer indicated a recently finished hot drink.

Maggie hesitated before she walked up to the bed, taking in what seemed to be an unaccountable transformation. Then, mother and daughter looked each other in the eye, and of course the daughter smiled. Her mother did not. However, this only emphasised a promising return to normality.

'I was wondering where you'd got to,' remarked her mother, without moving a muscle.

Maggie, who had found a plastic bucket chair from the corner of the bay and was pulling it over to sit beside her mother, had to think quickly; she had to remember how to engage with this style of conversation, how to brush aside barbed comments and divert the flow of words so as to neither ignore nor offend the speaker. Since her mother's fall and the operation, their manner of communication had been quite unfamiliar, where time had been spent trying to coax her back from the brink of incomprehension and loss.

Maggie could smell the coffee dregs in the cup. 'Oh, you've had some coffee. That's nice. I didn't think you liked it much.' She leaned over to kiss her mother's pale, lined cheek.

'Well, they just came with the trolley and asked if I wanted coffee, so I said yes. It was alright, I suppose. I would've preferred tea, though.'

'I'm sure they would make you a cup of tea, Mum. In fact, you had one the other day when I was here.' Too late she realised her mistake.

'I've *never* had a cup of tea here. They only serve coffee. Anyway, *you* wouldn't know as you're never here!' Her body, thin and fragile as an autumn leaf, bristled, and she turned her head ever so slightly away towards the bed.

In this situation, Maggie thought, she had a choice: she could protest and inform her mother of the truth about her regular visits; that she was here nearly every day and that until now she, the mother, had been too ill or frail to remember. Or she could dance around the words like hot coals beneath her feet, and let some imagined joyful music carry her through.

'You seem really well today. Are you walking any better?' she asked, smiling and forcing brightness into her tone.

'Of course I am. I've only had a little operation, you know, and I bounce back really well.' She lifted a wagging finger to underline her answer.

'You certainly do, Mum.' Wondering if she might be able to get to the bottom of this seemingly miraculous improvement, Maggie asked, 'Have you been walking with the physiotherapists today?'

'With the *who*?' A truly puzzled expression filled her mother's face. She turned back towards her daughter. 'I haven't been walking with anybody. I can walk by myself perfectly well, look...'

Two elderly hands wrapped in tissue-paper skin unfolded and stretched out towards the top of the metal walking frame, just to the side of the chair. Indigo channels tracked along from the wrists down the length of the protruding bones; her rose-gold wedding ring ran loose around the saggy flesh of her finger as she gripped the frame. The daughter knew that this was not the best way to achieve a standing position. Nonetheless, it was an instinctive manoeuvre which proved the intention to walk.

'I think it's best if you put your hands down here on the arms of the chair first, Mum, so you can push yourself upright.' The daughter patted the arm of the chair nearest her. She knew her mother wouldn't like being told what to do. But her reaction was not as bad as she feared.

'Oh yes, I forgot. Of course, that's what I meant to do. I'm only just getting back on my feet, you know. You must have some patience with me.'

The fact that this was a complete contradiction of what her mother had just been saying was neither here nor there. Maggie was only glad that, after all, somewhere in her mind, her mother had taken it all in; if the information jostled out in bits and pieces, then no matter.

The elderly woman placed her hands on either side of the chair and drew her feet in closer beneath her. The daughter, who had moved around to stand beside her, instinctively put her hand in the small of her back and gently felt for the movement of muscle mustering its forces for the coming charge. The warm body tensed and her mother, in silence, in slow motion, stood.

'There,' she declared, out of breath but triumphant, and plumped back down into the chair.

The daughter wanted to say, 'I thought you were going to walk?' but she stopped the words from coming out. The disappointment Maggie felt at her not actually walking by herself, as she had so brazenly claimed she could, was incongruous. She knew that her mother had already made a huge leap in her return to health just by her demeanour and alertness, so why she should feel it was a setback that she hadn't taken any steps was something she couldn't explain. Perhaps it was because it still left them in limbo as to where to go from here. The fact that there was potential for recovery was now clear, but how far would that run? Moreover, if her progress stopped short of reaching her previous mobility, then could they manage at home as they had done before?

'You seem so much brighter today, Mum,' Maggie remarked, as both of them sat once more; her mother's hands, with fingers interlocked, returned to their original position in her lap.

'Well, I decided...' her mother began. Then she halted, distracted by the patient in the neighbouring bed who had begun to call out for indiscriminate, indefinable help. 'She does that all the time, you know. There's nothing wrong with her, just making a fuss.'

'What did you decide, Mum?'

Her mother looked blank for a moment, then her eyes brightened with recollection. 'Yes, as I was saying, I decided that if I want to come home, which of course I do, then I have to get back on my feet, *mobilising*.' The last word was spoken with deliberate emphasis; a special, new discovery. And all at once Maggie saw a chink of light; a realisation as to what might have prompted this altered state of affairs. It seemed that perhaps someone had had a word with her about how the future could look if she were not able to walk again; someone who had used the word *mobilise*.

Before she left that day, the daughter and her mother had prayed together. The daughter had spoken the words and her mother had remained silent but she had nonetheless prayed, uttering a defiant 'Amen' at the end. The mother was not the sort of person who divulged the secrets of her faith; nevertheless, the daughter was sure that between herself and God there was a solid understanding and belief. They had ended with the Lord's Prayer, 'Our Father…,' and as Maggie had begun to speak the well-known words, holding her mother's hand as they sat beside the hospital bed, she recalled, with a firework of joy, the brilliant moment that had occurred two evenings ago, when she had shared the takeaway meal with Rachel.

The food had been surprisingly good. Maggie had not known what to expect owing to her scanty knowledge of the local gastronomy and had presumed that the dishes might have been swimming in grease, luminescent with artificial colour. In fact, they had been rich and flavoursome and had tasted like the genuine article. Together with a bottle of rosé, the meal had been a treat. They had chewed over their own particular worries and had discussed a variety of possible outcomes and ways to move forward.

Afterwards, lying in her bed in the almost darkness, Maggie had thought about what they had said. She had found it both remarkable and wonderful that they *were* looking forward. In the face of their individual difficulties and upheavals, which were emotional as well as practical, there was a determination to meet the obstacles head on; the sharing of these circumstances only served to strengthen resolve. However, there was a difference between them. On first inspection, she thought, you may think that it was Rachel who was the stronger of the two. She had only herself and her own wits and wisdom to rely on, neither of which were in short supply, and that was clearly evident given her openness and frankness of character. But at some point, these qualities would run dry; as with all human efforts, eventually their finitude would be revealed.

This was no criticism, as Maggie could only admire Rachel's ability to seem easy and at one with the world around her. However, ultimately, she knew that self-reliance was a false road to be travelling along. It was also a wide road where everybody rushed, scooting by, living for the moment, because, 'You've only got one life, you know;' a road where every moment was crammed full of experience and newness, while the knowledge that there would be an end to it all hovered like the malicious shadow of a highwayman. And yet, in the face of such knowledge, this lust for life was still considered to be worth the ride. That was the difference between them, Maggie thought; it was not based on personality traits, or talents, or achievements, or goodness even, but rather on whom they were living for.

At a suitable lull in the conversation that evening, after lying back in her chair, Maggie had declared, not for the first time, what a great meal it had been and how stuffed she felt; she had checked her watch and decided, for her part at least, to end their evening. They both had to get up for work the next day.

'Shall we pray before you go?' It was Rachel who had suggested this, much to Maggie's astonishment. 'Well, when I say *we*, I mean you really... if that's OK?' she had added.

Maggie, who had stood up ready to leave, sat back down. 'Absolutely, of course we can. I mean, I will if you like.'

Rachel nodded with sudden eagerness, as if for her this was dessert.

Maggie thought for a moment then suggested, 'Shall I pray about the things we've just talked about and, do you remember the Lord's Prayer, did you ever say it at school or anything?'

Rachel appeared hesitant; perhaps with concern about what was implied or simply because she wasn't sure if she knew what her friend meant.

'It starts with "Our Father..."' Maggie prompted.

Rachel's face lit up once more. 'Oh yes, that one. I think I remember the words; mind you, it's been a while,' she laughed.

'OK, I was thinking, then,' Maggie shuffled to the edge of her seat, a little unsure of her suggestion, 'after I've prayed about everything we've been talking about, then perhaps we could say the "Our Father" prayer together?' Her face prepared itself for a rebuttal.

Although Rachel pursed her lips and frowned a little, she nodded in agreement. 'I'll give it a go, then, but I can't guarantee I'll make it to the end in one piece!' she joked.

So Maggie had prayed about their respective situations. She had kept it as simple and straightforward as possible, making a point of not just presenting their list of requests but rather of thanking God for His promises, His care and His unending love. Then she had said, 'Now we can both pray together, Rachel, here we go...'

As they had begun to speak the first few words aloud – "Our Father which art in heaven" – as predicted, Rachel hadn't made it past the first line. And it wasn't because she couldn't remember the words. With huge sobs, which welled up from her sturdy, genial soul, she had wept. As an old, rusty key turning in an equally ancient and decrepit lock, something had moved within her; a sharp strand of light had pierced the gloom.

It was now Saturday lunchtime, and as Maggie left the ward and walked through to the main hospital entrance, it seemed as if the whole world were gathered there. Large, glass, revolving doors, acting like a giant microbial capsule, constantly rotated; a gateway from outside to inside and vice versa. Visitors, loaded down with paraphernalia – in and out. Staff, in a host of different uniforms – in and out. Patients, either aided or unaided, some for a smoke or into waiting transport – in and out.

At one side of the entrance hall, a small café staffed by volunteers, which operated amid an aura of welcoming smells and sounds, was bulging with customers. Most of those already seated, smug behind their coffee cups and newspapers, feigned ignorance of those still wandering with laden trays and who were now bemoaning the fact that they had not bagged a spot before queuing and paying. Chairs scraped and clanked across the mottled tiled floor, steam shot and hissed from the coffee machine, and the large grill plate behind the counter sizzled.

Maggie was glad to escape the throng, thankful that for today her visit was over and that she was not one of those whose current circumstances required them to be eternally waiting, forever without end, it would seem, among the clatter and hoo-ha of the café.

Outside the air was fresh and a gusting breeze played with the debris in the gutter. Crinkled and fine like tissue paper, a loose collection of rose-white cherry blossom had succumbed to the sharp and sudden winds; like insects, their short-wired lives had been busy but brief. Forgoing the bus, Maggie walked slowly along the pavement with the definite intention of stretching her legs until she reached the town centre.

She thought about her mother. For the moment it remained a mystery exactly who had spoken to her, with the resulting transformation. Maggie had tried to mention it to the staff on the ward before she had left, but as it had been lunchtime, it had not been so convenient. There had been very few people around who were free to talk. In fact, in her most recent experience on the ward she had found that there rarely seemed to be a good time to talk things through as staff were constantly busy. They beetled around, chasing their tails, jumping through hoops which appeared to be set far too high. Even today, a Saturday, it had all appeared to be too much, and so she decided that on Monday she would ring up and try to make an actual appointment (if such a thing could be made). Perhaps some light could be shed on the future: her mother's and therefore her own.

In actual fact, she thought, I have made decisions about quite a lot of things over the last few days. Only yesterday at work she had grabbed a moment with her manager to fill her in on the situation with her mother. No, she didn't think she needed any more time off just at the moment, though it was going to be hard to predict. Within a few short hours things could change. They may want to discharge her mother, especially if this semblance of perkiness continued. Then if she did come home soon, Maggie imagined that she would need time off to sort out a new care regime, which in itself would be a whole other issue, both expensive and complicated. It could be, she had told her manager, that she may have to leave work altogether; the situation may demand it. On the other hand, it may not. She needed to be prepared. As yet she had no idea how any of this would make her feel. The only certain element about the whole thing was the unpredictability of the outcome, in regard to both timing and logistics. Her manager had arranged for her to have a meeting with the HR team on Monday so that they could at least outline some helpful ideas and be well armed when a decision had to be made. Before she knew it, she found herself right in the centre of town.

Here was another rabbling fray: scarves, hats, T-shirts and faces of red and white hosted all and sundry in the central square, as folk were gathering before an afternoon football match. Raucous groups of fans patched together for moments at a time before splitting off. Over the heads of the shoppers who minced their way between them, they hollered to their fellow devotees, before swarming off in further batches, in the direction of either the pubs or the football ground. Theirs were the only colours to be seen and one could only suppose that the opposing team knew better than to flaunt their painted faces in the thick of enemy territory. Maggie did not feel particularly intimidated; nevertheless, she kept her distance and wandered through the crowds aimlessly until she reached the far side of the central town square. Life in full colour was washing around her like hot, soapy bubbles in a bowl. She sensed herself mingling with the sparkling cacophony as she ambled along the edges of the square, not wanting to be drawn in but just to absorb a little of the atmosphere.

After a quarter of an hour or so Maggie realised that she was hungry, and that if she stayed in town she could catch up on a bit of shopping and have something to eat before heading home. Light-heartedness was not a sensation she intended or expected to feel; however, there was no escaping it and she realised that she was just thankful for many, many things. For the freedom to walk around town, taking in the life of the city, unhindered by time constraints; for the safety and care of her mother in hospital; for the sudden upturn in her mother's demeanour and the promise of recovery. She was also thankful for the opportunity to make decisions, even though they were more like pre-decision decisions. She was thankful for her friend and neighbour, Rachel, and for new possibilities; for her Father in heaven who, she knew with only fleeting doubt, had His mighty hand on her life. She was also thankful for understanding work colleagues.

Then she remembered: had she really forgotten? Surely not! They had an arrangement; they had even exchanged numbers. Mike had not been in work on Friday, and since the plan had first been talked about they had not met or made contact to confirm. Perhaps it didn't matter either way; she would still go to the main cathedral Sunday service anyway, and if he was there too, then that would be fine.

Soon, after completing a full circuit of the crowded town centre, she found herself walking back down the street, passing the building where she worked and the café where they had had lunch together. No, she knew she hadn't forgotten because everything – the food they ate, the things they had talked about, the simple ease and happiness she had felt – came rushing back to the forefront of her mind. It was as if she had needed to file all this away because the issues with her mother, which pretty much signified her whole life at the moment, were of paramount importance. Though there was, of course, another reason; a reason hardly acknowledged but which now shone through clearly in her mind with stark strangeness. Was it foolish to entertain the thought that *her* life might be even slightly interesting to somebody else? This was far too dangerous a topic to be mulled over at leisure. Instead, she needed all her sense and strength to deal with the real issues concerning her current circumstances.

No, she would not go into the café and have her lunch there. She would just get the bus and go straight home. She was suddenly very tired.

The Son

'Surely this man was the Son of God!'

This was the verse that many years ago had sparked his journey along the road to conversion. Mike, the colleague from Maggie's work, read it again now with a renewed, gilded remembrance of that time; a one-liner from an amateur production of an Easter outreach service. As a teenager he had heard those words and had then heard nothing else.

The rather plump, short man, dressed in a makeshift outfit (old curtains and cardboard put to imaginative use), intended to represent the tough and stalwart figure of a Roman centurion, had by any standards been a minor player in the whole affair. His only line was not expected to be the one on which the story pivoted, and yet for Mike, it had. It was a well-rehearsed line, delivered in the true military style of a commander, and his voice had carried through the prefabricated, post-war church hall, where afternoon tea and cake rubbed alongside jumble sales, Boys' Brigade meetings, Sunday school parties and mother-and-baby groups. Mike's mind flew back to that tin-hut evening when he had been dragged along by friends in the youth group to see the production; there had also been the promise of some interesting girls who hung around. Despite the anticipated attractions, he had come away with an altogether unexpected and unforeseen collection of thoughts; thoughts that had stood to attention, immovable, like the Roman soldier himself.

Up until that point, the Son of God, Jesus Christ, had been relegated in his mind to purely historical and seasonal categories: His existence merely helped to pin down certain points in the calendar – Christmas, Easter, Whitsun – and not much else. To Mike's unprovoked mind, this character from children's Bible stories served no other purpose apart from somehow being neatly boxed in with being Christian and British. The Bible was the Bible, and that was all well and good, as long as it and its contents didn't impinge on his life; and why would they? Why would some words from ancient history have any relevance to his own? And who would presume to suggest that they did? That had been his thinking back then.

After the play had ended and a jolly song had been banged out on the piano in the corner, as the lights had lifted and folk had begun to file away in chattering, comfortable groups, he had understood one thing: the answer to that last question – who would presume to suggest that what had happened two thousand years ago still mattered? The players in that amateur production did; especially, it had seemed to him, that short, fat man mimicking a centurion. It had almost been as if he had been standing alone on the stage speaking to an audience of one. 'Surely this man was the Son of God!'

On this bright, new spring day several decades later, much water had flowed under the bridge and this solitary man, Maggie's colleague, sat on his sofa with an afternoon mug of tea and a freshly opened packet of biscuits, preparing to flick through the TV sports channels. Before that, though, he had read the verse that had resurrected the memory. He had found the passage in an old book of daily devotional readings and had of late begun to use them on a fairly regular basis. The current readings corresponded with the run-up to Easter and he had found himself inexplicably eager to read ahead.

Today on his sofa, in his own living room, in front of the telly, he had read the verses from the Gospel of Mark chapter 15, and especially verse 39. He remembered how as a teenager the whole Easter play experience had caused him to think: if this man had truly been the Son of God, then that was more significant (although he would probably not have used words like 'significant' back then) than any fictitious superhero who could only ever exist in the imagination, on paper or on film. If Jesus was who He said He was, and who others began to say He was – including the Roman officer who would have no other cause to comment on the situation, and millions of believers ever since – then that could and should have an impact on his own life after all. It was then that he had decided, almost with compulsion, that it was worth investigating.

Lately he had started to think that somehow, all these years since, he had lost his way along that road. He had been caught out and tripped up and aimlessly lost in the face of unending barriers that had blocked his path. And yet here he was, back on the right road once again, and he had reached two conclusions: first, there was so much to catch up on; second, and most reassuringly, he had actually not wandered very far at all. Either that or someone had moved the path deliberately closer so that with a few simple steps he had turned his heart back to God. He strongly suspected the latter; he walked in the sunlight once more.

Because it was a spring afternoon, when the rain clouds were far away bothering another part of the country, crowds of people were out in force. The bold colours of numerous bulky jackets, which could easily be more than just a fashion statement if the weather called for it, dotted the cobbled area surrounding the cathedral. The waterproof element of such jackets would surely not be required today; however, they were assiduously worn, nonetheless; from experience the wearers understood the fickle climate.

It was one of the first Saturdays in the season when the cathedral was open for tours. As well as the main body of the building, this now included the crypt and the tower, the cloisters and the gallery. The cathedral represented the main place of local interest; the city did not have much else to attract in the way of tourism.

The Canon knew the routine. There would be two tours that afternoon: one at 2.00 and another at 3.30, and as he crossed the stones he was pleasantly surprised to see how many people were gathered there, eager to book up for the allotted times. Then a different thought struck him: why was he glad to see a large group of people waiting with the intention of touring an ancient building? Yes, he knew it was good for the city to have a buzz of interest about the place; it was reassuring to see that folk in general still had an interest in historical monuments and were keen for their children to discover the wonders of their heritage. Nevertheless, he felt a sadness that they were here for the past and not for the present, and probably not for the future. And he presumed that perhaps it was very unlikely that they were here to meet with God. Maybe he was wrong, too quick to judge. Maybe the significance of a magnificent structure such as this cathedral, which had been purposed centuries before to glorify the Church of Christ, *could* ignite a flame in an open and unprejudiced heart. It was moments like this that the ice-cold finger of cynicism prodded his heart, trying to catch a hold on an unguarded train of thought.

He smiled with each 'Excuse me, please' as he passed through the knots of waiting people. After he had reached the far side and was walking along the neat pathway that curved towards the back of the cathedral, he thought about another way he could have done things. Instead of smiling and just being generally pleasant as he passed the people by, what if instead he had acted like one of the early apostles and presumed the folk had gathered there to hear about God? For a moment he imagined himself like Paul, jumping up on a stone step or a perfectly placed bollard, flinging his arms wide with the welcome news of Jesus, the Son of God; proclaiming 'freedom for the captives and release from darkness for the prisoners'. His voice would be raised like a colourful standard, caught in the atmosphere above their heads as they listened, captivated by words of life. But he had not done any of that and he was reminded again of the heavy weights that pinned his feet to the ground; shackles of fear, timidity, anxiety and the need to remain sensible and acceptable.

Hurrying on to the chapter house where he needed to locate some very important information, the purpose of which had for an instant quite escaped him, he realised he was not completely at a loss. Just a short while ago he had had a vision as he had prayed and led the faithful few through the truths of Scripture. So perhaps, despite his feebleness, God still had something planned for him.

The falcon, which then appeared above all of their heads, both the Canon and the crowd, glided along its invisible, windy highway created by the tumble of lively spring air. It wound around the topmost spires of the cathedral, looping and listing between the ornamental features, announcing the details of its mission with calling squawks and cries. People screened their eyes and pointed upwards at the additional note of interest promised by this great stone structure.

The Canon knew they were all watching the bird of prey, yet another biblical image sprang to mind: Jesus, the Son of God, had ascended into heaven and with strained vision the crowd had searched the sky, wondering what could have happened. Angels had appeared as they waited:

> Why do you stand here looking into the sky? This same Jesus, who has been taken from you into heaven, will come back in the same way you have seen him go into heaven.

Words from the first chapter of the book of Acts.

It seemed unreal and irrelevant. He shook himself. It was anything but. It would prove to be the most real and concrete thing ever to happen in this world. And here he was, a man of the Church, so close to forgetting it. The next day, Sunday, he would be there, leading the service from the front. Everything he was going to say had already been planned; the same faces would be there, expectant or otherwise. Perhaps there would be another vision.

It was then that he made his decision, and yet he could so easily not have done. He could have let his feet carry him along the pathway skirting around the back of the cathedral; then the waiting crowds would be out of sight and therefore out of mind. But he didn't.

The Dean would not approve, he was sure of that. However, the Dean was not here this weekend. With a deeply physical effort, the Canon turned his body and marched with sudden conviction back towards the people, who were watching for the tour guide or for another glimpse of the falcon.

It was just before the early evening Saturday news programme, after the sports round-up but before the family blended mix of talent shows and drama series, when Maggie's mobile phone rang. For a brief moment she just stared at the little silver-grey gadget as if it had materialised onto her small dining table out of a science-fiction fantasy. Nobody ever really *rang* her mobile. She received text messages, naturally, but she rarely expected it to actually fulfil its primary function. The house had a perfectly good landline and she wasn't one to change her habits or the habits of the homestead so easily. As a mobile device it was a comparatively old-fashioned piece of technology because it wasn't a *smart* piece of technology, but so far that was not something she felt she was lacking. Her laptop served that purpose. So when her phone rang, she almost didn't recognise either the sound or the scenario. Breaking from her daze, she picked it up.

Mike had waited for several hours that afternoon before he called Maggie. A crippling concoction of nervousness and self-doubt had held him back until finally the oppressive constraints of time dictated his move. He was expected at a family birthday party across town at seven o'clock, and with the minutes ticking on he didn't like to be late; the timeframe within which he could make his call was shrinking. The call itself was simultaneously the problem and the desired goal of the evening; the courage he so badly needed eluded him.

What was so difficult about calling her? He made calls all the time, so why should this one be any different? The reason was obvious but unwanted: unwanted because he was so very much afraid of where this might lead, and even more afraid of where it might not.

In the end, after glancing yet again at his watch, he had given himself a tough talking to. With gritted teeth he had found her number and dialled. She hadn't answered immediately. That meant he still had the opportunity to hang up and pretend he had never called. Then again, she would of course see his number on the screen and realise he had. That was presuming she was anything like him and had, with a sense of urgency, added his number to the list of contacts as soon as possible. Perhaps she wasn't like him. Perhaps she hadn't done that and it would only come up as an unrecognised number or, worse, caller unknown. He didn't want to be unknown, not by her. He didn't think he was; however, the thought that he might never get the chance to get to know her better frightened him. All these awkward, disconcerting notions paraded before him in the short time it took for her to answer the call.

They exchanged brief greetings, familiar and friendly, and he began to wonder what on earth he had been so worried about. At first, she had seemed surprised to hear him on the other end of the line, as if she had forgotten they had exchanged numbers. However, very soon her voice sounded more relaxed; their conversation was easy and comfortable and he pictured her face as they chatted.

'I didn't catch you at work this week, sorry about that,' she added, moving the conversation along.

'Yes, I'm sorry too, but I was on a course most of the week, a bit of a last-minute thing. Somebody dropped out and, you know, I got roped in, so I didn't get the chance to mention it...' He screwed up his eyes, wondering why she should be bothered either way.

'No, that's fine. I just wondered.' There was a bubble of hesitation between them; would she ask why he was calling or just wait for him to explain? With much trepidation, he took the lead.

'So, I was just thinking about a couple of things…'

'Yes, of course, go ahead.' Maggie took the phone with her over to the small sofa where she usually sat, next to her mother's big chair, which also had a view through the bay window. The last of the afternoon sun was still evident, tainting the almost empty sky with a few scant rosy streamers. She heard him clearing his throat at his end of the conversation.

'Well, first things first: how's your mum?'

'Oh, thank you for asking, that's really kind.' It *was* kind and it was meant to be exactly that. He was relieved. Maggie continued, 'I saw her today and I think… I think she's picked up.'

'You don't sound sure.'

'Yes, I know, but it's her mindset, I think. She seems to have come out of the sort of fuzzy world she's been living in since her fall. She was in a dream before and it was as if no one could get through to her. I was beginning to think she would never improve and that we'd have to completely change our whole lives. It was a bit scary, to tell you the truth, because I suppose I felt, I feel, really alone in making any decisions. Who on earth can tell me what the right one is?'

'That must be really difficult.' He didn't say more.

'Yes, it is. Even though I know I'm not *really* alone in this, sometimes it really feels like it!' Maggie let out a sigh, almost a little burst of laughter. Voicing her thoughts in this moment – a moment above any other moment – lifted her spirits and lightened her load. Then all at once her heart plumped back down onto the harsh, cold ground below: *Was she talking too much?*

'You say she's picked up: how do you mean?' Mike asked. The question and the concern it revealed set her back on her feet again, as if he had reached out a hand, grabbed hers and pulled her to standing.

'Well, when I was there today, she was so much more aware of her surroundings. She was contradicting me, which believe it or not is a good sign, back to her old self!' This time she laughed a little more because the irony was true. 'Although from a physical point of view there doesn't appear to be a great deal of improvement, now she's back with us, so to speak, I think, I hope, she might respond to the physio a bit more. I guess we'll just have to wait and see. There was some talk of moving her to a less acute environment to really get her going but I haven't heard anything more about that yet. Maybe I'll hear something on Monday. So anyway, that's where we are, I suppose…' She nodded as she spoke as if agreeing with herself, confirming her own statement. Looking down at her dark cord trousers, with her free hand she scratched at a small dried patch of something indistinguishable which was suddenly all too visible; it was intruding on their conversation. Then she recalled that he had said 'First' – so what was the second item on the agenda?

'Was there anything else?' She cringed at her words, which sounded like a trite customer service platitude: *Is there anything else I can help you with, sir?*

'Yes,' he answered, and even she could sense the deepening nervousness with which he spoke. 'Yes, I was just wondering about tomorrow, the service at the cathedral. Are you still going?'

The whole conversation reeked of that charged yet reticent adolescent mix of awkward new beginnings. He felt like that gawky teenager once again, and the thought amazed him that such an ancient, immature feeling could be so easily resurrected.

'Yes, don't worry,' she said, not sure why she needed to say something reassuring, but she did. 'I certainly plan to, hospital calls notwithstanding. I'm really looking forward to being able to go on a Sunday for a change, not that going on a Sunday is the be all and end all, but you know what I mean.' It never really crossed her mind that he wouldn't understand. The common undulating features of life that marked both of their lives – sharp ascents and dark troughs; joyful highs and empty lows – were part of their respective landscapes. Nevertheless, these landmarks were now behind them, never to be revisited in quite the same form. There would always be more of the same ahead;

however, the future could be faced without fear because of the promises of God.

At the other end of the conversation, with sudden resolve Mike halted one train of thought and diverted his mind to another. It was about more than just his friendship with Maggie (he didn't want to use the word 'relationship', not yet). He shook off the schoolboy mantle. It *was* about a relationship but not a transient, finite, human one, although he would be the first to admit that that would be welcome. He had met with the Son of God many years ago. He had wandered away and now he wanted to end his drifting state. Walking hand in hand with Jesus Christ once more was like having his life back again, and in going to church with Maggie, well, it would be all the sweeter.

'Yes, of course,' he answered. 'I know what you mean – the actual day is not as important as going there in the first place and meeting with others who believe the same. To be honest, though, I'm pretty nervous about going, so to go with a friend would be enormously helpful. Tomorrow seems like the obvious choice, if you don't mind.'

'Not at all – as it's not the usual service I attend it'll be new for me too. So we'll both be handholding.' It was a risky comment but also a standalone one and she felt it was worth it.

The details were arranged and they finished by each hoping the other one had a pleasant evening: she at home, with a new DVD to watch and an easy pasta dish for dinner; he at his family celebration, where he hoped his sister would not be continually plying him with plans to set him up on a blind date.

The rich, abundant colours of the evening sky had completely given way to the darkness of the final act. Streetlights glowed, marking the route along the road, illuminating the dull shades of the parked vehicles and sombre front doors. Maggie stood up and drew the curtains, touching the low radiator to check that the heating had come on, before heading back into the kitchen, where she gathered the ingredients for her meal. Switching the radio on while she worked lent a kick-your-shoes-off feeling to the atmosphere in the house. Everything was settled, even the things that weren't; everything was comfortable and at home for the night. Deciding to avoid analysing her most recent, enjoyable, unusual, unnerving, conversation with Mike, she sang along with the tunes she knew, and shuffled her feet and hips a little to the ones she didn't. Although all the words, spoken and unspoken, could be left aside for now, she realised that it only signified a postponement of the inevitable review process; this would probably begin when the darkness of sleepless hours pervaded her bedroom, when she would be hemmed in by silence.

As the onions were slowly sliced and the water put on to boil, as her voice and body responded to the music, she recalled once again the golden moments that had broken into her life just the week before. The heavens had unfurled before them, there in the cathedral, wrapped up in ancient stone; the words of the prayer had rung out above their heads. At the same time, they had pierced her soul, not leaving her untouched.

'And the blessing of God Almighty, the Father, the Son and the Holy Spirit...'

The Holy Spirit

The Spirit you received does not make you slaves, so that you live in fear again; rather, the Spirit you received brought about your adoption to sonship. And by him we cry, 'Abba, Father.' The Spirit himself testifies with our spirit that we are God's children. Now if we are children, then we are heirs – heirs of God and co-heirs with Christ, if indeed we share in his sufferings in order that we may also share in his glory.

The Canon read these words to himself, from the book of Romans chapter 8, one more time as he heaved on his jacket and collected his papers, notebook and Bible. They were visible, open on his desk, printed out on a sheet of paper in bold, large print. He had come across them yesterday and the significance, the acute sense of perfect timing, with which he had flicked through the pages of his Bible and rediscovered them once more was not lost on him. It was no surprise that things happened in this way, not to him at least, because living words that daily jumped off the page towards him were the essence of a believing relationship. In the heart of one whose life was hidden in God, His Word would flourish; encouraging, equipping and embellishing the whole. No, he wasn't surprised, but was his heart set on fire? Most definitely. And even though that fire was sometimes an insubstantial flame, often wavering, it still burned with steadfast courage.

His recent study of the Gospel accounts and the days leading up to the Easter story had furnished his heart and mind for this Sunday's sermon. However, these fresh words suddenly seemed to convey the message so completely; they were now at the forefront of his mind, and he wanted to let them colour the picture of Jesus' walk towards Jerusalem. A walk towards brief honour, recognition and cries of 'Hosanna!', chased by last words and a last meal shared with friends; towards the painful, wrenching burden of prayer and betrayal in a garden; onwards to a sordid, fumbled trial, where the earlier cries of praise would be trampled in the dirt; towards a common, brutal execution.

'But of course,' he had thought, 'death was not the finale. The goal had been adoption, God's Spirit living with us and in us to make us family.'

His wife was just about to knock on the door of his study, wondering whether or not he had forgotten that he was preaching that morning, when he pulled it open. Just for a moment they were equally startled even though logic told them, in simpering terms, who else would they expect to find on the other side of a door in a house they both shared?

'Ready?' she asked, being the first to recover her wits.

Her husband nodded. 'Ready.'

The decision about whether or not to ring the hospital to check on her mother's condition had played on her mind since first light. After a few hours of solid sleep, Maggie had lain awake, waiting for the darkness to fade and watching for the golden dawn of morning light to break the horizon, like the distant, faint silhouette of an approaching traveller. The possibility that no defining bands of light would ever appear if the sky were filled with cloud had not occurred to her.

She had no doubt that it would be a dazzling day, heralding a new vision of glory and splendour. It wasn't because she was eternally optimistic – she certainly wasn't – rather, it was more a sense of anticipation. Though she was nervous about the planned events – she was not sure how to behave; she was almost overwhelmed by a sense of guilt that she had decided to go anywhere at all – somehow, she could only imagine that the day *would* bring brightness. When the morning finally came, it was in reality a good, clear, spring morning.

If she called the hospital then it would be compounding her guilt, which she felt at one and the same time to be unnecessary. Yet if she didn't call and something *had* happened, then the burden of guilt would be too much. Nevertheless, she reasoned, it would be a burden brought on by circumstances beyond her control. On no other day since her mother had come through the operation – now supposedly in the process of rehabilitation – had she sensed such a compelling need to phone the ward, and it puzzled her as to why today should be different.

What would solve the problem, taking it out of her hands altogether, would be that the hospital would phone her and inform her of some downturn in her mother's condition. If that were the case, then the plans for that morning would be thrown out of the window; she would resume the all-consuming life of a daughter who cared for her mother, and nothing else. This alien thought shocked her and she berated herself for entertaining the idea of fresh calamity. Sometimes, she said to herself, it is very difficult being human.

After showering and dressing, a process which carried the added intrusion of indecisive thoughts – should I make an effort to dress well? If so, would that be for the company or because it's a Sunday? Should I just wear what I would normally wear and be myself? And why is this suddenly such a problem? – Maggie began to make some toast and more tea (she had already drunk several cups).

She watched the news on the television, which was another thing she didn't normally do. Everything she did that morning lay outside her normal routine. All at once a mad march of panic, like cavalry lines, steaming and champing at the bit, ranged before her, ready to attack any hold on reality. The expectation of good weather was the only thing that seemed to be true, and from her earlier certainty she felt herself sinking away to nothingness inside.

She was ready in plenty of time; the arranged lift was not due for another half an hour. Maggie ran back upstairs and collected her Bible. Her intention had been to bring it downstairs to take with her. Instead, plumping down on her bed, she opened it again to Psalm 28, which she had read that morning; she wanted light, vision and the glory of God.

> To you, LORD, I call;
> you are my Rock,
> do not turn a deaf ear to me.
> For if you remain silent,
> I shall be like those who go down to the pit.

Despite the comfort of her outward circumstances and the triviality of her position, a cry, deep and passionate, flooded her soul. It was echoed in the words before her and she knew their honesty brought her close to God; to a place where He could fill her with confidence and strength. As she prayed for the day ahead once again (asking for she knew not what), a gentle covering by the hand of God descended and she understood that she was loved.

The knowledge of a good day with blue sky, sunshine and puffy cloud was restored. Gathering her thoughts and her belongings, she went back downstairs to wait for Mike. With a momentary, wistful expression she touched the arm of her mother's chair and then turned to watch through the bay window for any activity along the street. She would not call the hospital. Rather, she prayed for her mother. Then the prayers extended, unfurling as she thought about Rachel next door, about the imminent service and her colleague, about the man in the shop, and all at once the car was there.

Mike's car was a dark grey, generic-looking hatchback; she didn't know exactly which make or model. Clearly it was quite new and in immaculate condition, yet somehow, although she presumed that many people would find this impressive, it made her feel the opposite. Was he perhaps a person who valued expensive objects, a person who prioritised cleanliness, perfection and luxury? If so, then she felt sure she would never fit in, that she would never meet the standard. Shaking her head to rid herself of such irrelevant, purposeless thoughts, she stepped out through her front door. She pulled it shut behind her with a bold, decisive effort. She allowed a smile to briefly light up her face before stepping up to the passenger door and climbing in.

'It's good to see you,' he said straight away. His face looked as if he really meant it.

The car wound around, in and out, along the residential streets where a thousand other cars were parked, still undisturbed on this spring Sunday morning. Maybe in an hour or so the inhabitants would stir, and in the decided leisurely mood that really only belonged to the weekend, their pliable plans would take shape – perhaps going out for breakfast, or to the pub, or mooching around the retail parks, or taking the kids out to the park, or for a bike ride, or watching sport, or visiting family, or just preparing a big roast dinner – plans that would kick into play. The modern British Sunday would be in full, lazy, swing.

There were a few other cars already on the move, and as they drove along, Maggie wondered how many of them were going to worship. In no sense did she think these things out of smug piety; who was she to question how the rest of the world lived? She was nothing compared to most, or at least that was how she saw herself. The idea that there were others who would be going to church to meet with the family of God just made her feel a little less of a misfit.

She glanced across at Mike. She didn't want to break his concentration, despite the minimal amount of traffic. He had a face that appeared older than hers and his chin was sagging, but he had a lively look about him, as if he were eager to please, eager to bounce back.

'Did you enjoy your film?' His question broke the silence and Maggie was embarrassed; perhaps he had noticed her watching him and it had made him feel uncomfortable. She was also not sure what he meant at first and then she remembered her DVD.

'Oh, yes, thanks. It wasn't bad, really. Although halfway through I remembered I'd seen it before.'

'Oh, I know what you mean. I'm always doing that.'

They had pulled up at a red traffic light, a pedestrian crossing where someone a few seconds earlier had pressed the button. Then, seeing that the road had been clear, they had crossed anyway, making fools of the drivers, who now had to wait for nobody.

'How was your party?' It was her turn to ask.

He rolled his eyes and laughed a little. 'It was fine, the usual antics, the usual conversation. Saying that, we all get on really well, even with my sister in the mix!'

'Oh, I see.' Maggie didn't really see but wasn't sure how else to respond. She was thankful when he clarified the situation.

'So my sister is lovely, she'd do anything for anyone, but she tends to go a bit overboard. She tries to fix everybody, and then gets really upset when they can't be fixed, at least not straight away, or by her.'

Maggie nodded. 'I'm sure she's very kind.'

'Yeah, yeah, she is. She certainly kept me going when my wife died.'

They were nearly in the centre of town, and finding somewhere to park was not at all difficult. Maggie had been concerned that she would have to help him find a spot and, not owning a car and therefore being out of practice, this had worried her, but he managed without a problem and they left the car just one street away from the cathedral.

Rising up before them like a shard of volcanic rock forced through the earth's crust, the spurred structure of the building, elaborate and yet so at odds with everything around it, stunned them into hushed, awed tones. They had seen it so many times before, Maggie especially; however, today, on this sparkling Sunday morning, it was more breathtaking, hugely monumental and resplendent.

Quite a few more people than she had expected to see were filing in through the main entrance. It appeared as if they were glad to be swallowed by the dark, gaping doors of the cathedral. With similar thoughts in mind, they both halted, lapping up the spectacle, then they turned to each other and smiled.

'Shall we?' Mike held out his right hand, the hand furthest from her so that there could be no mistaking the fact that he was purely indicating the way forward rather than inviting her to take it. Maggie nodded. Companions in happiness, they joined the others.

Was it perhaps an odd thing to be excited about, going to church? Was it a foolish, pathetic, weak thing to be meeting with the few other people on the planet who still supposed that there was a God, and that that God had an interest in them? Maggie often thought that this was how the majority of other people saw it, yet she would then remind herself of the truth. 'Going to church' was a set phrase that people understood; it was linked in with tradition and culture and the way things used to be done. The Church had been one of the focal points in communities down through the ages, and as such it had used its power both for good and evil (yes, even that). Putting aside these facts, going to church was now much more a matter of choice; but why would you choose to go to an old stone building, magnificent in and of itself, unless it was to admire the architecture?

The truth was that the building did not matter. The Church exists wherever people exist in common belief and faith in God, Maggie thought. And this led on to her next thought: is it really the case that there are only a few other people who involve themselves in church? No, it is not just a handful of people who still manage to scrape themselves together, huddling in shame and irrelevance against the rest of the world. There are many who gather together, yes, sometimes in fear, and there are many, many who make up the Church of God worldwide. Not an organisation, or a denomination, or a contrived hierarchy but rather a beautiful, victorious, courageous, faithful body; a blend of humanity and spirituality.

To the watching world, Maggie pondered, the Church may appear to be a feeble thing of frailty and worthlessness (maybe even of corruption and abuse), because it is difficult to spot the genuine article unless you are really looking. To her mind, the true Church of God should never be brash or brazen, flaunting itself or competing with the fleeting adrenaline rushes of the world. It would be absurd to attempt it, and pointless, when the cornerstone on which it is built is sacrifice and the cruellest form of execution.

Maggie had often thought that in a very real way, going to church meant meeting family. It meant encouragement, praise, a place to be nurtured, to be enlightened and to be refreshed and, above all, a place of openness to God, where your heart cannot hide. When the Church met together, whether in a towering cathedral or a dark cellar underground, in a secret cave or a borrowed school, the promise is sure that the heavens will open and the Spirit of God will fill the seeking hearts and minds of those who love Him. It is a most invisible thing, and yet it is the purest, the strongest and the most enduring.

Maggie was sure that this was not everybody's experience of going to church. However, this was the promise, this was the intention and this was what she believed in as she walked with God. It looked like an inane thing to do on a Sunday, on any day, yet she knew it was quite the opposite.

Although this was not the style of service her colleague had been used to in the past, he seemed to fit right in. He found that following the words in the prayer book was surprisingly helpful; he could focus his mind on recognisable themes and concepts, and so many memories of God's goodness rolled over him as he prayed and sang and listened. The structured service gave him confidence and he realised that it had been a long time since he had experienced such a sense of belonging. The Bible passages that led them forward towards the Easter story were simultaneously unmistakable and novel, as if he had heard them all his life yet, like a character in the scene, he was experiencing them for the first time. He sensed the mounting tension between the religious authorities, the people and the person of Jesus Christ: God made man for us. It was all at once tangible and, on several occasions, he found that he was on the edge of his seat leaning forward so that he wouldn't miss a thing. It filled him with wonder and hope as well as a kind of sadness.

If he had allowed that deep sorrow he felt at realising how long he had been away to completely overtake him, then he would have broken down and cried right there in the pew next to Maggie, who, he supposed, would have wondered what she had let herself in for. No, she wouldn't, he thought, she wasn't like that. She was kind and she understood.

The Canon was coming to the end of his sermon. You could tell by the rounded sense of completion that they had come full circle. In a short journey of twenty minutes so much ground had been covered; so many fresh truths, with as many old ones, redressed and reaffirmed. To her right, Maggie glanced across at Mike. His gaze was intent and his eyes were jewelled with tears, almost brimming over. The Canon was not a great man and his words in themselves were not strident. It was not like the other day – she remembered *that* day, when they had been caught up in the vision of heaven and the splendour of God – nevertheless, this morning, a power invisible and unimaginable had taken hold; 'full of grace and truth' he had spoken the Word of God, and the Holy Spirit would take those words, those seeds, to water and establish them.

They were almost finished. Taking their breath as at the end of a satisfying meal and just before they stood to leave came the final flourish, like the last sip of dark, sweet coffee. The Canon read the words from Romans 8:

And by him we cry, '*Abba*, Father.' The Spirit himself testifies with our spirit that we are God's children.

Maggie watched from the corner of her eye as her colleague dropped his head, and she saw his shoulders as they gently shook. In her bag she found a packet of tissues and, with as little rustling as she could manage, she undid it and handed him one. He took the tissue and then squeezed her hand just for a moment. Going to church was more than just something to do on a Sunday.

'Maggie,' the Canon called as he made his way over to where they were standing, tucked inside the entrance, their figures stark against the bold sunlight. 'It's so good to see you here, today!' He shook both their hands. 'How's your mum?'

Maggie updated him on the situation with her mother and thanked him for his concern, reassuring him that if she needed any further help, she would be certain to ask. She knew that his original offer had been genuine and she hoped that, likewise, her response would be taken as such.

'This is Mike, a colleague.' Maggie turned to introduce the man stood beside her.

Although the Canon did not appear to be a confident man, he smiled and shook Mike's hand once again, as if doing his best to form the beginnings of a conversation. 'It's great to see you both here today. So you work together?'

'Yes, that's right,' Maggie answered. 'Just down the road from here.' She pointed back over her shoulder in the general direction of their office building, which they all understood to mean the centre of town.

Mike added, 'I'm so glad I came today. Thank you, it was really good, really good to be here, and...' He trailed off; he didn't know how to continue or put into words what it had meant to be there that day, or how significant it had been for him; 'good' seemed such an inadequate word. He wanted to tell the Canon, whom he had never met before, all about the Easter play he had listened to as a teenager, how the centurion had spoken to him – just to him – and how he had understood everything. Then he would go on to tell him about how he had drifted away and forgotten the Roman soldier's statement, and how he had been carried along with the trappings of an ordinary life until his wife had died, and he had come face to face with death once again. That was what he *wanted* to say. Nevertheless, although an ominous landscape of emotion again threatened to overwhelm him, he decided that what he *had* said was enough for one day.

He reiterated his thanks and the small party of three parted. In two different directions they set off across the cobbled stones. Birds breezed overhead, surfing the currents, their particular species indistinguishable to the comparatively poor-sighted humans on the ground.

'Thank you for coming with me today,' Mike ventured, as they ambled back to the car. 'I don't think I would ever have gone alone.'

Maggie nodded and said that obviously she had been going anyway. However, she knew he meant more than that and she wanted to let him speak. After a few minutes, with a sheepish glance and fearful speech, he picked up the thread.

'I was a bit overcome, you know? I wasn't expecting it to be like that, not at all...' There was another pause. 'Thanks for the tissue, by the way.' They both laughed. 'I don't remember church making me feel like *that* before, except years ago, the very first time I got it, when I really understood... that God loves me, loves me enough to give Himself... I don't know how I could have drifted so far away.'

Maggie had been thinking about this, and although the words were jumbled in her mind, she attempted to respond. 'I think that it's because your heart is open to God. You've been seeking Him, you want to come back to Him, to renew your faith. I suppose, perhaps, that in the close setting where other Christians are gathered, and we are all speaking the same language, as it were, all wanting to meet with God, then the Holy Spirit is there, helping us, urging us on towards a deeper understanding of Him.'

'I don't think there's any *perhaps* about it; I think you're spot on.'

'Well, sometimes I think that if our minds, hearts and souls are closed off and we don't want anything to do with God, then

He gives us what we want. So of course the opposite must be true. It says somewhere in the Bible, I can't remember exactly where, that those who seek Him will find Him when they seek Him with all their heart.'

How original and wonderful it was to have a conversation about God. Maggie could not remember the last time this had happened. They approached the car with a shared, unspoken reluctance, as they knew that the morning was soon to be over. They and their thoughts would go their separate ways, the pair finally breaking down to its composite parts.

'Are you going to the hospital?' he asked.

'Oh yes, absolutely,' she answered.

'I'll give you a lift.'

Be Among You

The vinyl floor of the hospital corridors was flecked here and there with black scuff marks, mostly from the constant steering and braking of rubber wheels. At ground level, this same rat-run of corridors was also broken every now and then by glazed partitions on either side, which opened out on to small garden squares, and Maggie wondered at their purpose.

These outside areas had been somebody's bright idea once upon a time. Perhaps their intention had been to spruce up the shroud of dismal surroundings; perhaps they were designed to uplift and inspire the weary visitor, anxious patient or overworked member of staff with greenery, invention and meaningful modern sculpture. With passing years, these small, structured cubes of flora and creativity had lost much of their charm, and consequently their purpose. The slimy flagstones were splattered with mounting moss, and somehow the small pieces of sculpture had not stood the test of time; the only marks of recognition or appreciation were those left by the occasional pigeon, crow or seagull. On warmer days the doors to the garden areas would be unlocked; nevertheless, these outside areas were rarely investigated by the public. Whoever did choose to step over the threshold and wander outside found themselves marooned at the bottom of a shadowy pit, where only a few hardy plants sprouted in the meagre sunlight; where tired gravel mouldered, permanently sodden. To Maggie, they did not appear to be the once-promised pockets of organic vitality.

At her mother's bedside, Maggie sat down in the spare chair she had found at the entrance to the bay and had since placed next to the bed. It was not in her character to prattle on about herself, as if it were inconceivable that the other person would not want to be swept up into her wave of happiness and positivity. Even so, with her soul still full of the morning's residual grandeur, unstoppable joy oozed from her smile and her manner.

The elderly lady was dozing in the hospital armchair by her bed with the remains of her lunch dispersed across a blue plastic tray. Today it was obvious that, drowned in gravy, the standard roast dinner had been on offer. Maggie was pleased to see that most of it had been tackled. There was a plastic beaker of orange juice, however, which remained untouched. It was a drink her mother rarely enjoyed and Maggie wondered whether it was something she had actually requested. Reaching across the table, she touched her mother's hand; she was taken aback by how cold it felt. The six-bedded bay seemed stiflingly warm. The narrow-banded gold rings on the cold hand hung loosely and looked as if they would jangle like bracelets if shaken. At the daughter's touch the mother opened her sticky, tired eyes.

'What day is it?' Her frail voice, like the tinkle of transparent china, posed the all-important question, the question to anchor the mind and so the person.

'It's Sunday, Mum.' With a light touch, Maggie rubbed the skin stretched across the fragile hand and squeezed it. She wanted to kiss it but thought that would look odd. Instead, she stood up and kissed her forehead, which she was pleased to discover felt warmer than the hand.

'Where have you been? I was looking for you earlier.' Her mother's remark was a little puzzling as it displayed some of the previous week's confusion and dreaminess. Then again, Maggie thought, she had just been roused from the beginnings of an afternoon nap so it was more than understandable.

'I've been to church, Mum, to the cathedral service.'

'But it's Sunday, you don't go on a Sunday.'

Maggie was relieved and amused by this comment. 'Yes, it's a funny day to go to church, for me at least,' she laughed. Stepping away from the joke that her mother wouldn't necessarily get, she added, 'I just thought I would go for a change, you know. It's a beautiful day.'

They both turned their heads towards the wall of windows which, although to the side, were almost behind them, spanning the width of the bay. The clouds shifted by in clumps, rearranging the sunlight as they passed.

Her mother murmured, 'I've forgotten what it's like outside...'

An idea dawned, and Maggie was all at once annoyed with herself for not having thought of it before. 'Wait here a minute, Mum, I'm just going to ask the nurses something.' She realised afterwards that the danger of her mother *not* waiting was minimal: where would she go?

After some polite wrangling with the staff on duty – she had almost felt that she had been disturbing a quiet Sunday afternoon – Maggie had got hold of a wheelchair and, still driven by the glory of the spring day, she undertook the process of taking her mother out for some fresh air. There was a jacket and a thicker cardigan to ward off what would seem to her mother's constitution a cold wind; and she could, if necessary, forego her own green-grey scarf, sacrificing it to wrap around her mother's head and shoulders. The blanket from the bed would do to cover her knees.

The table with the derelict dinner tray was pushed to one side and the walking frame was placed in front of her mother's chair. The daughter waited while her mother pushed herself to standing. With slow, delicate side shuffles she achieved the intended goal, landing without grace in the sagging dip of the wheelchair seat. There was no cushion and Maggie realised too late that she could have used a pillow. It had not been a sharp operation but it was nonetheless successful, and with the beginnings of a smile, her mother was wheeled through the ward, displaying an air of royalty.

Merely for her to see beyond the confines of the six-bedded bay was as much an outing as any. They moved through the hospital, travelling down a few floors in the large, busy lift; then along the lengthy corridors with their sunken, dingy box-gardens swimming in shadow, out into the noisy, brazen concourse domed in glass, where the elderly woman discovered that she was not the only one to be taken out for an airing. Altogether, these scenes were enough of a treat for her dulled senses. Maggie wondered whether she even need bother with taking things further, and head out through the main hospital entrance.

Stopping for a few minutes beside a bank of cushioned benches, upholstered with wipeable fabric, they paused. Here was a moment to catch their breath, although neither of them was actually breathless, and reconfigure their plans. Maggie watched her mother's face, alive with novelty as she scouted the area for human activity, of which there was plenty. She thought of her mother's chair at home beside the bay window and how she always found the people-watching pastime so fulfilling. Compared to that limited suburban vista, the hospital lobby was teeming with abundant life.

After a short while, Maggie broke into her mother's reverie. 'Would you like to go outside or shall we have a cup of tea?'

At first there was no response. She followed her mother's gaze, which pitched from the main doorway across the public area, past the information desk, towards the lifts at the back. Her eyes were following a tall figure in rolled-up shirtsleeves and a wayward flapping tie, which jostled with an identity lanyard. He was a young man, a member of staff, who clearly had popped out for some lunch. He was clutching a roll or a sandwich in a white paper serviette and was carrying a takeaway cardboard coffee cup with a lid.

'That's my doctor.' Her mother lifted a skin-and-bone hand from underneath the blanket and pointed to the fast-moving frame. As Maggie had suspected, the gold rings did indeed jangle as she moved her hand. Squinting after the retreating figure, she wondered how on earth her mother could tell one quick young doctor from another.

'Are you sure? He was walking very fast.'

'Yes, that's him. He does walk ever so fast, I've noticed.' With a definite nod she confirmed her statement.

'Well, would you like to go outside for some fresh air?' Maggie tried once again to get an answer but soon realised that for her mother, this bubbling pool of human activity was thrilling. Instead, she sat back and listened to her running commentary: 'Look at her... I should watch out for that, if I were you... Look! Someone's brought a dog in... *They* don't look very ill to me.'

On the whole, her remarks did not require a response, for which Maggie was grateful. They were merely an observation on the meeting of two worlds: the sloppy freedom of private lives publicly displayed and the imperfect management of all that ails us.

It was a good while before her mother finally answered the original question.

'Yes, a cup of tea would be lovely. Put the kettle on, please.'

Maggie smiled and stood up to wheel the chair towards the small café area that was closer to the glass front of the building. There was now an extra dimension to add to the current circle of interest, as the comings and goings at the main entrance were visible, both inside and outside. The daughter parked her mother near the windows next to a low trough of artificial ferns, and went to stand in the queue for some tea.

At first, Maggie had found her mother's command to put the kettle on amusing, also noting that she had not forgotten her manners. But waiting in line, she thought about it: did her request hide something more? In her mother's head there was still a muddle, an inaccurate jumble of truths, like the puzzle pieces from a child's toy in need of a shake-up. Naturally this could be attributed to the whole hospitalisation process, ever since she had first been admitted. The infection and the operation, together with some degree of disorientation, and today's sudden change of environment, all had their part to play. However, she also wondered whether this was a worsening of an underlying downward trend.

As she moved along behind the people in front of her who were now ordering at the till, she sighed. She understood, or at least she thought she did, the inescapable paradox between the need to go into hospital to have the broken hip fixed and the detrimental effect of such a stay. Perhaps that was why her mother had not wanted to go into hospital in the first place; perhaps that was why so many elderly people were terrified at the idea; perhaps they knew that the odds of old age were stacked up against a good recovery?

She imagined herself in a similar position – having a broken limb. As she was now, she could only conceive that, although it would not be a welcome occurrence, getting into hospital would be a priority, a good thing. Strength, comparative youth, robust health and full independence were all on her side; the odds *would* be in her favour.

Bringing two cups of tea over to her mother, she placed them on a small table, next to a stool where she could sit, and together they waited for the tea to cool. A familiar figure was walking towards the hospital building through the banks of parked cars, their windscreens winking in the sunlight. He was walking with purpose which, of course, thought Maggie, anybody would do. A hospital was not usually somewhere you stumbled across on an afternoon's stroll and would then decide to pop inside and view. He was a visitor, perhaps, a relative or a member of staff, but she recognised the gait and the sense of awkwardness, as if the person were not quite there where everybody else was. As he approached it all became clear. She waved a tentative hand to greet the Canon if he should happen to glance in their direction. She did not want to grab his attention; on the other hand, she did not want to appear churlish or standoffish. He did glance across just before he stepped inside the entrance; although he looked momentarily surprised he grinned and seemed thankful to see a friendly, unreserved face.

'Maggie, hello...' He strode across with an outstretched hand and shook hers. Then, taking the elderly lady's hand in both of his own, he crouched down beside her chair. 'It's lovely to see you looking so well and enjoying the sunshine this afternoon.'

Her mother's answer surprised them both. 'Yes, thank you. We were waiting for you. I suppose you must have been held up.'

Both Maggie and the Canon exchanged bemused expressions; the former shrugging her shoulders and shaking her head, while mouthing the word 'Sorry'; the latter briefly raising his eyebrows. Making a quick recovery, he pulled up another stool and sat down next to the wheelchair.

'Yes, I didn't intend to be this late, I do apologise. How are you today?'

More than a few minutes had passed in which the Canon had, with complete patience and grace, devoted his attention to Maggie's mother. She had told him things about her stay in hospital – about the food, the staff, things Maggie had tried but failed to ascertain – then she continued by saying that now she had decided she was ready to leave; that she was just waiting for her daughter to come and fetch her.

The Canon looked across at Maggie but said nothing. Maggie felt a stabbing sadness though she also said nothing. For a moment they were all quiet together. The mother stared out of the huge windows before them.

Gathering his thoughts and experience as a minister and a shepherd, the Canon took a hand each. They made a neat group of three drawn in together.

'Now, just before I go, because I don't want to be any later for my next appointment, we can pray together and although we are just three people here, we are greater than that. God is here with us; He is among us, even with all these other people wandering around too. God is here and He is close to us, of that we can be sure; and no matter how sad, or confused, or worried we are, He has promised that we are never alone. We don't need to be in a church to talk to Him, we *are* the Church...' He continued in an effortless stream that flowed with all the beauty of sparkling water running over stones. His words became prayer. They were talking to their heavenly Father because He was right there with them.

Squeezing their hands, the Canon stood to leave. He spoke a few words aside to Maggie as her mother reached for her cup of tea. 'I'm sorry I can't stay. I had a call over lunch to make an urgent visit.'

Maggie swelled with guilt and a tumble of apologies began to spill out of her mouth. He put up a hand to stop her. 'You didn't call me over, I chose to come and see you, and I'm so glad I did. Maybe this was another reason I was meant to be here today, because I suspect you wouldn't have wanted to ask me, not really.'

'Well, no, because you're so busy, you have so much to fit in and we're fine really...' Maggie put a hand on her mother's shoulder.

'Are you sure?'

Maggie nodded but she was alarmed at the sudden warm roll of tears that filled her eyes.

'I think we should talk some more and arrange a proper visit soon. Again, I'm sorry but I must go.'

The Canon weaved his way through the crowded concourse and joined a gathered group beside the lifts. The daughter sat back down beside her mother and found a tissue to blow her nose, and they drank their tea.

'He was a nice man,' said her mother as she placed her empty teacup back on the table.

Maggie had made a decision that as soon as they got back to the ward, she would find a member of staff and fix a time to talk about her mother. She could come in first thing Monday morning; it didn't matter about work, she knew her manager would be sympathetic and would give her the time off to sort things out. The changes ahead for them both could well be major ones, and she sensed that she had dallied around for too long waiting for someone else to kickstart the process.

Not long after the Canon had left them, her mother requested to use the toilet and so it seemed sensible to head back to the ward.

'I thought I was going home,' queried her mother in the wheelchair as they traced their way through the tangled throng towards the lifts. 'I'm just waiting for my daughter...'

At the lifts, Maggie crouched down, bringing her face level with her mother's.

'I'm here already, Mum. We can't go home just yet; there are a few things that need to be sorted out first.'

Just what exactly could be sorted out she didn't yet know; however, if some sense of normality could be restored – a renewed idea of home, a circumstance that would enable them both to be firmly established once again – then whatever the state of her mother's recovery and health, they would face it together.

They travelled in the crowded lift that would take them up the few floors to the ward. It was a necessary inconvenience; filled with the breath and bodies of bunched-up humanity, their proximity unavoidable. The jerking, wheezing transportation carried them together, high in a box above the ground. Patients in chairs like her mother; visitors and the thin spread of weekend staff; everyone shuffling, squeezing while trying not to make significant eye contact: it was all part of life, but a part that few enjoyed.

Her mother appeared to be the only one who had foregone the respect of social boundaries. She imagined herself to be in a bubble, safe from scrutiny while free to scrutinise. Without lowering her voice, she commented on the other passengers in the lift and pointed a scrawny finger here and there. Maggie attempted to make amends by placing her hand on her mother's shoulder and whispering gentle, though futile, reprimands in her ear. Through facial expression, she tried to communicate as much apology as she could to those who had been singled out for criticism. There was no one more relieved when, finally, they exited the lift.

During these recent weeks, Maggie had come to realise how many of her own boundaries had had to be broken. Having led an undisturbed life of routine, with only a restrained and stable circle of social contact, she had had to step outside that circle. The neat and simple pattern had been shattered and now she felt like she was running around trying to gather all the shards back together. This had meant far more interaction with others, and therefore far more courage had been required.

The corridor running through the ward was clean and tidy, though there was still a retentive shabbiness pervading the structure; the flooring, handrails and borders along the walls were tired and scuffed. What had once been modelled to the latest design now gave the appearance of a style that lagged behind, jogging along in last place.

'There he is. I told you, that's my doctor,' stated her mother as they approached the central hub of the ward. Here, some of the staff congregated, making the most of the comparative quiet.

The daughter was more than surprised to see the same young man whom her mother had pointed out earlier walking at a brisk pace through the concourse, now perching on the edge of a desk, coffee cup in hand. Astounded that her mother had got the right person after all, she was speechless, as even to her the junior, fresh-faced doctors all looked similar. Maggie was also amazed that her mother had recalled their brief conversation about it.

The picture her mother presented was at best confusing. Out of the blue she could display a sharpness of mind, accentuated beyond her previous character traits, and yet so often the mist of muddle descended, clouding her from view. It was exhausting to observe and relate to. Maggie longed for clarity, both for herself and her mother.

They stopped and chatted at the desk for a moment, her mother holding court, before Maggie remembered that she had needed the toilet (although since that first request it had not been mentioned). This inelegant operation completed, she eased her mother down into the high-backed armchair beside her bed. Once reinstalled in her temporary realm, with everything to hand, the daughter kissed her mother goodbye, promising to visit the next day.

Before leaving the ward, she returned to the nurses' station to talk with the staff about her mother's future. It seemed that she was not the only one who needed things to move on, and although her mother was not troublesome, the general feeling was that hospital was no longer the best place for her. At least she had been able to make a Monday appointment to discuss this further.

At the door at the end of the corridor, where Maggie halted for a moment to rub her hands with the antibacterial gel, pumped from a plastic tub on the wall, the thought of her mother coming home was all of a sudden immense. A monstrous tsunami, rising from the deep, it shuddered before her as after a terrifying earthquake. Maggie froze. She felt helpless and weak-limbed.

'... *and the blessing of God Almighty, the Father, the Son and the Holy Spirit, be among you and remain with you always.*'

And Remain with You

At the corner of the street where Maggie lived, the afternoon shadows were swallowed up in the enveloping cloak of a greater shadow, as a bank of heavy cloud ranged across the sky. Maggie tightened her scarf around her shoulders and was glad that the walk from the bus stop to her own front door wasn't far. The day had started out so well and now darkness had descended, but that, she had noticed over the years, was often how it went. Sometimes it would be the other way around, darkness turning to light, but it was rare that a day would hold only one or the other in complete domination. She pondered the seasons of life: they are already marked out for us on a daily basis, she thought, and yet why are we so often surprised, incredulous even, that life should treat us with such disappointment, with such seeming unfairness?

Some things had been established, in her own mind at least: her mother would soon be leaving the hospital. She, the daughter, would meet with the relevant staff and talk through some options the following day. She would give some notice at work on an indefinite basis until some sort of pattern could be established. And the care company would need to be informed, although on the ward it had been mentioned that there could possibly be a care package organised from their end for a short time; a kind of overlap period where hospital care was continued at home; in cases like her mother's, this was often put in place. Monday morning would hopefully bring clarity and action, however terrifying. All at once she needed Monday to arrive.

Maggie was almost at her house when she noticed a figure bundled up in a bright fleece sitting on the neighbouring doorstep. Rachel was there, smoking a cigarette and looking like she had just got up. In the light evening breeze, her tousled hair was gusting in wayward fashion and her pink slippers looked grubby at the toes.

As Maggie approached and smiled before saying a simple 'Hello', Rachel took a heavy drag on the diminishing cigarette. She stubbed it out on the doorstep next to her. She didn't smile in return or say anything; rather, she let a steady spout of exhaled smoke speak for her.

'Hi, you OK?' Maggie smiled again. She really wanted to say, 'I had no idea you smoked!' She had never seen any evidence of this at all, but thought that might sound judgemental and that was not how she wanted to sound.

Rachel was silent for a moment as if unsure either how to answer the question or whether she even wanted to. Maggie turned in from the pavement towards her own front door and, as she approached, to her complete surprise, Rachel answered the other question, the one Maggie had not dared voice. Her arms opened out from their taut position, wrapped around her torso, and she yawned, stretching like a cat after a long doze.

'Yes, I used to smoke more than this but I still have the occasional one every now and then, when I really need it...'

'Oh...' At first this was all Maggie could find as a reply; nevertheless, she nodded as if she understood. It was not that she hated smoking or anything remotely like that; it was something to do with Rachel's manner that caught her off guard. Over recent days and weeks they had crossed the polite social boundaries that defined them purely as neighbours, and had stepped out into deeper, uncharted, territory – it was almost adventurous – and she had supposed that a genuine friendship had been established. However, this doorstep moment seemed to have them both on the back foot; Maggie sensed hesitancy and defensiveness.

'Yes, that's fine. I mean, not that you need my approval or anything, just that...' Maggie found herself stumbling over clumsy words that did not seem quite right as a response.

Rachel stared at her. Perhaps she was glaring, even. Some urgent reparation was required.

'I'm sorry. I didn't mean that at all.' She shook the awkwardness from her head and, sitting down on her own doorstep beside Rachel, she tried a different tack. 'How are you, really?'

Rachel heaved a great sigh. Then, at length, she appeared to let all signs of defence drop at her feet like empty gloves, lifeless and limp without fingers to fill them. She didn't seem to be angry with her neighbour, with Maggie; perhaps it just so happened that she had come along right now. Rachel looked a touch dishevelled, unmanaged even, as if the twists and turns of bitterness and despair were, like mangled roots, gripping her mind; as if her neighbour, her friend, Maggie, had caught her unawares. And yet here she was, thought Maggie, sitting outside on her own doorstep, not hiding away. Maybe it had not been a conscious decision but maybe she had wanted to be found.

'I'm really fed up, to be honest.' She had meant it to sound light and jokey but it was a flimsy façade.

When Maggie reached over the low wall separating their properties and put her hand out to touch her shoulder, this bold front shattered, and all at once Rachel knew that she had missed her kindness. Also, she had missed her openness, a way that made her feel easy about being open in return. She had missed her caring comments which always made her feel encouraged and never squashed down; and she had missed the steady quietness of Maggie's soul leading her forward into hopefulness; underlining the fact that not everything ended in a black hole. She cried there on the doorstep. Maggie handed her a tissue from the already much-called-upon packet. At that moment they were both glad of the relative seclusion provided by the overgrown hedging around their respective front gardens.

'It's just so hard...' Rachel began, the words wrenched out of her in between sobs. 'It's just so hard to live through this. Everything's changed, I don't know whether I'm coming or going. I don't know how to move forward, or even whether to move forward at all, or whether to try to make things work as they were. Then again, he's disappeared off the face of the earth after promising he would go to counselling with me, so I presume not... If things were clearer, more straightforward and I could see which was the right path to take, then I would be fine, I would be able to handle it, you know?'

Maggie found herself wondering if these were the very words she had been silently voicing in relation to her own dilemma: the right path to take.

There was no sign of any return of the earlier sunshine. It was already later than they had both realised. Even with their outer layers on they shuddered; the combination of inertia and vulnerability had left them exposed to the gloomier elements.

'Shall we get inside? I can put the kettle on,' Maggie offered.

Rachel, all at once awake to their circumstances, responded, 'No, I will. You've been out all day and my house is already warm. Come on.' With unexpected alacrity, she stood up.

Herding wild clumps of curly hair, ordering them together with a red hairband until they were gathered in a bold bush at the back of her head, she pushed open her front door – the door that had taken many a beating, and which had been held closed on the latch while she smoked. She urged Maggie inside.

The house was in a great muddle. Maggie supposed it was more so than normal because of the ongoing state of flux in the domestic arrangements. Then again, she realised that until recently she had hardly ever been inside Rachel's house, except for their shared meal the other evening, so perhaps this was quite run-of-the-mill for her.

'Take your coat off, sit down,' Rachel called from the kitchen. 'Tea or coffee?'

Maggie hung her coat on the finial of the banister rail where there was already a knot of jackets, bags and cardigans, before calling back her preference.

It was in the small back kitchen, which had a layout similar to that of her neighbour's, that Rachel filled the kettle and wondered about Maggie. She could see her figure reflected in the large mirror that spanned the fireplace as she wandered about the front room; this reflection then ricocheted across from a glass-framed print on the opposite wall, into the dining area beside the kitchen.

Maggie was a simple soul, she thought, and by that she didn't mean dim.

As a neighbour, Rachel would not have made any particular effort to be her friend. On the face of it, Maggie was completely underwhelming as a human being. There was almost nothing there at first glance and you could be forgiven for thinking that she was one of life's mishaps. Her unimpressive clothing was a humdrum collection, seemingly acquired decades ago. She was just the sort of person, Rachel thought, that a budget women's magazine would be eager to get their hands on, just to prove the value of a good, solid makeover. Her hair was unremarkable and her features bland. Nevertheless – *nevertheless* – there was something to be discovered beneath that dull surface and Rachel was as surprised as anyone to have found it.

The chance to talk about how she felt had done a world of good; like a deep-sea diver finally breaking the surface, Rachel's gaze had been lifted above the depths, upwards and outwards from her own concerns. Although troublesome undercurrents were still there, Rachel felt able to survey her surroundings and gauge her bearings; for the moment at least, her perspective was restored.

Together in the lounge on the sofas, they sipped at their steaming mugs. Rachel prattled on about what she suspected would be facing her at work that coming week, and about family members whom she had since informed about her domestic traumas, yet who appeared to take little interest. They also talked about what practical projects she might tackle in the house during the coming months, when the hope of better and brighter weather spurred thoughts of activity on.

After a while, Rachel stopped and looked at Maggie as if she realised that she had held court long enough. She asked, 'Have you been to the hospital today?'

It was the pivotal question that had been waiting in the wings for its proper cue, and now the tone of the scene before them changed; a new act commenced.

Maggie held her mug in both hands; despite its waning heat it was still a comfort. 'Yes, this afternoon. I took Mum out in the wheelchair, although we didn't actually go outside, just around the hospital foyer, you know.'

'Did she enjoy that?'

'I think so, it's never easy to tell with Mum,' Maggie laughed half-heartedly. 'I suddenly thought she'd been cooped up in that ward for days. I was annoyed at myself for not thinking of it earlier.'

'So where were you this morning, then, because I noticed you've been out all day?' Rachel smiled. Had she surmised anything in particular? Because it sounded as if she had. Perhaps on opening her bedroom curtains that morning, she had noticed Maggie getting into a car.

Maggie sensed an apologetic explanation sitting on the tip of her tongue, because surely this neighbour, this sharp, worldly wise woman, who was so utterly different from herself, would be disappointed that her jaunt had only been to church. However, after she had weighed up this thought in the briefest of seconds, she did away with the apology and answered plainly.

'I went to church. I got a lift, which was great, and as I never go on a Sunday normally because of Mum, it was brilliant.'

She noticed that Rachel sat back in her chair, crossing her legs as if putting a little more distance between them. It was probably an unconscious movement, but as she then raised her eyebrows and threw out the additional comment of 'Never thought of describing church as brilliant', Maggie realised that that was exactly what she was doing.

Had it only been a few days since she had sat in this same room with Rachel and they had prayed together? Then, like today, her neighbour had been overcome with emotion and they had talked about God.

Maggie remembered two things: she remembered that emotional issues lie close to spiritual ones and that they can often be muddled up; and second, she remembered that if anyone without a background or established understanding of the things of God were to suddenly show signs of interest, then there would be a call to arms in the spiritual realm: where a soul had been sleeping in ignorance they might awake to the shock of a battlefield. To both heaven's armies and the raging opposition, Rachel was now a prime target.

After a few seconds, Maggie responded. 'Well, I suppose for most people *brilliant* wouldn't be quite how you would describe it, but for those of us who believe, it's like being at home with family, a get-together, like a party...'

'Like a party, *really*?' Rachel shook her head as if disbelief and derision were the only sensible responses.

All thoughts of Maggie suggesting they should pray together about their respective situations had flown out of the window, but she would not hurry away defeated or, worse, offended. Instead, she altered the course of the conversation and began talking about her mother – the proposed meeting the next day and the probable changes that lay ahead for them. Rachel seemed to listen and their mugs were soon drained. Maggie leaned forward to place hers on the coffee table in readiness to leave.

'I think I ought to be making a move.' She glanced at her watch. 'I can't believe it's gone six o'clock already!'

Mimicking her actions, Rachel uncrossed her legs and leaned forward too. Then she said, 'I'm sorry about just now.'

Maggie was a little puzzled. 'About what?'

'Well, I wasn't exactly…' she hesitated as if searching for the right word, '*supportive* just now when you were talking about your day and going to church and all that sort of thing.'

All that sort of thing. Maggie found herself wondering what it was she thought she did at church! 'Honestly, it's fine. It's what I do because I really want to. I don't expect other people to understand necessarily. There are lots of strange folk like me who go to church, all over the world,' she remarked. Her response didn't seem adequate but it was all she could manage.

'All over the world? I thought it was just a British thing.' Rachel's question was genuine, and for many, thought Maggie, it was a more than reasonable one.

'We didn't invent Christianity over here. It was brought to us centuries ago.'

'Oh, I see,' Rachel muttered.

The conversation was clearly at an end and Maggie stood. 'Thanks for the cuppa, and it was good to see you.'

'No, thank you for listening; you just seem to turn up at the right moment and it really helps.'

As Maggie was lifting her coat from the mound on the banister, Rachel waited with her hands in the back pockets of her jeans. She looked awkward, as if something was missing.

'You're not going to suggest we pray or anything, then?'

This caught Maggie unawares; she had begun to sense something like disappointment between them. Of course they could pray, she thought, but after their conversation it hadn't seemed to fit.

'Yes, if you want to, of course. I would never force you into anything you weren't OK with.'

Rachel laughed. 'I don't think *you* could ever be accused of forcing anybody to do anything!'

Although Maggie was unsure how to take this, she answered, 'So, let's pray, right here, if you like?'

In the dim light of her bedroom at the back of the house, where no streetlight could paint its amber glow, tracing the edges of the curtains; where no passing headlight could throw a transient pattern against the papered walls; where the only chance of an alteration in the darkness was when a backyard security light would be triggered into action by a cat or a fox (although hopefully not an intruder), Maggie lay surrounded by the thoughts of the day.

In the morning she would call her office and request the time off. Then she would head to the hospital and wait, she suspected, all morning until the appropriate people could be gathered together for the meeting about her mother: a meeting which she also suspected would reveal a very fluid situation.

To say she was prepared for the outcome was not exactly true; she had never had to deal with this situation before because when her father had died suddenly at home, there had been no question of nursing homes or care, and her mother had been much younger. Nevertheless, she *was* prepared to be prepared for whatever circumstances prevailed. Maggie was tuned to focus on the best outcome for her mother and she was thankful, oh so thankful, that her livelihood and her home were not in immediate jeopardy. There would be fine details to work out and she would need to adapt, but it would not be beyond her ability. But that very thought made her stop in her tracks: in her determined self-reliance, would she not be in danger of forgetting her dependence on God?

The chance meeting that afternoon with the Canon had, of course, not been by chance, of that she was certain. He had brought to them, to her and her mother, the grace of God as if served on a golden platter, delicate, sumptuous and fine. It had been the added reassurance of a heavenly Father's care; a token in the midst of a heaving throng of people lost without it.

Then her thoughts stole back to the morning, and it did really seem to have been a long time ago. They had been to church, she and Mike. In their entering into, sitting down, standing up, singing, praying, reading and listening; in the passing of a tissue and the brief touch of hands, they had partaken of the richness of the family of God. Yes, she imagined that many, like Rachel, would scoff at her thoughts on the matter, as if taking part in those things could in any way be fulfilling or abundant. But she knew, although she could not describe how, that this was true.

All around her it was dark and filled with shadow. 'God is light; in him there is no darkness at all.'

Where was Rachel in relation to darkness and light? Was she, Maggie wondered, perhaps skirting the edges, drawn to the soft but unknown, unfathomable light, though nevertheless afraid of leaving what she knew? How strange to be stumbling around in the darkness when there was light to be had, and yet, she observed, how much safer we feel with the devil we know.

I could be afraid of the dark, Maggie thought; I used to be as a child. I could so easily be again and I am surrounded by the night... But I am a child of God and today He has shown me so clearly. I can't, I mustn't, slip so easily into forgetfulness.

'Be among you and remain with you...'

His love remains.

Maggie – the daughter, the neighbour, the friend, the child of God – rolled onto her side. Hugging the duvet up to her neck she noticed a silvery hue, like a sprinkling of dust, shimmering around the edge of the curtains. She imagined that the moon had broken free from a bank of cloud and was now shining, vivid and resplendent, outside her window. For a moment she was in two minds: she could race from the warmth of the bed and open the curtains to stare at the moon in all its glory, or she could let sleep win, leaving her dreams to imagine its beauty. The decision took too long and she fell asleep, unafraid.

Always

High above, the edifice of the cathedral was interspersed with carved, stone figures depicting heroic saints of long ago; those who had played their part in building the Church. Not in the structural rendering of stone – masons, labourers and architects had already laid down the evidence of their worth – but rather the establishment of God's kingdom in that particular part of the world. Although their solemn, hood-eyed, open-mouthed faces gaped down upon all those who entered and exited, they were nothing to be wary of; their gaze could not penetrate the devious, duplicitous human heart. No indeed, their ghostly expressions held no sway over the animated figures below.

It was instead the pinnacles, the spires, that sung from the top of the building, dominating the skyline – they were the ones to watch out for; they were the ones beneath which to tremble; at least, this was how they viewed things from their own, lofty perspective. What of the mean figures that scurried beneath, scavenging for the titbits of life? What could they do against the backdrop of splendorous stone? Granted, the spires had been created by human hand, but they were now so far removed from any taint of mortality that they felt more like geographical features, which had emerged from the ground in another age altogether. In their disdainful, distant posture, the spires assumed they were far more influential and significant than the chiselled, futile figures that clung to the solemn arches like crusty barnacles on the bottom of the ship. The pinnacles scoffed in the blank faces of stone; faces that would always be overshadowed by their own towering splendour.

The Canon and his wife had taken the day off. In a burst of decisiveness, they had driven out of the city, parking their car halfway up a hillside in the properly designated area. With solid walking boots laced up to the ankle, boots that still retained evidence of a similar expedition several months before, they strode out across the road that sliced through this quiet beauty spot towards a convergence of gravel pathways. A walker could choose any of the possible routes on offer, or even strike out across the rough-brushed terrain, though naturally that would not be wise, especially for anyone who had to lead a chaplaincy Bible study meeting that evening, without having turned an ankle from a reckless venture off-piste.

Reaching this hub of various tracks, his wife stepped out first, choosing the central path, which led immediately down through a low copse of pretty trees, before promising a steep climb up towards the summit of a hill. The silver-barked dell of saplings and larger trees – rough and gnarled, mossy and dented – were so full of texture, light and shade that anyone with a hint of the creative would instinctively reach out and run their fingers over their tactile surface. Lacy streamers of lichen hung trailing and snagged in ashen veils across the branches.

'I've missed this...' said her husband, a few steps behind her.

'Yes.' His wife needed no clarification on what exactly it was that he missed; it was all too obvious, and a simple affirmation was all that was necessary. They walked on in relative silence, lapping up every precious moment of other-worldliness offered by this little grouping of trees. Caught in a tiny capsule of mythical delight and fairy-tale wonder, they could almost hear the tinkle of mystical voices from an age gone by. It was purely imagination, yet that in itself was a beautiful thing.

All too soon the ground beneath their feet began to curve upwards, leading them out of the hollow. Dry, chalky stones protruded; a haphazard staircase carved by a thousand feet. Leaving the storybook scene behind, a sharp breeze took them by surprise on exiting the dell. Even though it was just a weekday rather than a weekend, they were not alone on the flat, open flags of grass and rock, which sloped gently onwards towards the top of the hill. A number of dog walkers and a few small groups of people were either heading up the hill, like the Canon and his wife, or coming back down having already achieved the summit.

Nobody was in a hurry. The bright stretch of sky was just as it had been the previous day, and despite a steady wind, which swept across from the west, there was still some discernible warmth from the sun. It was the perfect day for climbing a hill; if the collective thoughts of all those out in the elements that day had been analysed, that would have been the unanimous conclusion.

The couple stood at the edge of a broad sweep of open grass, with their backs to the trees; they surveyed the scene before choosing their upward route. It was good to breathe in the air as it whistled past them. The breeze, the exercise and the enjoyment lent a rare blast of both colour and shine to their expressions. Conjured by physical exertion, warmth soaked down through their limbs, and not wanting to halt the process, they continued, taking the most obvious route.

Maggie had had a phone call with her line manager. She had sent a brief email the previous evening, to the effect that she would not be in work that day, and probably not for the foreseeable future until some sort of pattern could be established at home. It was not quite that she had handed in her notice; she did not feel that she had reached that stage yet; nevertheless, although the outcome remained unclear, the scene was now set.

Another bus ride, a later one than her normal Monday morning routine, took her to the hospital, and she was there at the nurses' station by ten o'clock. She had been in two minds as to whether or not she should first go and greet her mother. If she did, then she would risk adding to an already confused situation, and if she didn't, then some might wonder at her seeming lack of interest in not greeting her mother first. These latter concerns, she thought, sprang from a more self-centred motivation, worrying about what other people thought; therefore, she decided it would be best to visit her mother properly afterwards; when she had something concrete to tell her, and when she could actually stay with her to chat it through.

That morning on waking, with her first cup of tea to hand, she had read from Psalm 33: 'He who forms the hearts of all, who considers everything they do. No king is saved by the size of his army; no warrior escapes by his great strength.'

One of her overriding thoughts as she had struggled from sleep into wakefulness had been of escape: how could she escape from her life, her predicament, her responsibilities? Was this all that the rest of life had in store for her? Was there to be nothing else? This was not the kind of conscious thought with which she was usually beset, yet through the night, in her dreams, it had dug its claws deep within and was not easily shaken off. She wanted to escape; yet she also wanted to win through.

The psalm ran ahead of her and she chased over the words, lapping them up as sure nourishment for her soul: 'But the eyes of the LORD are on those who fear him, on those whose hope is in his unfailing love, to deliver them from death and keep them alive in famine. We wait in hope for the LORD ...'

The promise was steadfast: in the face of death – although not her personal current state – and in the face of famine and destitution – again, this was not where she was at – moreover, in circumstances of trouble and pain, the answer was sure that the Lord would provide. He would carry through those who trusted Him to do so. The promise was not that she would escape but that she could live in hope; a surety of ultimate victory. With these words she had armed herself for the day. Her situation was unsettling but not hopeless.

'Do you want to step into the office? I think the doctor might be along any moment, but we can make a start.' The charge nurse on duty that morning, a thin man, probably in his late thirties, ushered Maggie into a small room behind the nurses' station. A myriad boxes and papers and drawer units, containing and propped up with items both administrative and clinical, cluttered the room.

'A bit of a health and safety issue in here, I'm afraid,' the charge nurse commented as he pulled out a seat for Maggie. She thanked him and said something to the effect of it not being a problem, and that she imagined it was very difficult to keep things in order, what with the practical work taking priority.

'Tell me about it!' The charge nurse exclaimed, in cynical exasperation. He shifted a heavy pile of papers from the middle of the desk that stood between them and, as if they were hallowed documents, placed her mother's notes ominously on the cleared space. He leaned forward but kept his hands in place on top of the file.

'Now then,' he began, 'let's talk about your mother…'

The town centre on this Monday lunchtime appeared to be in typical form for the start of another week. Although the weather was not a constant factor that could be relied upon, or could be said to be indicative of a typical Monday, it was nonetheless good, and ripe with the promise of continued spring warmth and airiness. However, this did not alter the heavy atmosphere that now encumbered those facing a long week ahead; those for whom the weekend hadn't been long enough. For others, though perhaps they were fewer in number, the chance of a busy day filled with errands and shopping and bustle brought a welcome break from the emptiness of a lonely weekend. At midday especially, people who fell into both categories were visible en masse.

After her hospital visit, Maggie had headed into town; she had not felt like going straight home. Despite rarely requiring the company of others, she sensed an urgent need to talk to someone, as if all she had had to digest that morning, little of which had been unanticipated, was weighing her down; stones in her pockets, dragging her below incandescent waves.

Her thoughts were neither clear nor decided; however, she followed her nose along the road, towards her place of work. Yes, she knew she would have to update her line manager but they had already agreed that a further phone call would suffice, certainly for the meantime. Also, she knew she needed to get home in order to make more arrangements: phone calls to a host of agencies so that her mother's move back home would run smoothly. Nevertheless, overriding all of this she wanted to talk to someone right then, and she wanted it to be her colleague, Mike; the one who had become a friend. She did not know how on earth that was going to happen.

Outside the office building, yet still on the other side of the road, she looked up, shielding her eyes against a banner of dazzling sky overhead. As if synchronised by delicate, divine precision, *his* figure was looking out of the tall windows that framed the communal office seating area, where they had shared their lunch break. Simultaneously they lifted hesitant hands in greeting; hardly waving; just an acknowledgement of each other's presence; a stifled disbelief that the very subject of their thoughts had materialised before them.

The windows of the little café were still steamed up despite the warmer weather. The gush from the coffee machine, which let gutsy aromas linger around them, together with the burnt-cheese smell of the sandwich toaster, were like dinner on a plate before they had even ordered. They joked about it all becoming a bit of a habit, these chance meetings for lunch. This time Maggie ordered and paid while Mike found a table. The ones at the window were all taken but there was still plenty of room further back. At the till, she turned round and smiled at him, her relief apparent. Pleasure at having found her again on this mundane Monday was written all over his face. Quickly flicking her gaze back around towards the person serving her, as if she had been swiped by a cold hand of blame, Maggie frowned, shocked at herself. This wasn't supposed to be about her, her satisfaction, her pleasure or her future well-being; this was all about her mother. It should be about her duty, and her desire as a daughter to fulfil that duty: to care, protect and watch over her.

This time there was a tray with two hot drinks to be carried over while they waited for their sandwiches to be ready. As she placed it on the table it was as if he had read her thoughts, and she nearly spilt everything.

'It's not just about your mother, you know.' He spoke as if he had seen the sudden frown that had clouded her face at the till and had understood its meaning. 'This is your life too; it has to work for both of you.'

To respond to that was impossible. He had good sense on his side, yet it was not a manner of thinking to which she was accustomed. Settling herself down in the chair and picking up her coffee, too hot even to sip, she sighed. Was there the possibility that she could be talked into selfishness? Or did his comment go even deeper: was he the one who was edging towards selfishness in expecting too much from her? How could she think that and why did these thoughts bombard her? Surely she had enough going through her mind without the additional twists and turns of further, more intrusive emotions?

'I'm sorry.' Mike, his hands clinging to the handle of his own hot mug, looked sheepish, as if he wanted to unsay everything. 'I didn't mean for one minute to tell you what to do. Well, in fact I know what you have to do, what you're going to do, and I'm glad you've got something definite at last, a decision. I think I was just letting how I feel interrupt all that, which of course is not what you need right now.' He chuckled just a little as if to make light of the serious things that filled his heart.

The arrival of the hot toasted sandwiches lifted them out of momentary discomfiture, echoing the youthful, carefree mood when they had first seen each other and had walked into the café just a few moments ago.

Changing tack, Mike mentioned the service from the day before. 'I can't tell you how good it was to be at church yesterday.' He had wanted to add *with you*, but thought it best to hold back from emphasising the whole truth. Then again, he wanted – he needed – to be honest, because it would still have to be said sooner or later. 'What I really mean,' he continued while they both waited for the hot, melted strings of cheese to cool, 'what I really want to say is that it was not just because I went with you that I enjoyed the service. Although, without doubt, you were for me the perfect companion to share it with. This is the most important part, and I want you to hear this and know that it's true: I feel that I have made my way back to God, and despite it being a bit stomach-churning, it wasn't as hard as I thought. He more than met me halfway!' His smile was genuine.

Maggie smiled back; her response sufficed, and they ate their lunch in perfect companionship.

Outside in the street, they wandered back towards the office building.

'So,' Maggie began as they were about to go their separate ways once again, 'I'm going to go home and begin to arrange everything.' She shook her head, shuddering a little at the prospect. 'And then we shall see how things go.'

'And then,' Mike reminded her, 'then you can tell me all about it tonight. I'll ring you.'

'Well, you don't have to…'

'But I do. We are friends, aren't we?'

'Yes, we are friends.'

He took hold of her hand and squeezed it and then turned to cross over towards the office building.

Catching a glimpse of the towering cathedral between the mismatched forms of the city landscape, Maggie stopped, caught in her tracks. This was a sight that never failed to bring a burst of joy into her heart. It was not because of anything particularly spiritual, not usually. Rather, it was because of the wonder of the architecture: spires that seemed to speak of higher things; stonework that whispered from ages past, when the limits to human creativity were not hindered by tools and materials deemed inadequate by modern standards.

The recollection of a vision (was it only just a matter of days ago?) came to her mind, and once more that day she let her footsteps lead her, this time to a building rather than a blending of hearts.

Inside the cool cathedral there was a chill, but it was not unpleasant. Tourists and visitors were few in number. It was a Monday and the Easter holidays were still a week or so away. Folk carried leaflets around with them, guiding them towards the various points of interest; muttering in the library voices demanded by the magnificence of the vaulted arches, elephantine pillars and gloriously worked windows.

Maggie realised, though, with a measure of resigned sadness, that it was history and architecture that inspired most of the worship within its walls, at least then and there, on that Monday afternoon.

Slipping into a pew, somewhere in the middle, she settled her mind and her heart and shut her eyes against the intricate beauty and splendour of the structure surrounding her. Calling out to God – her God; the God of many souls and nations; the God to whom all ultimately belonged; the woman, the daughter, the perfect companion – Maggie prayed.

Always; He had always been, and always would be; God eternal from age to age. Always; He was always available; never too busy, or in a meeting, or off on an expedition, or too important to be disturbed.

She could talk to Him, and although that did not have to be in a cathedral, or in any particular place at all, today in the face of all her emotions, in the midst of those wandering around her, she could talk to God. And maybe, she thought, others might see that God was not relegated to history and great buildings of stone.

Amen

It was well into April by the time the three falcon chicks finally hatched. Gawky with pale fluff, dark eyes and stick legs, knobbly and tough, they could not be described as beautiful. The young birds appeared ungainly and out of proportion; only with age and rapid growth would their true form emerge: the ugly duckling into the slender swan. With eyes only for their young, the falcon pair had no interest in the lifecycle of other beings. The fact that, for the most part, with newborn humans the situation works in reverse – babies are full of pink delightfulness with dark, button eyes, all cuddles and cuteness, with a sweet smell that lingers after a kiss; only to be replaced by blemishes and awkwardness in adolescence and adulthood – was neither here nor there.

The chicks were greedy, and daily film footage showcased their squawking and the endless, diligent parental focus addressing their most immediate need. At first, the larger of the falcons, the female, remained in the scrape while the male carried out most of the hunting. After several weeks, however, both parents would take to the air, hunting in mid-flight to sate the never-ending appetite of their growing chicks. In sunlight and showers, sharp spring breezes and cloudless skies, the cathedral spires radiated pride while nursing the fledgling family. With disdainful nonchalance they dismissed the limited though increasing activity of the local ornithological society, who put in appearances to tag the youngsters and check the cameras.

Speaking on a regional news programme, on location outside the cathedral, the Dean looked quite at home in the spotlight.

'It is so very good to have peregrines nesting in our cathedral towers once again. As custodians of this magnificent building and as part of our mission, we aim to share in the whole life of the church, including these new additions to the cathedral family, and we look forward to seeing them grow and develop over the coming weeks.'

The life of the falcons and their offspring brought some welcome media attention, but it was a focus of which they themselves were mostly ignorant. As long as pigeons and other small prey remained plentiful, then the business of any other form of life was irrelevant, not worthy of their attention; the cathedral spires could not agree more.

The Canon and his wife had several matters under consideration. It had been after that particular hike on a Monday, several weeks ago, that they had remembered what it really felt like to be themselves once again. The distance and the time taken away from the cathedral and its politics had, as they walked and talked, unearthed long-forgotten dreams and plans from earlier years. It was not that they had somehow missed the mark and had gone off at a tangent, in completely the wrong direction, or that those ideas and ideals had been sacrificed to a cul-de-sac existence, but rather despite being submerged in work and the business of everyday life, a fresh viewpoint had brought fresh impetus and revealed the possibility and challenge of change. As far as they were aware, they had not left God out of any of their past decisions, and they could faithfully say that, 'The boundary lines have fallen for me in pleasant places ...' They believed, and could testify, to a God who keeps His promises. Nonetheless, the experience of standing on a breeze-blown hilltop looking down on all they surveyed, including the apical towers of the cathedral, all at once distant and small, lent a new and sudden perspective.

Finally, it was the Canon's wife who had spoken. She merely remarked, 'Pastures new?'

For the moment they had decided just to put feelers out here and there; picking up on mission articles they might not have done otherwise; being careful not to dismiss ideas because of immediate or superficial impracticalities. Old connections were haphazardly rekindled, and the Canon embarked with a serious and diligent determination on his smouldering idea for a book. Now was the time to focus on gathering material and beginning some research, before the embers grew cold.

His wife, who had studied with him years before, when they had met as students, now saw fresh opportunity; she knew that she had a gift and, where the field of service had looked cold and abandoned, all at once it swathed before her with the promise of new life. Daily prayer developed a more specific focus, and they spoke often about the vision he had had that dreary Tuesday morning, only weeks before. If nothing else came of it, they felt that at the very least, whatever their circumstance, they could do no worse than take the words to heart: 'Go forth...'

Rachel ordered and subsequently had fitted a new, dark-blue front door. It had been an opportunity to smarten up the house; it made a change from the standard plastic white, which had become the norm along their street. As her partner had disappeared from her life altogether, she decided to take advantage of the counselling sessions alone. The impact that habitual thought patterns and behaviour had on one's life was something she had hardly been aware of, or had never dared to face before. With this dawning understanding came pain, but she sensed that it was constructive; it was pain of the necessary kind.

The friendship between the two next-door neighbours remained unsullied and undiminished; they regularly met just to chat and often for prayer. Rachel was in two minds about the whole spiritual side of this friendship: first, because although it was helpful – really helpful – she knew deep down that there was more; more to be gained and more to discover, and that at some point, more would be required of her. It wasn't like going for a massage or a spa treatment that for the short term did you some good, with the minimum of responsibility or consequence. Perhaps this was what led on to her second concern: as she prayed with Maggie, or rather Maggie prayed with her, there was someone else involved too. There was another person in their relationship, a person who reached out to her, Rachel, and promised to stand beside her, whether or not she had a kind and caring next-door neighbour. How much longer could she go on ignoring that fact? It was a thought that now bugged her each and every day.

Mike, the colleague from Maggie's work – the office where she *used* to work – was thankful that his sister had eased off on the whole match-making project. It was strange, he thought, now that he no longer worked with Maggie, they somehow saw an awful lot more of each other than when they had spent hours in the same building three times a week. As he worked full-time, he of course was there five times a week, whereas Maggie had been part-time.

A novel thought had begun to cross his mind; every day he tossed it back and forth, weighing up the pros and cons. There was nothing stopping him from doing the same. After being widowed he had continued to work full-time mainly because it kept so many hours of the day occupied, full with many important things. He was rapidly realising that such things were not as important as he had once assumed. His work pattern could change. Retirement was only a whisker away, and all of a sudden there were so many better ways in which that time could be filled. For one thing, there was a church life that, like new, green shoots, was blossoming out of dry, parched ground. Revival of the soul, mind and heart had taken place, and none of this had been stunted by the scorching heat of pressure or the blasting wind of disappointment. The soul awakened was his alone; there was no confusion with the promise of other human relationships.

Once a week he met with the Canon, who was surprisingly confident and full of wisdom, and between the two of them they scoured the Bible, foraging for the food of God's Word. Such nourishment was not difficult to discover when found by the appetite of a searching heart.

And then, of course, there was Maggie; their love was inevitable. Although they had only just set out along the road, everything fitted. Their relationship was not one that would have been picked out of the bag by his sister, or any other well-meaning buddy, but it was tailor-made nonetheless. He often found himself wondering: who could have designed such a perfect companionship? Naturally, the answer to the question came flying back at him so fast it stung.

The woman, the daughter, the friend, Maggie, was a person who carried these titles with truth emblazoned. After what had seemed like a long climb up a very rocky hillside, mother and daughter had re-established a workable domestic routine. Her mother was frail; frailer than she had been before the fall, and there was no surprise in that. It had made good sense to Maggie to relinquish her work altogether, for the foreseeable future at least. It was not altogether an acceptable decision and it was not without sacrifice. They could still afford to have outside help coming in several times a week, so that errands could be run, and so that Maggie could benefit from time alone, without the pressure or demands of caring. She could still go to church; she could still pop into town and she could still take time out for any other business.

From time to time, like mythical creatures from the deep, resentment and self-pity would rear their heads. At a moment's notice they would leer at her, while at the same time plying choice morsels of discontent: why should she not put herself first? Why had this happened to her? Was this to be the story of her life? She knew it was dangerous to entertain such thoughts. They were poisonous; they would only eat away at the foundation she had laid. Whatever the future held, however long this season endured, she knew that nothing lasted forever. Despite the possibility of many long years – a false landscape, an endless wasteland of self-denial – which threatened to stretch out before her, she reminded herself that it never proved beneficial to dwell on what those years might look like. For all her spiralling thoughts about being left desolate and alone, she was as far from that as she had ever been. Now she had a friend next door. Moreover, overwhelmingly so, there was also another friend who promised to be more, and he was due round for dinner that very evening.

The broad carpet of daffodils had begun to shrivel, turning brown; the glory of their short life ending. Across the freshly cut lawns of the park, their sunshine was no longer necessary; their straggling leaves and stalks were now pure fodder for the gusts that ranged through the trees, along the tarmacked paths that delineated the park. As the daughter pushed her mother in the wheelchair, she noticed the tulip beds, curving out and around in half-moons on either side of the pathway.

Like a little, scrawny bird, her mother was wrapped up in a hat, blanket and gloves. The sharp air made both their noses run and they stopped beside one of the flowerbeds. Maggie blew her nose and then helped her mother to wipe the dewdrop from her own, as she was reluctant to allow any warm air inside the cosy blanket to escape by lifting her hands free, even for a moment.

It was early afternoon and the bright day had drawn them outside. Maggie often thought that it was actually more beneficial for *her*, rather than her mother, to take a walk: outside she could be exercising whereas for her mother, physical activity was not on the cards. On the other hand, as long as there was plenty going on for her mother to observe and lap up, there was still benefit.

Maggie walked briskly, either searching for pockets of warmth in the sunlight or stopping at planned destinations along the way in which to warm up. One such place was the little park café, a familiar favourite. Today they had drunk tea and her mother had eaten half a biscuit. The constant battle against weight loss was of concern. As the elderly lady's interest in food and her ability to cope with meals diminished, so did her already shrunken frame. Increasingly, it was part of the picture but it was one they had to accept.

On their way back from the café, Maggie had thought that they could take a short detour and stop off at the little corner shop where they sold just about everything. Previously, her mother had turned her nose up at the place as it wasn't, in her eyes, neat or tidy or gleaming with modernity like a supermarket. Such an initial response bemused Maggie; she presumed the little corner shop rather resembled the stores of years gone by, where the goods – higgledy-piggledy – were stacked in boxes like a warehouse, or collected in piles on a sawdust floor. However, since her return from hospital, her mother seemed to have lost these prejudices. Arriving at the shop (being pushed by Maggie in her wheelchair), she often had a ready smile and a few words of greeting for the owner, who seemed to be there in permanent residence, like a flag fixed to a mast.

'Good afternoon, my dear.' The owner was also full of smiles today and came out from behind the counter. He took her mother's hand, which had readily crept out from beneath the rug covering her knees, and they exchanged a few words about the weather, her health and his family. During this little tête-à-tête, Maggie skirted around the wheelchair and trailed along the shelves. She searched for a jar of mustard, which she had forgotten on the last online delivery order, some gravy granules and a box of eggs. She had already picked up a couple of parsnips from the vegetable display outside.

'We're expecting company for dinner tonight,' remarked her mother, nodding at the items that her daughter laid on the counter. Maggie allowed herself a little grin at her mother's reference. Their usual Wednesday evening had of late become a regular event: a roast dinner where Mike would join them after work. She was not sure in what role or with what significance her mother understood his company, but so far, her reaction had never been anything but positive.

'Ah, guests for dinner, very nice, very nice...' The owner's response was automatic as he registered each item across the scanner. 'Are *you* cooking?' he asked Maggie's mother, out of politeness rather than presumption.

'I used to be a very good cook,' she replied, with an edge to her voice. 'But my daughter will manage that tonight. Thank you, goodbye.'

This was the signal that she wanted to leave, and Maggie, with an added 'thank you' of her own, grasped the handles of the chair, allowing the shopkeeper time to nip ahead and hold the door open for them.

'Have a lovely evening,' he said.

'Thank you, we will,' declared Maggie's mother.

There was nothing dramatic awaiting them. No sudden change in the weather; no unexpected crowds of people from which to extricate themselves. They had all they needed and they had met with no misfortune, and their story would go on. Perhaps there would be drama further down the road, where once again the practicalities of life would face the brunt of age and decay. For now, however, only the mediocre joys of a mundane home life lay ahead. Nevertheless, Maggie was thankful for all this and more.

She prayed for her mother as they crossed the road; she prayed for the shopkeeper as they passed back along beside the railings of the park; she prayed for Mike as they turned into their street and she prayed for Rachel as they approached the house. These prayers had all been silent, spoken from her spirit. Then, without thinking, she said, 'Amen,' out loud.

There was a resounding response from the wheelchair in front of her, 'Amen!'

Love must be sincere. Hate what is evil; cling to what is good.

Be devoted to one another in love.

Honour one another above yourselves.

Never be lacking in zeal, but keep your spiritual fervour, serving the Lord.

Be joyful in hope, patient in affliction, faithful in prayer.

Share with the Lord's people who are in need.

Practise hospitality.

Bless those who persecute you; bless and do not curse.

Rejoice with those who rejoice; mourn with those who mourn.

Live in harmony with one another.

Do not be proud, but be willing to associate with people of low position.

Do not be conceited.

Do not repay anyone evil for evil.

Be careful to do what is right in the eyes of everyone.

If it is possible, as far as it depends on you, live at peace with everyone.

(Romans 12:9-18)

List of Bible/other quotations

Into the World
Matthew 28:16-20
2 Kings 6:17
Hebrews 10:31
Philippians 2:7-8

In Peace
John 14:27

Hold Fast That Which Is Good
'Whose goodness faileth never' from 'The King of Love my
Shepherd Is'. Lyrics by Henry W Baker (1821-77).
Philippians 4:8-9

Strengthen the Fainthearted
Psalm 27:9
Psalm 27:11
1 Chronicles 22:11-19

Support the Weak
Mark 9:24

Help the Afflicted
Luke 9:37-43

Honour Everyone
Philippians 2:3

Love and Serve the Lord
John 6:68
Matthew 10:16-39

And ...
Galatians 5:22-23

The Blessing of God Almighty
Matthew 16:18
Mark 10:42-44; Matthew 20:25-28

The Father
Matthew 6:9, KJV

The Son
Mark 15:39
Isaiah 61:1
Acts 1:11

The Holy Spirit
Romans 8:15-17
Psalm 28:1
John 1:14
Jeremiah 29:13

And Remain with You
1 John 1:5

Always
Psalm 33:15-16, 18-20

Amen
Psalm 16:6